PRIMAL DESIRE

HEART OF THE HUNTRESS, BOOK 6

TERRY SPEAR

PUBLISHED BY:

Terry Spear
Primal Desire
Copyright © 2021 by Terry Spear
Cover Copyright by AM Design Studios

Discover more about Terry Spear at:

http://www.terryspear.com/

Print ISBN: 978-1-63311-073-1

Ebook ISBN: 978-1-63311-072-4

❀ Created with Vellum

SYNOPSIS

Selena Townsend has no idea what will happen after she kills a fellow hunter while protecting an innocent vampiress. She's ostracized, but acquitted of charges against her, but now she's looking for her sister who has disappeared. That mission takes her to a vampire club and all kinds of trouble.

Atreides has been in charge of the vampire clans, while his brother is off on a honeymoon with his new mate. He doesn't expect a huntress to walk into one of their vampire clubs, which is just not done, and then return later after being savagely attacked by a vampire. He has to take care of her before the League of Hunters learns of it, and then he wants to pawn her off on the hunters who can protect her pronto! But he finds he really doesn't want to give her up after all.

War between the hunters and the vampires could break out any moment unless they find the rogue hunters who are killing innocent vampiresses and the vampire who had attacked Selena and other huntresses at the same time—and terminate the rogues.

To Nancy Sipes, thanks for loving my vampire series and may you only have the best of bites in life. Primal Desire is dedicated to you!

Selena Townsend was supposed to meet with her sister at the Forest Grove Hunters Club in Portland, Oregon, but Rosa hadn't arrived at the off-the-lot parking area yet when Selena heard a man fighting with a woman a couple of streets away. Between a huntress's excellent hearing and the fact they were being so loud they had caught her attention. She wanted to wait for her sister, but when the voices escalated and she heard the woman say, "The baby is yours, Fenimore," Selena decided to investigate. It wasn't that she planned to interfere, but if a man and woman were going to come to blows, she wanted to prevent it. Especially if the woman was pregnant.

With her huntress abilities, Selena was stronger than humans, so there would be no contest for her. She grabbed her hunter's sword out of her car, when she normally wouldn't be taking it with her when entering the club, but since she was taking on a side mission, she was always armed, just in case.

"I can easily take care of that!" the man said.

Selena recognized the voice as that of a hunter—not just some human named Fenimore. She ran toward them, fearing the worst, hearing the hunter's sword drawn and reached them just as he was ready to kill the woman.

Selena saw not only Fenimore Thomason, but his brother, Cliff, and three of their friends—Perry Rochester, Harry Canton, and Lonnie Wilson.

She also recognized the woman—Charlene, a vampiress, and not one who caused anyone any trouble either. In fact, she'd helped the hunters find a hunter child who had gotten lost near a vampire club one night. Selena couldn't believe Fenimore, who professed hating vampires with a vengeance, would have created a baby with one.

"Stop, Fenimore!" Selena shouted, startling him, her heart beating wildly. They'd all been so wrapped up in this business that they hadn't even noticed her running to stop him.

Charlene was crying, when she should have just vanished. Selena could never understand how the vampires would stick around for a fight when they could just leave without being injured. But maybe Charlene felt Fenimore would not harm her and the baby. As angry as he appeared, Selena didn't believe he would stand down without some intervention.

She finally reached them and ran in between Fenimore and Charlene, acting as her shield. "Stop, Fenimore! You don't want to go down that path," Selena said.

Fenimore pointed his sword at her and she had hers ready to fight. The hunter would not intimidate her. She only wished Charlene would leave so that the confrontation would end. At least she hoped.

"You don't want to interfere in my business," Fenimore said.

Then he thrust his sword at Selena, surprising her, but the adrenaline already filled her with the need to fight—to save the stubborn vampiress who wouldn't save herself, and to protect herself even. She realized Fenimore wouldn't want her to live to tell the tale of how he had made a vampiress pregnant. This would be a fight to the death.

She parried, knocking his sword away. "You don't have to do this."

"You should have minded your own business," he said, his voice filled with hatred.

The other hunters watched but waited to see how this would end.

"Tell your brother to stand down, Cliff." Selena hoped his younger brother by a year would convince Fenimore to listen to reason.

"Fenimore," Cliff said, halfheartedly, not forcefully like Selena wished he'd sounded.

"Shut up, Cliff. You know this has to be done." Then Fenimore stabbed again at Selena and she jumped back and swung her sword at his, the clanging sound of the swords reverberating off the buildings.

He came at her again, and she backed up, staying out of the reach of the thrust of his sword while Charlene moved away. Selena could see the red haze in his eyes. He was in killing mode. First, it was Charlene, now he had to rid himself of a huntress who knew too much. She knew once he had decided something, no one could talk him down. His parents, both hunters, were both dead at the hands of rogue vampires. They would have turned over in their graves if they knew he'd impregnated one.

But she couldn't believe Cliff and the others would allow Fenimore to kill a huntress in a coldblooded way.

He thrust again, and she parried, defending herself, not attacking, hoping someone would stop the madness.

Then she heard footfalls in the distance and saw a couple of male hunters running their way. Good. Maybe one of them could talk Fenimore down when his brothers and friends couldn't or wouldn't.

Instead of ceasing his attacks on her, he appeared to be controlled by bloodlust like some kind of berserker of old. When he cut her sword arm, she knew she wouldn't survive this if she didn't fight back. She thrust her sword as he swung his sword back to strike her and stabbed him straight through the heart.

It seemed everything was in slow motion at that point. He looked shocked to the core that she would fight back. She pulled her sword out of his chest, feeling no victory, the other hunters finally reaching them before Cliff and his friends could retaliate against her. She felt horrible about killing a hunter, no matter that he'd turned rogue and was trying to murder an innocent vampire. She was still a hunter like him. She felt terrible when she heard Charlene crying her heart out, broken up over losing the hunter, the father of her unborn child, even if he had intended to murder both of them.

"What the hell happened?" Mack MacPherson asked. He was one of her brother, Daniel's friends, so he knew she'd always been honorable in her fights against rogue vampires.

She'd never expected to fight a hunter to the death.

Selena explained what had happened and Charlene finally gathered her composure to corroborate her story. Which was a good thing because if Cliff and his friends had been the only ones to witness the fight, she was certain their version would be a hell of a lot different from Selena and Charlene's. She realized then that Cliff had his sword out and he was giving her the evil eye.

He had looked up to his brother in all things, and she was afraid she would have to watch her back whenever he was around now.

"We'll have to take this to the League of Hunters Council now." Mack looked sympathetically at Selena, but with disdain at the vampiress, as if it was all her fault.

Charlene said, "I will speak on your behalf with the Council, Selena. Thank you for saving my life."

Two more hunters arrived, though Selena thought they had seen the action, but were just farther away than Mack and Donovan when she killed Fenimore.

"Take care of your brother," Mack said.

Then her brother came running to the scene of the fight. *Great.* Daniel looked at Fenimore lying on the pavement dead, and Selena's sword dripping with blood. He might not have seen the action, but he could put two and two together. She hadn't had time to process all of it—and realized she could even be put on a rogue hunter list—scheduled for termination, worst-case scenario, or be ostracized by the hunter community for killing a hunter instead of just letting the whole matter slide. In other words, allowing Fenimore to kill the vampiress and pretend none of it had ever happened.

Which she would never have done.

But now she had to face the League of Hunters Council, her parents, her disapproving brother, and who knew how her sister would feel about it. One little act of kindness had turned her world inside out.

CHAPTER 1

*S*ix weeks later, Portland, Oregon

Atreides, prince of the vampire clans on the west coast, had seen his brother, Daemon, and his mate, Tezra, off at the airport to go on a well-deserved vacation a week ago. He couldn't be more thrilled to be in full control of the clans instead of serving just as his brother's subleader. Daemon was even taking his bodyguard, Voltan, and Maison, his advisor, so they could also have a vacation. Atreides was in seventh heaven. As long as no other trouble presented itself, he would prove to his brother that he could be in charge and not screw things up. And then Daemon and his mate could take more trips away from home without any worries.

But what he couldn't believe was when a huntress showed up at Tamblyn's Dance Club—walking through the vampires who had been laughing, conversing, drinking and dancing prior to that. A hush fell over the whole crowd. Even the band stopped playing, everyone looking to Atreides to deal with the huntress.

No hunter entered a vampire club ever. Just like no vampire in his right mind would enter a hunter club. Most hunters and vampires stayed clear of human clubs too.

Was the huntress crazy? A rogue? She wasn't armed at least, which was good, or he would believe she was here to terminate a rogue vampire who might be on her terminal list. Atreides would not harbor a rogue vampire, but there was no way a hunter was coming into their club to kill one either.

He watched as she continued on her way to the bar, her chin held high, her gaze taking in a few of the vampires and blood bonds filling the place. He sat on his chair at a table where he waited for Iconia, his girlfriend, to show up, who was late, as usual. He waited to see what the huntress was up to, but if he had to remove her bodily from the club, he had no qualms about it.

* * *

As soon as Selena Towson entered the Portland, Oregon dance club, disco lights flashing over the dark room making everyone look surreal, she knew it was a mistake. Then again, if she knew how to do anything extraordinarily well of late it was making mistakes. Not that killing the hunter was a mistake, but it sure had cost her when it came to having any friends now within the hunter community.

Clueing her in right away that coming here was the wrong thing to do, she saw that everyone visible to her in the packed place turned to stare at her. As loud as the thunderous beat of the New Age music was, no one would have noticed her, unless they were vampires or hunters. But this *wasn't* a hunter club.

Fans circulated the air through the high-ceiling building and the scent of bloody cocktails drifted overhead. If that wasn't enough to convince her where she'd ended up, two of the women standing nearby bared their extended canines at her in a sinister taunt.

Selena's skin prickled as if thousands of stinging nettles had suddenly punctured it. Straightening her shoulders, she wouldn't give up now. Had she known the woman called Twilight meant to meet her at a vampire hangout, Selena would have insisted on going to another place. Hunters did not enter vampire establishments, nor did vampires violate hunters' space, not unless either intended violence. Just the hostile look from the vampiresses in the group was enough to prove at least one side was itching for battle.

Everyone wore black—satin, silks, taffetas, leather, the most dressed down—denim. Selena's silky creation stood out like a red rose among a bed of black roses full of thorns. She had dressed appropriately for a human's club!

Quashing the irritation that spiraled in her blood that she hadn't had enough foresight to ask her friend more about this meeting place earlier, Selena proceeded to the bar. She had assumed Twilight was a human—unless she was a blood bond who offered sustenance to vampires for the sexual intrigue. The woman ought to have known a hunter would never enter a vampires' lair unless he or she had no other choice. Well, Selena supposed she had no choice if she was to find her sister. This was the first lead she'd had.

Making her way through the crowd of men and women observing the dance floor, Selena felt every eye on her now. Faint unease skittered along her nerves—a necessary evil or she would be just as cold and heartless as a rogue vampire, who had long ago dispensed with any emotions. But she would not show how she felt in front of a bunch of vampires and their blood bonds. As much as she could fight it. She didn't have any control over her heart rate, or the tiny smattering of chill bumps that erupted on her skin.

Wishing she could read their telepathic communication, she guessed at what most of them were thinking. What was a huntress, who was trained to take down rogue vampires, doing in one of their clubs?

The thing of it was she wasn't like other hunters. Trained, yes. Always ready to take down a bloodsucker who was bad news—

yes. But she wouldn't always play by the League of Hunters' rules. Too much corruption and politics for her. She did it her way—and had been ex-communicated for the latest infraction again—after killing a hunter in self-defense and protecting a vampiress this time. The punishment meant that she couldn't legally carry a hunter's weapon or have a list of vampire rogues to take down.

She ignored that rule too. Not that she was armed at the moment. Her weapons were waiting for her back in the car because no club allowed weapons inside. But being a hunter without her sword was like being a surgeon without a scalpel. They were just tools of the trade. And if a rogue vampire tried to kill her, she wasn't going to let him just because she didn't have a list of rogues she was allowed to eliminate!

She was halfway surprised a bouncer in the club hadn't tossed her out on her ear already. But she suspected they were dying to know why she was here. Like...to take down one of them? That would be suicide.

"Huntress," a vampiress hissed at her through clenched teeth, her vampire canines fully extended.

Selena pitched a perfectly fake smile at the woman whose red curls were stacked high on her head, her green eyes crystalline daggers. Selena brushed past the vamp, bumping her aside, which prompted another hiss. Selena *wasn't* going to be intimidated.

Selena continued walking toward the bar with purpose and an air of ease, even though deep inside, her heart beat *way* too fast, while she continued to look for any sign that one of the blood bonds watching her might be Twilight.

If Selena located her sister, Rosa—who could do no wrong when it came to hunting renegade vampires—*maybe,* Selena wouldn't be so ostracized by her family. But Selena wasn't certain whether Rosa was in harm's way or if she was just being her usual inconsiderate self, letting everyone think she'd disappeared without a trace, not of her own free will. Since her sister had vanished three times in the past two months, then sheepishly returned home after a hunter tryst didn't work out, Selena shouldn't have been worried this time either.

But she was. The fact that Twilight, whoever or whatever she was, had passed on the note to Selena's friend that she knew something about Rosa's disappearance set Selena's nerves on edge. No one else bothered to look for her sister this time. Not her friends, family, associates, no one, because they all assumed Rosa was missing on purpose once again. Don't cry wolf came to mind.

"Huntress," another vampiress hissed, stepping in front of her, blocking her path. This one's hair was black as a darkened well, and her ebony eyes flickered with flame.

Thank God the males didn't seem to be annoyed with Selena's presence like the females did, but instead seemed highly intrigued. Which, come to think of it, could be a bad thing.

With determination, Selena steeled her back. She was here now, and she wasn't running away. How would that look? Like she was afraid of vampires. Which she was not.

She sidestepped the vampiress and was sure if she looked behind her, the woman's gaze would be boring into the back of Selena's head. The rest of the vampires moved out of her path as if she were the queen walking down the red carpet to her throne.

Sighing heavily, she was sure her human friend, Tara Green, had gotten her information wrong. Selena glanced around the crowd, looking at individual female faces, all eyes on her, no one saying a word, though they might have been telepathically communicating up a storm with one another. One of the women watching might be this Twilight person. Everyone seemed unduly interested in Selena, blood bonds and vampires alike, so she couldn't tell if any of them might be the woman. What if she had changed her mind and decided it was too dangerous to tell Selena the truth? At least, while she was among the vamps?

Tara probably hadn't even known this place was a vampire dance club. Then again, maybe a vampire had brainwashed her into luring Selena here. Which sent a trickle of dread down her spine. Was she being led into the vampire's lair for some dark purpose and this had nothing to do with locating her sister?

It wouldn't be the first time. And she was certain it wouldn't be the last. Vampires lived so long, they often needed a diversion in their lives to break up the monotony. Any huntress who hunted alone and by her own rules was fair game. Was that what she was? A mouse for the long-fanged cats to play with?

Glancing around the large building that seemed small because so many people were crammed in here, the fragrance of perfumes and colognes wafting in the air, she kept a watchful eye out for both someone who might be Twilight and any vampire threat that might occur. She wasn't sure what she would do if a vampire decided to attack her. Not when she was without weapons. She couldn't hope for anyone to come to her rescue if she began to fight one of the vampires. She could only hope that if she didn't provoke an attack, no one would initiate one either.

Surely, others would not permit a rogue's unprovoked attack against her here. Though several of the women looked like they were having a devil of time reining in their more primal instincts.

The notion a vampire might have put Tara up to bringing Selena here, put a new spin on the situation though. At once, the unease that she'd tried to contain while she flaunted herself in front of the club full of vampires began to take its toll. Her hands grew clammy and perspiration collected between her breasts. Her heartbeat quickened no matter that she tried to slow its pace by breathing in more deeply. The sound of the blood racing through her veins served as an enticement for ravenous vampires. So, she really needed to calm her frantic heart.

She took several deep breaths and when she reached the edge of the dance floor, she searched for the bar through the myriad of dancers. Desperately, she wanted to quit the place, but she couldn't. Not without appearing to be a coward. Hunters already looked down on her. She wasn't about to be treated the same way by a bunch of blood-drinking vamps.

Scanning the dance floor where men and women began to get back to the business of dancing, rubbing their bodies together in sexual bliss, Selena raised her brows. She'd never witnessed them dancing before. Not intending to show any interest but to get a drink, observe the crowd for as long as it took to finish her drink while waiting for a sign from Twilight, then vamoose, she couldn't tear her eyes away from the dancers. From one couple in particular—the man dressed in a black tux, his black hair curling to the edges of his white collar, while his fingers stroked the woman's breasts covered in a black silk dress—in front of everyone. The woman responded by slipping her leg between his legs and rubbing.

Selena had never seen anything so bold, so indecent in public, and so intriguing. She knew she should look away and concentrate on the whereabouts of the woman named Twilight.

Before she could shift her attention from the erotic dancers, Selena moved away from the dance floor and ran straight into a solid figure. Jerking her gaze from the dancers, she turned to see what immoveable, warm-bodied force she'd stumbled into. Her eyes caught the man's icy blue ones, which proceeded to darken to nearly black. His lips remained noncommittal, but his eyes held hers with such determination, she almost felt he could read her mind, or he thought he could control her. Neither of which vampires had the ability to do with hunters. She scoffed silently to herself. All vampires were totally conceited.

Mumbling an apology, she tried to go around him, but he blocked her path.

"Would you care to dance?" he asked, in a typical vampiric voice, deep, dark, and seductive.

Both males and females used the timbre of their voices to lure an intended blood bond to them. But Selena wasn't a normal human, and thankfully she couldn't be lured in that manner.

"Thank you, no." She managed to slip around him and headed for her intended destination. The bar. A drink. Another quick survey of the crowd. And an even quicker departure. Though she intended to make it look like she wasn't departing quickly because she was bothered by any of *them*.

Reaching the bar, she found all the stools had been taken. Not that it mattered. After she got her drink, she could slip closer to the door and leave as soon as she was done. If this Twilight woman wanted to approach her, maybe she would do so if Selena was nearer the exit and not quite so conspicuous. As if a huntress in a vampire club could be inconspicuous, she chastised herself.

Then again, maybe when she left the club, the woman would attempt to meet with her in the parking lot.

The music shifted to a slower tempo, but the erotic moves of the dancers couldn't get much more sexual without the dance partners stripping off their clothes and doing it on the floor. Sure she was experiencing an early hot flash after getting an eyeful, Selena leaned toward the bar and ordered a Tom Collins. The blond male seated next to her, slid off the barstool, gave Selena a wicked look, then floated away.

Still intending to get a drink and leave, Selena ignored the available seat.

"Sit," the man with the vivid blue eyes said. He motioned to the barstool. "I'm Basil. And you are?"

"Thirsty." She gave a small smile but didn't take the seat. She assumed now that Basil had telepathically told the blond guy to vacate the seat for Selena. Was he attempting to get her under his spell?

"I'm the owner of this dance club. I'm curious as to why you're here."

Ahhh, so he wanted to ensure she didn't cause trouble.

Most of the conversation in the club ceased and even the music piped down. As long as the club owner didn't force the issue, she didn't intend to explain her business and risk losing her contact. But everyone seemed to want to know just how she would respond.

The bartender reached across the counter and slid the drink to Selena.

She handed him a ten-dollar bill, but Basil shook his head. "Drink's on me."

"Thanks." But she didn't mean it.

The guy made her uneasy, although she knew why he had targeted her. For his patrons' peace of mind, she was certain he was determined to learn if she had come here looking for a vampire on her terminal list. Except he wouldn't know she didn't have a terminal list...for now. They were handed out only by the League, and she was on their no-hunt list. Still, it was nobody's business that she was a huntress without backing from the League. The vampires would look upon her with as much disdain as her own kind did. Some might even test her resolve not to take them on.

But she had no trouble with fighting rogue vampires. Or renegade hunters, for that matter. Even if the League said it wasn't fully convinced the hunter she had killed had been a rogue. Yet, she knew differently, or they would have terminated her for killing the hunter.

Her mind still mulling over her choices, she watched the dancers and listened to the beat and rhythm of the music stirring up the heat. Against her express permission, she moved slightly to the music, then caught sight of a couple of blood bonds whispering to each other while their gazes remained glued on her.

She frowned. Even most humans, if they knew the truth about her, wouldn't have anything to do with her. After all, what good was a huntress who couldn't terminate vampires legally if the humans needed protection? At least that's what she'd heard a few say.

As much good as a dentist who wouldn't take care of someone's bad teeth, or a lifeguard who wouldn't save a swimmer in distress.

Tara Green was the exception. For whatever reason, the human liked her.

Basil, the club owner, lingered near her as if he was a bouncer, waiting for her to reveal wrist daggers or pull out a sword from her silky dress, then he would toss her out of the building. Did he think she had a death wish? And heck, couldn't he see she was totally unarmed? Nowhere to hide anything in this clingy creation. Besides, that was one rule she didn't violate—the no-weapons-in-a-club rule. Drinking and weapons could be a dangerous—and deadly—combination.

It was bad enough that vampires carried their own weapons intact.

Once she realized this was a vampires' place of entertainment, she really wouldn't have been that stupid to walk in armed to the teeth anyway.

Coming here had to have made her more of an enigma in the vampires' eyes. Any hunters who were different should be warily watched. Who knew what crazy things a person who wasn't like the others might do?

Before she could take a sip from her drink, she noticed a man sitting at a table observing her. Not that most weren't already, but something about him caught her attention.

Maybe it was his dark brown eyes the color of Brazil nuts narrowed in dissatisfaction, bordering on contempt, or the way his body language shouted at her to go away, or the way his umber hair was cut short, making him look roguish in appearance when all the other vampire males wore theirs pulled back in tails and looked much more vampirish. Not only that, but when most of the males were a bit dressed down compared to the women who were dressed to the nines, the vampire was dressed in a tux, like the one who had been dancing with the vamp. She was…impressed.

Though somewhere in the crowd she'd seen a guy who looked like a cowboy—one of the bad guys all dressed in black—that had caught her eye also.

"Who are you searching for?" Basil asked, as if he were her friend and wished to help.

"I came for a drink," Selena said, sliding a look at him.

"Yet, you are not drinking it." His mouth turned up slightly. This time his eyes sparkled with mirth.

He was right. She tried to raise the glass to her lips, but she couldn't. What if the drink was laced with something that would make her pass out? Make her more vulnerable than she already was in a dance club full of vampires, any of whom could possibly be renegades? Any one of them who might think he was on her terminal list?

"The drink is safe," Basil said, as if reading her mind.

But she knew he couldn't. Her hesitation at drinking it was what clued him in.

Human males were so unobservant, she had concluded early on. But vampiric males and hunters had the same intuitiveness that nearly all females had, whatever their kind.

She was not afraid. Trying to keep her hand from trembling, she lifted the glass to her lips, but the man with the dark brown eyes and the short-cropped hair suddenly appeared beside her and bumped against her arm. Before she could stop herself, she dropped the glass on the floor, shattering it into a hundred pieces and quashed the swear word that rose to her lips.

"You will leave here, huntress," the man whispered harshly into her ear, his hand grasping her arm in a decisive grip. "And never return."

Having been thrown out of so many hunter establishments over the years because of constantly being on the outs with the League, she wasn't surprised to be treated similarly here. Well, especially here.

She raised her chin and gave him a slight smile. "Apology accepted."

His eyes widened slightly, and for an instant, his threatening posture dissolved.

Seeing his surprise, she couldn't help that her smile broadened. As a kid, she'd learned to deal with other hunters who treated her meanly, just by doing the opposite of what they expected. It threw them off-guard. It seemed the trick worked on vampires too. Glancing at Basil, she found him glowering at the other man, but she assumed whoever the roguish-looking guy was, his spilling her drink saved her from some kind of trouble.

Yet, defiance stirred deep inside her, and she would not be bullied into a hasty retreat.

"Wanna dance?" she asked the man she assumed had saved her butt.

For an instant, he stared at her with a modicum of disbelief, but then the condemning look returned. "You would not do the moves justice." Yet despite his harsh words, he took her arm and led her to the floor.

CHAPTER 2

*W*hen the vampire took Selena to the dance floor —*led* would not be quite the way to describe it, more like he practically lifted her off her feet to get her there— his action surprised the hell out of her. She'd expected him to sneer at her, then move away. And when he didn't, a strange quiver of intrigue raced through her blood when his fingers held her arm tightly in his grasp.

Did he think she would change her mind? She wanted to. She'd been a fool to enter the dance club once she'd figured out who the clientele was despite wanting to meet Twilight.

Walking onto the parquet floor, the colorful strobe lights shining greens, blues, yellows, and reds dancing across its surface, she felt her nerves tingle with apprehension. The notion had flitted across her brain that if she had to do this, she'd expected other dancers—as crowded as the floor was—to hide the two of them from view. Not that she couldn't dance. But dancing like some of the others had? And with a vampire? No way.

She reminded herself the vampires had probably been with their mates, and this one wouldn't expect her to dance in that manner with him. She didn't care one whit whether she had any of a vampiress's exotic moves or not. She would not back down.

Everyone cleared the floor as if they were specters fading into the mist—or in this case, the dark building where colorful lights flashed all over them, the dance floor, Selena, and her dance partner.

She was left standing in the middle with tall, dark, and vampiric, and no matter her bravado, she wanted to melt into the parquet. Even the music had stopped, and she felt her lioness heart shrivel into a mouse's as the whole building was cloaked in absolute silence.

The man's mouth turned up slightly at the corners, but the humor did not reach his darkened eyes. She knew then he laughed at her, as much as everyone else did. But when she glanced at the others, vampires and blood bonds alike, she didn't see a smirk among them, just intrigue, anticipation, wonderment. Well, except for the vampiresses. She saw a lot of rabidly, venomous looks from them, and she was certain they were barely keeping their fangs hidden.

She wished she wouldn't disappoint her admirers, but unless she was sloppily drunk, no way could she rub herself against a man, a vampire on top of it, in some base, seductive dance in front of a club full of onlookers. Killing rogue vampires was tons easier.

Taking a deep breath, she figured she might as well introduce herself and get it over with. "I'm Selena."

"Atreides." He bowed his head, then turned to the band.

Several of the band members smiled, their gazes shifting from Atreides to Selena.

She was in trouble now.

The music played just as seductively slow as when she'd first entered the club, the mood enticing lovers to bare all. She tentatively touched Atreides's waist with her hand and reached for his with her other in a formal distant way, but he pulled her hard against his body.

She gasped and instantly the temperature in the room elevated to sauna level—or at least her body heat had.

Murmurs filled the club, but she couldn't make out what was being said. Probably that the huntress was out of her element, and her boldness served her right. Which about now, she totally agreed with.

Atreides gripped her hand, keeping her tight against his body, then moved his leg between hers, and that was the last thought she had about how others viewed her. His free hand roamed down her back, sliding the red silk against her skin, slipping lower until he caressed her buttocks. She should have kept her huntress calm, but she lost whatever huntress sensibility she'd been born with and melted against the rogue's caresses. She knew he had to be a rogue to want to seduce a huntress. Or maybe he didn't want to seduce her but was just toying with her for being so brash to enter his world.

Determined to show him she could do this too, as much as it went against everything she was, she leaned against his thigh and gave a tentative rub. It would have been much more effective if she hadn't been trembling when she did it.

The vampire's eyes blazed with heat, and his neck muscles tightened. She swore a low growl rumbled in his throat. It was then that she felt his arousal hard against her hip. She barely noticed that he was moving her along the floor at a snail's pace. Her every sense was attuned to the way his hand cupped her buttock, the way his thigh lifted higher, connecting with her damp mound, and his smoky eyes devoured her with ardent attention. He might not like her at all, but he was definitely lusting after her.

Closing her eyes, she savored the erotic feeling and pretended she was on another planet, that her misbehavior was perfectly acceptable there, and that the man who had freed her from her earthbound world was her lover.

She tossed her head back and laughed.

The other hunters were right. She was insane and needed to be locked away for everyone's good. But not until *after* she'd had her dance with the hot vampire.

* * *

ATREIDES WOULD SHOW the woman how wrong she was to have entered the vampire's lair. He truly didn't think Basil had ordered the bartender to lace her drink with drugs, but he couldn't be certain. However, if it made the huntress wise up that she risked her life by coming into the place, spilling her drink was well worth the effort.

Who knew if any of Tamblyn Dance Club's patrons might be renegades? Any of them might be on the huntress's target list, and any would be ready to fight her if she made a move to take him or her down. Hunters were as arrogant as the vampires, though this one was more so if she thought to come to a vampire club and leave unscathed.

What Atreides hadn't expected was her offer of a dance. Did she think getting in thick with the vampires who weren't rogues would give her a way to locate those who were?

He grunted under his breath. It was the hunters' jobs to locate and terminate the renegades. They got paid for it, not the vampires.

But the feel of her soft buttocks and the way she moved against his hard body enticed him to want more, made him forget what she'd come here for, made him forget his own mission. Or that she was a huntress.

Hell, all evening he'd declined every offer from vampiresses to blood bonds alike to dance when Iconia was so late coming to the club, so why had he accepted the huntress's offer? To show her that she could not dance like the women here, that she didn't belong, and she should give up whatever game she was playing?

He released her hand and planted his free hand on her other buttock, lifting her higher against his thigh. God, she felt good, yet he tried to concentrate on his reasoning for dancing with her. To scare her off.

Yet some dark part of him remained intrigued. She'd offered herself to him like a blood sacrifice, yet if he moved in that direction, he was certain she would have wished she was armed. No huntress had ever offered to dance with a vampire in the club. Hell, none of the hunter kind would be so forthright as to walk into a vampire's dance lair. Something deep inside him wanted to experience the sensation. Not that he thought she would live up to the way his usual partners danced. However, Iconia was late, and what the hell, he was always looking for some new diversion in his life. After having lived so long, life did get dull at times.

He could barely move on the floor he was so enraptured with the feel of the huntress, the way her jasmine fragrance tantalized him, the whisper of her breath against his neck, the racing beat of her heart that sent his senses reeling. All her soft curves pressed against him, molding to him, making him all the harder. He fought the insane urge to taste the huntress's blood. He hated the hunter kind, he vehemently rebuked himself.

Many hunters loved their job too much when terminating rogues. Some killed vampires who weren't even killers. And then the hunters had to eliminate their own kind. But sometimes the hunters got away with the deed, the murder covered up, or explained as an accidental killing. Vampires who were on the right side of the law tolerated the hunters, but that was about it.

Although he had to admit, he did feel a brotherly affection for his brother's mate, a huntress turned vampire, and her younger sister. But she and her sister were exceptions to the rule.

Most of the telepathic communication between the vampires had stopped because they were so intrigued that he would accept a dance with the huntress. Iconia was not happy. He'd seen her enter the club right after he'd taken the huntress to the floor, and she was glowering at the both of them at the edge of the dance stage. The vampiress would have words with him later, which might help to spark their dreary relationship of late.

The huntress leaned into him, pressing her soft body against his hard one, rubbing her mound against his thigh, and he nearly lost it. She had no business using her feminine wiles to attempt to ensnare him. He'd meant to scare the huntress off with his erotic moves. Normally a good judge of character, he hadn't believed she would have the fortitude to dance like this. What else had he mistakenly misjudged about the woman?

Instinctively, he knew she had to leave before she became a rogue's target. But part of him wished to know why she'd come here. He refused to get sucked into caring. Getting rid of her remained his priority.

If she'd been Iconia and heated him the way the huntress had, he would have left the club and finished the dance moves in private. Still, he couldn't rid himself of the elicit thoughts of taking the huntress away from here and showing her some new moves to see if she was as willing to play the game further. Which was downright madness. He despised the hunter kind, every last one of them, except for Tezra and Katie, he reminded himself.

"Why are you here, huntress?" He meant to sound forceful, gruff, but his voice sounded husky and drenched with lust, which irritated him all the more.

She looked up at him with eyes as luring as green emeralds sparkling in the sun and she smiled in a not-so-innocent way. "I asked you to dance and you accepted."

Yeah, but she wasn't supposed to react the way she had, nor was she to feel this provocative.

He wanted to talk some sense into her and warn her to stay away again for her own good, but when she reached around his back and clutched at his butt, his arousal jumped.

Hell, woman, he seethed. He had no intention of allowing a huntress to turn his body into a raging fire. With every stroke of her hands on his chest and ass, she was turning the heat up higher.

Brushing his lips against her bare shoulder, her skin satiny, begging for his ministration, he felt his bloodlust rising. In a hundred years, he hadn't felt such desire, such an uncontrollable thirst. The huntress shivered when his tongue licked at her throat, spurring him on. Sensing everyone in the club waited for him to lose control, to take the hauntingly seductive creature for his own, Atreides bit back on his natural inclination. His brother, Daemon, who was in charge of the vampires in this region, would have had a conniption if he'd seen Atreides dancing with the woman like this.

Atreides glanced in the direction of the band, knowing damn well the song should have ended several minutes before this. The band leader bowed his head with a devilish glint in his gray eyes, but the music played on. The huntress tilted her chin up and gazed into Atreides's eyes. If he hadn't known better, he might have thought she *had* been drugged. Every one of her actions, the innocent, sweet lure of a huntress, beseeched him to take his fill.

"Thank you for saving me," she said breathlessly.

Her silky voice entranced him, held him hostage.

Saved her? For an instant, his hand stilled on her breast, the soft mound begging for his touch, the nipple peaked and straining against her silky red dress. Red, the color of fire and burning straight through him all the way to the core.

"Thank you for knocking the drink out of my hand," she said, her full red lips turned up just a hint. Lips that tasted as sinful as they looked, no doubt.

He preferred blonds to brunettes, he reminded himself. And vampiresses, never a huntress, not even a human. He'd seen his brother agonizing over a human who didn't wish to be turned. And then Daemon found himself falling for a borderline rogue huntress. No one in their right mind messed with a huntress, normally. Vampiresses on the other hand were willing and available. A much more suitable match.

In truth, this woman appealed not in the least.

The huntress pressed against his groin again, and he groaned. Okay, so she slightly appealed, at least to that male part of the equation that stood up and took notice.

Her dark curls drifted over bare shoulders in an avalanche of silky tresses, and her floral fragrance tempted him, but that's all that interested him. Well, and the way she fit so snugly against his body and tilted her head up to face him, her expressive eyes locked on to his like a vampire's gaze would try to mesmerize a blood bond.

He dipped her back, wanting to feel her pressed tight against his rigid cock, to see if she would expose her throat willingly to him. And she did. Arched her back, exposing her sensual throat, her hair falling away from her shoulders, so vulnerable, so enticing, the vein in her neck calling to him, begging to him to take a taste. He dipped his face to her throat, licked his lips, took in the heat of her skin, the fragrance, listened to the drum of her heart, the rush of blood through her veins.

Grinding his teeth to keep his canines from unsheathing, he turned his head and telepathically snapped at the bandmaster, *"Enough!"* It would not have been chivalrous to end a dance before the music was finished, but he would have no more of the bandmaster's wry sense of humor. Atreides was not here to entertain the masses. And he didn't want to fight the bloodlust escalating in his system any longer.

The music wrapped up, and in the ensuing silence, everyone waited to see what Atreides would do now. The huntress still clung to him, every inch of her naked skin covered in perspiration, the softness of her form pressed against him. He knew what he had to do. Force the huntress to leave the place, never to return. But she'd stirred his blood and sexual lust beyond reasonable levels, dictating him to choose another course—take her home and prove to her how vulnerable a huntress could be who dared play with them.

With as much dignity as he could muster, he released her and bowed his head. "You dance better than I thought your kind would." He meant to sound cruel, daunting, but his voice was drenched with arousal.

He thought she would frown and give him a smart ass reply like most any huntress might with his goading, but instead, her teeth shown in a sparkling grin. "Why thank you. I thought you danced well also. Want to do it again?"

Before he could hide his surprise or say hell no, Iconia shoved the vampires in her path out of her way.

"Get lost," she said to the huntress, her voice dripping with poison, low and menacing, "if you know what's good for you."

The black gown she wore wasn't half as appealing as the red dress the huntress wore, now that he could compare the two. And the huntress's coloring made her stand out more, while he thought Iconia looked a bit washed out tonight, her blond hair paler, not as thick, or long, or seductive.

Ignoring the vampiress, the huntress waited for Atreides's word on the matter, which amused him. "Another time, perhaps," he said with as much aplomb as he could manage. Although, he had no intention of ever touching the seductive woman again.

Selena gave him another brilliant smile, then nodded. "All right. I'll take a rain check."

She couldn't have been serious.

Then she turned and waited for the vampires to move out of her path.

"A dance?" Basil asked her again, when the crowd parted, and she stood face to face with the owner of the club.

"Thank you, no," she said again.

Which for some reason pleased Atreides when it shouldn't have mattered in the least. But he couldn't help but wonder why she had danced with him, and no other. Then again—he *had* saved her. He snorted. *Right*. Basil would have a word with him next about breaking the lady's glass and implying he had drugged it. They had been friends for too many years that Basil wouldn't wonder what was up.

The huntress made her way to the exit like a queen among her courtiers while Atreides, like everyone else, watched her disappear into the dark.

An unbidden feeling swept through him—like the effervescent bubbles in a glass of champagne suddenly vanished and left a flat, lifeless form in its place. Both anxiety for the huntress's safety and the lingering arousal she'd left him in, compelled Atreides to follow her. He doubted anyone here worried about her safety like he did. Which didn't make any sense as much as he hated hunters. But she wasn't armed for one thing, like her kind would be, and she'd stirred up a hell of a lot of vampiric interest on the dance floor that he was certain she couldn't deflect if she was forced to outside.

"Maybe I should see her safely to her car," Iconia said with a hint of malice.

Atreides saw the venom in the vampiress's blue eyes and seized her wrist. "We'll dance."

But when two of his friends exited the dance club right after the huntress left, Atreides forgot all about the vampiress he held stiffly in his arms. What the hell were Renault and Colt up to?

He had no reason for concern, he told himself. But he released Iconia so suddenly, she stumbled backward, and he headed for the door anyway. The music instantly stopped, and the telepathic communication began again.

"Atreides is not so immune to the huntress as he attempts to pretend," a vampire Atreides didn't recognize said.

"Can you blame him? If she'd been grinding against my body like she did his, she'd have been with me in my pad next," another male said.

Atreides had no intention of taking the huntress to his home. He merely wished to see her safely to her car and on her way with one last warning to stay away. But when he exited the dance club and heard Renault and Colt badgering the huntress somewhere in the dark near the edge of the parking lot, his teeth instantly extended.

Like a raging bull, Atreides charged into battle.

CHAPTER 3

*S*elena wasn't as much worried about the two vampires attempting to seduce her as the eerie feeling someone watched her hidden somewhere in the trees flanking the parking lot on the misty night. Was it Twilight?

Not one of the blood bonds had approached her in the dance club, and she still wondered if her friend, Tara, had gotten the information wrong. But if it was Twilight, Selena needed to rid herself of these men—who were not making it easy—so she could speak to the woman alone.

"Are you sure, darlin', that ya don't want to go with me?" the grizzly bear of a man asked, his blond hair tied back, his blue eyes expressive.

He wore black denims, though the rest of his outfit was more like something from the old west: a satin vest, a black shirt, a red neckerchief, and cowboy boots. She imagined he thought he was a cowboy without his horse. After giving it another thought, she realized he might have been a real cowboy in the old west. Woe to the horse who had to carry such a big man.

The other vampire was tall and lean, darker hair and eyes. He dipped his head and gave her an uplifting smile. Dressed in classy formal black attire, he was much suaver. "The lady would prefer a gentleman rather than a bowlegged—"

"Renault, you uptight, French milksop!"

"Or maybe the lady would like to share?" Renault said. A brow rose while he waited for her response.

"I was..." She almost mentioned Twilight, but then thought better of it.

"Yes?" Renault asked, his interest piqued.

The other man looked just as intrigued. She figured if she told them what she was doing here, they would inform the rest of the vampires at once and make points for themselves. But what if one of these guys, or someone they talked to, really did have something to do with her sister's disappearance? What if someone tried to silence Twilight?

Normally, Selena wasn't that suspicious of people. Then again, she didn't have a lot of experience dealing with vampires either socially or otherwise. They were the stuff of legends—able to control mere mortals with their vampiric charms and though they couldn't control her, as far as she knew, she didn't want to prove herself wrong.

She shook her head.

Renault reached for her arm, but before she could push him aside, Atreides swooped in for the kill, his wicked canines bared. Startled out of her skin at his deadly intervention, Selena screamed.

* * *

TACKLING RENAULT with as much force as he could muster, Atreides knocked him to the asphalt. Colt bellowed with laughter.

Finally getting over the shock of Atreides's forcing him to the ground, Renault cursed out loud. "What the hell do you think you're doing?"

A car door slammed, then an engine roared to life.

Leaping to his feet, Atreides watched the cherry red Firebird speed away. Part of him was relieved to see the huntress tuck tail and run. But the other part, he couldn't account for as his blood still coursed through him like a raging river, his anger smoldering beneath the surface.

Renault rose from the pavement and brushed his clothes off. "I never would have wagered your interest in a huntress, Atreides," he said darkly, though a glint of humor touched his serious expression.

Colt snorted. "She's fair game comin' here like she did, wearin' that blood red, silky dress, stirrin' us up. There wasn't a vampire in the joint who didn't want her."

That's what had concerned Atreides, though he told himself he shouldn't have cared. If she was witless enough to enter the lion's den, it served her right. Yet, her vulnerability touched him somewhere deep inside in the place he attempted to hide his darkest feelings. The same innocent susceptibility reminded him of his cousin, whom he'd felt brotherly toward, when she had lived. But then again, he didn't feel in any way brotherly toward this woman.

"Who's she after?" Renault asked. "Did she tell you?"

How the hell would Atreides know? From the beginning, the woman was a puzzle.

"She came to the wrong place." Atreides gave his friends a hard look. "Being a huntress, she was too proud to admit it. Anyone could have seen from the expression on her face when she first walked into the club that she *hadn't* realized it was one of our hangouts to begin with."

Colt shook his head. "I'll buy that she might have ordered the drink, but dancing with you?" He cocked a brow.

"She was grateful."

"Did Basil lace her drink with drugs?" Renault asked.

"*No*, Basil did *not*," the owner of the club said, joining them.

"What the hell was that all about? In the over one-hundred years I've been running this establishment, even in the days of the speakeasies, not once has a hunter so boldly walked into the place."

"She got lost," Renault said and gave Atreides a half smile.

Basil cast a questioning look at Atreides, who shrugged in return. "I have no idea why she came here. Your guess is as good as mine. Though I still suspect she thought it was just a human dance club."

Basil didn't look like he believed it any more than Atreides did. "And why would she go to a human club? Hunters notoriously stick with their own kind."

Atreides rubbed his chin and considered the notion further. Basil was right. If she was in the mood for dancing, she would have found a hunter club to go to. And she would more than likely know where they were and not have mistaken this one for one of her own. Unless she was new to the area.

His brows pinched in a frown, Basil looked more than a bit perturbed. "Why the hell did she dance with you?"

"He saved her," Renault shared with a smirk, "from the drugs you laced her drink with."

Basil shook his head and glanced at the club. "I don't have to drug my women."

"You think this one could be your woman? Atreides has already claimed her for his own." Renault brushed at his skinned-up satin shirt sleeve, looking somewhat miffed.

"Hell, looked to me like the huntress claimed Atreides. You sure you're not on her terminal list?" Colt smugly asked.

Everyone judged Atreides's reaction.

No, Atreides didn't believe so. "She danced with me, even offered to do so again. Hunters don't dance with their intended victims, as far as I know."

"She wanted another dance with you?" Renault whistled.

"What in the world did you do to attract such a hot-blooded huntress?"

"He saved her," Colt reminded him. "Women like that sort of thing. A knight rescuing a fair damsel in distress, though I wasn't around quite that early. My greatest adventure was saving a young girl from rustlers in the Texas Panhandle."

"Yeah, yeah, she was five years old and too young to keep for your own." Renault gave him a wink. "But this one, she's definitely the right age."

"Huntresses are better left alone," Atreides warned.

"Especially this one, eh, Atreides?" Renault's mouth rose in a grin.

"I guess Iconia put a bit of a damper on your blossoming relationship with your new girlfriend," Basil said.

"Good thing, too. I don't think any of us could have lasted if we'd seen the two of them dance again." Renault fanned himself.

"It wasn't any more risqué than what anyone else was dancing," Atreides countered, though he'd meant to keep his temper corralled and his mouth shut, not flame his friends' speculation further.

Colt slapped him on the back. "Right, old man. Like every afternoon we have a chance at a huntress like her. Hell, as long as most of us have lived, finding something unique to do is the name of the game. And watching a huntress dancing with one of our own kind is definitely damned different."

Something moved near the edge of the woods and all four men turned to look. Atreides made out the human host half hiding behind an oak. The impish woman was a dance club addict, and if she wasn't here, she could be found at any other dance club in the city any time of the day or night. He suspected a vampire was keeping her, or she would have to have a job to earn her way.

"Twilight?" Atreides called out. "What the hell are you doing skulking around in the dark?"

* * *

SELENA HAD NEVER BEEN in this area before and in her haste to leave the vampire fight behind, she'd taken the wrong road, she thought. Her cell phone wasn't working. Sometimes nearby vampire telepathic communications, if there were a lot of them going on at once, could mess with cell phone reception.

With her overhead light on as she drove down the dark road, she tried to read her scrawled script map and watch the road when her car hit something with a thump. Her heart nearly stopped, and she slammed on the brakes. She yanked the car onto the narrow shoulder of the deserted road.

Peering through the rearview mirror, she couldn't see anything in the dark. What if it was a person? A dog? Maybe just a bit of rough road. But from the way the car had thudded against something, she was certain it was more than just a bump in the road.

If it was a wounded animal, it could be dangerous. But she couldn't leave someone's beloved pet injured on the road. Or an injured person behind.

With resolve, she opened the car door. The security warning dinged, reminding her she'd left the keys in the ignition. Grabbing her sword, she left the door open to afford her a little more light, then walked along the road in the dark, searching for whatever she'd hit. She saw nothing. She peered into the tall grass bending in the breeze on the shoulder on the right side of the road, looking to see if the body had been thrown off the pavement. But she didn't see anything.

"Hello?" she said, feeling rather foolish. But if someone was hurt and could respond to her voice...

Her heels clicked on the asphalt while the warm, misty Oregon breeze plastered her dress against her body, even at this late hour. The wind whipped through the pine trees a few yards back from the road. A pale half-moon hung against the black velvet night and cicadas sung their noisy music all around her. Otherwise, she heard nothing—no sound like a wounded animal or person. Nothing at all.

Her skin prickled with apprehension. This had been a night of mistakes. But she saw nothing amiss, dismissing what she'd thought she'd hit as just a bad bump in the road that wasn't visible to her in the dark. She turned to head back to her car.

And gasped. In the glaring red taillights of the car stood a large gray dog. No, not a dog, a wolf. Or a wolfdog that was mostly wolf.

Its amber eyes watched her with a cold, calculating, predatory stare. The fur on its back rose. His mouth hung agape as he panted, his teeth exposed, but he didn't move away from the car. Had she hit him? Stunned him for a moment?

She stood very still and tried to calm her racing heart. Unless someone owned a wolf or wolfdog in these parts, which might be true, and the beast had gotten loose, there was yet another explanation that could be just as viable. And lots more dangerous —for her.

It wasn't a wolf at all, but a shape-shifting vampire. Or maybe a wild wolf. Some had been spotted in various locations in Oregon.

If it was a vampire, had he—or she—come from the club? Although as big as the wolf was, she assumed it was a male.

One of the two men outside of the club who had tried to talk her into going with them maybe? Or someone else who had been intrigued with her dance? Even Atreides, who had warned her to stay away?

If it was a real wolf and she ran, it could pounce on her and kill her quickly if it was starving. Then again, wolves didn't normally attack people. If it was a rogue vampire, and he meant to eliminate her, she would have a real fight on her hands. Particularly, if he was an ancient. They had lived so many years, often two hunters would team up to take one down.

"Hello," she said.

The wolf tilted its head to the side a little.

Maybe it *was* someone's pet after all. She'd always been able to befriend animals.

She took a step toward it. His fur stood on end, making him appear even bigger. His eyes kept contact with hers, an alpha male, challenging her, but he didn't move one way or another. By keeping her eyes on his, she was challenging him right back, when she knew to look away or chance incurring a fight. He clamped his mouth shut as if she'd surprised him, but she noticed now his tail stood like a pike straight out from its body. Stiff and on edge, he was ready to react quickly.

Yet, she had no other choice. She couldn't abandon her car and try to walk home. Hell, on top of everything else, she was sure she was lost. What a disaster this night had been.

She took another step toward the car, swinging her sword at it, trying to make the wolf run away. The wolf's jaw dropped open, and he gave a low throaty growl, his wicked canines bared. The growl was a warning, and heeding it, she stopped. She really, really didn't want to kill a wolf, if she could even manage.

Okay, damn it, she was probably only three or four miles from the dance club. Or five or six. She wasn't certain how far she'd gone in her haste. Maybe Atreides, since he had wanted her to stay away from the club and since he had not propositioned her outside but had instead rescued her, maybe he could help get rid of the beast guarding her car.

Unless Atreides was already gone. Which meant she might have to fight off the other vampires' attentions again. Only this time she wouldn't have a car to flee in—if anyone would even entertain the notion of helping her.

In a last-ditch effort to take matters in her own hands, she tucked her sword under her arm, clapped her hands together, and yelled, "Hah! Get out of here! Bad dog! Well, bad wolf! Hah! Go home!"

The great gray beast merely stood its ground.

Great, just great! Grabbing her sword, she swung around and headed down the dark road, hoping that no one would find her car sitting idly, the keys in the ignition, the engine turned off, but the door wide open, beckoning, "Take me, please!" She could just envision explaining to her insurance agent what had happened.

Hopefully, no one would miss seeing her on the dark road—should someone happen to drive by—and run her over because she wasn't visible enough.

She glanced over her shoulder and glowered at the beast. He hadn't moved an inch. "Bad wolf!" she tossed back and stomped in her wobbly heels along the dark road that grew darker as the car grew smaller in the distance.

Before it was out of sight, she looked back one more time. The wolf still stood guarding her car. The headlights reflected off the mist, making him appear eerily ghostly from this distance. Letting her breath out in a huff, she stormed in the direction she thought she'd left the club behind.

With the way her luck was going, the club wouldn't be there when she got back.

CHAPTER 4

*I*n the parking lot of the popular century-old vampire club, Atreides asked again, "Twilight, what are you doing out here?" Though he suspected she was meeting with a vampire, who didn't wish his mate to know he was having a fling with the human host.

She shrugged. "I was about to enter the club when I saw the huntress heading for her car and Renault and Colt hassling her. I just wondered if they..." She smiled. "She needed my help."

Atreides knew the woman would have aided the vampires and not the huntress, as much as she wanted to be accepted by them. She looked like a Goth from the black clothes she wore, to the body piercings and the ebony eye and lip makeup. But as much as she wanted to be like the vampires—even having dental work to add vampire-sized fangs—she was afraid to become one of them. She loved having them feed off her, but she didn't have the stomach to do the feeding.

Though Atreides knew that would change once she was turned, but Twilight had never wanted to go that far.

"So, who is she and what did she want?" Twilight looped her

arm through Atreides's while he and the other men returned to the club.

"Do you have another question? She's a huntress. That's all I know."

"I'm surprised Basil didn't throw her out of the club."

Basil turned and lifted a brow. "The most intriguing creature we've had here in ages and definitely the most entertaining? Not on your life."

When they entered the club, Twilight giggled. "Looks like Iconia's mad at you, Atreides. She's dancing with—"

"I see." Atreides bit back a swear word. Of all the vampires she had to hook up with tonight, did it have to be Ragnar? Dating back to the Viking raiders, the man was still little more than a beast. The blue-eyed, blond Norwegian caught Atreides's eye and smirked.

Atreides bowed his head and noticed several watched to see his reaction. The Norseman would not provoke him this evening. Atreides motioned to Colt, Renault, and Basil. "A word."

The four men entered a private lounge area furnished in black leather couches. Basil locked the door, then proceeded to serve the men wine. "What have you learned about this group of rogue hunters, Atreides?"

"That the League of Hunters denies such a group exists. The League insists that the vampire killings were warranted."

Colt cursed. "They killed four of our women who were no more rogue than any of us are."

Atreides curled his hands into fists. "I couldn't agree more. That's why we're taking it into our own hands this time. The League be damned."

"And your brother?" Renault asked. "Surely, Daemon won't permit us to do anything about this outrage until he returns. He doesn't want to cause a riff between us and the hunters."

Atreides scoffed. "He is busy with his huntress." He shrugged.

"While they are away, I'm in charge. By the time he returns, all will be resolved."

Renault's lips turned up slightly. "Many years have passed since you were in command of our battle strategies, Atreides. What's the plan?"

"Five hunters are involved. But we need a lure."

Colt leaned his bulky figure forward. "I'll be it."

Atreides shook his head. "Something sweeter."

Colt looked at Renault and smiled while Renault scowled back at him.

"You mentioned a huntress before," Basil offered.

"Yes, a huntress. She'll be working with our vampiresses, ready to defend them. Of course the vampiresses will warn us. When the men come, they will have us to face, not our vampiresses, who are too weak to fight the hunters' combined strength. Let them take someone on who is matched in strength and see how superior they are then."

"And the huntress?" Basil asked.

"She will fight alongside us, to corroborate that we had just cause. I've already located the right one." At least Atreides hoped. If so, he and his brethren could stop the rogue hunters before any more of his kind's blood could be shed.

* * *

FOR ANOTHER HOUR, they discussed plans, but when Atreides heard Iconia screech in the area of the dance floor, he threw open the door to the lounge and hurried to protect her from the Viking brute, Ragnar.

The music had stopped, and everyone was gathered around Iconia so that he couldn't even see her or what was happening.

"She has returned," one of the vampires telepathically said.

As soon as Atreides and the others entered the dance floor

and he could see what the matter was, his jaw dropped. Iconia was dressing down the huntress, Selena, who glared back at her with contempt, a sword clutched in her fist, the tip resting on the floor.

The huntress said in a high tone of voice—though she needn't have as the place was deadly quiet and their hearing enhanced, "I have to see Atreides."

Iconia hissed and grabbed for the huntress's throat.

The huntress's eyes flashed hot, but she didn't raise her sword, and in fact, she looked as though she could barely hold onto it.

"Hold!" Atreides shouted and jerked Iconia's hand from the huntress's neck. Grabbing Selena's wrist, he stalked back to the lounge, though she stumbled after him in her high heels, and he thought he was going to have to carry her. Hell, did the huntress have even more of a death wish than he had first suspected?

Renault winked at him. Colt grinned. Basil swore under his breath and shook his head. Telepathic communication buzzed so thickly, Atreides could only imagine what the frenzy of vampire voices were saying.

He shut the lounge door and then released her. "Didn't I tell you to stay away from here? What the hell are you doing bringing a hunter's sword in here? Are you suicidal?"

He noticed then that she looked like she'd had a good tumble the way her cheeks were flushed, and her hair tangled, hanging loosely around her face. The color in her cheeks quickly receded, and she looked hauntingly pale.

"Why are you here?" he amended, trying to calm his rage. How would it appear if he had the hots for one of the hunter kind? How could he lead his people if they couldn't trust him?

"Are you through being pissed off?" she asked, her brows pinched in a tight frown as she pressed her sword into the floor, using it like a cane. No one abused a well-crafted weapon in such a manner. A hunter's sword was often passed down through the generations, a special weapon that could dispatch a vampire in a permanent way.

She swayed a little and he looked down at her strappy sandals. His gaze met hers again. "No."

"Fine. *Whatever.* I need your help." Her words were breathy now.

He wanted to tell her to find some hunter to help her, but he kept his comments to himself, studying her, trying to determine what was going on with her.

Her eyes gazed into his and though he saw anger, he also saw the same kind of vulnerability as before and a tiredness he hadn't noticed during their first encounter. She didn't look well.

"What's the problem?" He poured her a drink, then offered it to her.

She leaned against the arm of one of the sofas. "My car...I—I thought I hit something on the road."

His brows lifted and his gaze raked over her appearance again. She didn't seem to have suffered any injuries in a car wreck, but her dress looked a little dusty.

"Where's your car?"

She took a weary breath, then drank a goodly sum of the wine. "A couple of miles back that way." She motioned with her free hand, which seemed to throw her off balance, and she wobbled backward a little.

He frowned at her unsteadiness. Was she not used to drinking? She hadn't been able to drink the one Basil had tried to serve her.

"You walked." He glanced down at her sandals again and couldn't imagine limping for miles in those things.

In an unlady-like manner, she collapsed on the nearest sofa as if finally realizing how much her feet hurt, spilled some of the remaining wine on her dress, and he swore under his breath.

He went to the bar and jerked off a handful of paper towels. Returning to her, he handed her the towels. She held them limply at her dress, not blotting where the wine had spilled, just sitting there, staring at his waist as if she couldn't lift her head to even look up at him any longer.

"So, you said you thought you hit something. But you didn't? Why did you abandon your car?" The woman wasn't making any sense, and he needed to get her out of here pronto.

"I—I need your help." The glass slipped out of her hand and fell on the carpeted floor, spilling the wine all over it. The sword fell from her other hand. Her eyes slammed shut, her head rolled back, and she collapsed against the seat back of the sofa.

What the hell? He quickly leaned over and felt the pulse at her neck and found her pulse shallow and uneven. He withdrew his fingers. Sticky warm blood coated them, and he smelled the sweet iron that called to him. "Hell and damnation."

Sweeping her hair aside, he found the telltale bites of a vampire. But the attack had been sadistic. Bruises covered the area, and the bites were jagged, not neatly confined as they would be if a vampire had fed and pleasured a host. He hadn't even sealed the wounds, and she was still bleeding freely.

As much as he hated the notion of tasting the huntress's blood, he leaned over and licked the wounds, sealing them, memorizing her sweet blood, wanting more.

"Damnation! Basil!" he yelled out.

Though he'd only called for Basil since the club was his, all three of his friends rushed into the lounge. He assumed they'd been listening at the door as quickly as they entered the room.

"What the hell," Colt said, his steely gaze giving Atreides the evil eye.

"Someone bit her. She abandoned her car on the road in a southwesterly direction and walked all the way here. She didn't manage to explain what had happened before she passed out."

"She needs blood." Basil smelled the scent of her blood in the air. "I've got B-positive in the fridge." He vanished.

"I'll search for her car," Colt said, his teeth clenched, and Atreides knew he was trying to keep his fangs in check, her blood calling to him, like it was to each of the vampires in the room.

Atreides turned to Renault. "Go together. I wager the huntress wouldn't have permitted a vampire to feast on her. He has to be a rogue. She said she thought she had hit something. She must have left her car. But she didn't say why she had walked here. I want the two of you to go together."

"Gotcha," Colt said. "Come on, Renault. Let's find the little lady's car."

Renault eyed the huntress. "I'd rather watch over the lady." He smiled casually, then he caught Atreides's glare and bit back a dark chuckle.

Once Renault and Colt disappeared, Atreides pulled off Selena's high heels, then rested her legs on the couch. Small feet, shapely legs.

Grasping her wrist, he felt the feather-light pulse. All they needed now was some damned rogue vampire attacking huntresses. And for the huntress to die in the vampire club.

When Basil returned with a bag of blood, he said, "She'll need an I.V. I've sent one of my girls to the nearest hospital for one. But it will take a while. Are you sure you don't want to take her to a hunters' clinic?"

"And have the League come down on all of us, trying to determine which one of us did this to her? You'll know they'll question every one of your patrons."

Basil rubbed his chin and nodded. "All right. I'll ask around to see if anyone had left the club who might have had the opportunity to attack the woman while we were here discussing plans. Don't let her die in the meantime. I wouldn't want to have to close down my establishment on the account of a huntress's death here." Basil stalked out of the room.

After removing a plaid blanket from the arm of one of the other couches, Atreides covered the huntress. "Did you see the vampire who targeted you?" he asked, not expecting a reply. Her hands were ice cold, and he took them in his and attempted to warm them. "Why did you leave the car, Selena? You would have been safe inside your vehicle."

Twilight poked her head inside. "The word's out that she was bitten. Can I see her?"

"I don't think she would appreciate being viewed as a curiosity," Atreides said too harshly.

Twilight shrugged. "I saw the two of you dancing. It didn't look to me like she was too uncomfortable being on show."

The Goth was a strange woman, and there was no figuring her motives, but Atreides sensed she was more than just curious about the huntress.

Twilight moved into the room and crouched beside the huntress. "Some of the guys are saying she asked for it."

His gut clenched. No woman deserved to be abused. "She was preyed upon."

The slight woman nodded. "I didn't say I agreed. It's just what I heard. And some of them, well those who were speaking out because I can't hear their telepathic conversations, said you were more than intrigued by the huntress."

"Don't you have someone to dance with?"

"The music has stopped."

Atreides turned and listened. All he could hear were people talking.

"Basil's questioning everyone concerning who left the club about the time the huntress was gone. No more dancing tonight."

"So why don't you go home?"

She shrugged. "Nothing to do there for me. It's more interesting here. Iconia's pretty pissed. I would have figured she did it."

"The bite marks are too deep. Too vicious. It had to be a male."

"Well, I only meant she had the best motive."

"A rogue doesn't need a motive."

Reaching over to Selena, Twilight touched her dark hair. "Iconia was here the whole time dancing with that berserker, Ragnar. I might have thought she sent him after the huntress, but he hadn't left either."

"You were keeping pretty good tabs on everyone?"

"My life is dull. I find your world fascinating. So, yeah, I watch people a lot."

Atreides had never noticed. The woman was an oddity, and yet she faded in the background. Every once in a while, she would catch his eye, and the way she smiled at him, he assumed she was interested in snagging his attention. He wondered if she was afraid of Iconia's wrath. Only other vampiresses dared to entertain hope that he would show any interest in them.

Twilight sighed heavily. "I thought you didn't care anything about humans or huntresses. In fact, a lot of people were surprised tonight. You'd better believe that you and your huntress are the talk of your kind this evening."

Atreides gave her a harsh look and addressed the real concern. "Who left the club after the huntress left?"

"Three male vampires I didn't know but I gave a description to Basil. Some of the others probably know them."

Selena groaned but she didn't open her eyes. Twilight touched her cheek. "I'm Twilight, if you ever want to talk." She winked at Atreides and stood. "Where are you taking her after you give her blood?"

Hell if he knew. He didn't want to return her to her family looking like this. In a couple of days, the vampire's marks would have faded because the hunter genetics, just like a vampire's, meant they healed from their injuries faster than humans.

The woman smiled. "Your place. Has to be because you wouldn't trust anyone else to protect her. Maybe I can drop by tomorrow. See how she's doing? She might want to talk to someone other than just a bunch of vampires."

"The hunter kind don't associate with humans either."

"Maybe—being that she came to a vampires' lair in the first place unlike others of her kind—she does. You'd better watch out for Iconia though. She has already told some of her friends if you take the huntress home with you, you'll both live to regret it."

Basil walked into the room to see what else he could do.

Atreides studied Twilight and then forced her to tell him what she knew about the huntress because he knew something more was going on with her—especially when they'd found her skulking around the parking lot.

"Okay, okay, the truth is a human named Tara Green told me to speak with Selena," Twilight said.

"Why would a human tell you to speak to a huntress at a vampire club? Why at this one? And what were you supposed to talk to her about?" And why hadn't she told Atreides right off the bat?

"I don't know." Twilight shrugged. "Her sister?"

He couldn't believe it. He was beginning to wonder if Twilight and the other female human had been compelled to tell Selena to meet them at the club.

Twilight frowned. "You know, I can't remember. I was thinking Tara Green told me to go there, but now I don't know."

So Tara might have been the one brainwashed to tell Twilight to meet Selena at the club. But if Twilight couldn't exactly remember… She very well could have been also.

Atreides telepathically told Ragnar, *"Find me this Tara Green woman. Bring her here to me."*

"On my way."

"You're thinking a vampire compelled the women to send Selena to the club?" Basil asked.

"Yeah. It doesn't make any sense that two humans would think it would be acceptable to send a huntress to a vampire club."

"My vampire club," Basil said.

"Right. That I frequent the most," Atreides said.

"I'll go see if I could learn anything else." Looking like she might have done wrong, Twilight turned and hurried out of the lounge.

CHAPTER 5

*A*treides didn't know what to think as he took the huntress home with him. He kept feeling he was making a mistake in doing so, but he really didn't want to give her up to any other vampires, and he was sure turning her over to the hunters would be even more of a mistake.

"Even though we couldn't find the huntress's car, we did find blood on the pavement, a pile of ashes, and clothes. She must have killed the vampire who bit her," Colt said.

"An ancient then." If it had been a newly turned vampire, he wouldn't have turned into ash, and the body would still be on the road. "He couldn't have turned her then, if she was able to kill him." That had worried Atreides. That she had been turned into one of them. The person a vampire turned couldn't kill the vampire. He was glad the vampire wasn't free to injure or kill anyone else then.

But the woman's car had simply vanished. Basil had drugged her—*this time*—to ease the pain while she healed. She would heal faster than a human, but Atreides didn't want the League to know she'd been attacked by one of his kind until she was well enough to tell him more about her attacker. He had every intention of taking the bastard down himself. While Daemon was away, Atreides, his twin brother and a prince in his own right, had every authority to police their own people, if warranted.

Atreides's staff never went to the club, yet as soon as he drove into the garage, they were there to assist. They had learned all that had happened. As much as he understood, anyway.

He knew as soon as he had seen the huntress enter the club, she would be trouble.

* * *

THE BLEAK DARKNESS surrounded Selena and her heels clicked endlessly against the asphalt, the soles of her feet sore, her calves tired, but she had to push on, had to keep moving until she found the vampire dance club. She had to get Atreides to help her. She wasn't certain he would though.

She envisioned the way they had danced, their close moves, the way the heat of his body turned hers into an inferno, the way his smoldering, dark gaze had mesmerized her. She remembered the way his lips had turned up slightly, but the feeling behind his expression had eluded her. Had he been amused at her boldness? Or something else?

Then a low rumbling growl sounded behind her, and every thought of him instantly vaporized.

The wolf had moved, and he was damned close.

Heart thundering against her ribs, she couldn't look back. The dance club was straight ahead. Another half mile. She thought.

She could make it.

She stumbled along as fast as she could in the high heeled sandals. She would never wear the blasted things again. She was afraid to attempt to run, was certain the wolf would pounce on her as soon as she did.

Another low threatening growl. He was stalking her. Keeping the same distance between them, but it wasn't enough.

Everyone in horror movies always looked back at whatever evil stalked them. And then they would be torn to shreds, devoured alive. If she didn't look back, he wouldn't attack, she tried to convince herself.

A quarter of a mile. She could hear the boisterous music in the distance, and the glowing lights served as a comforting beacon in the night. She was almost there.

Yet, the hair stood on the nape of her neck. She couldn't fight the fear escalating in her blood that the wolf would soon pounce on her and kill her. That he was only letting her believe she would make it before he lunged at her.

He had not attacked all this time. Maybe he wasn't stalking her but corralling her back to the dance club for some dark purpose.

Every breath she took chilled her lungs. Goose bumps trailed down her arms and legs. Instinctively, she rubbed her arms, trying to warm them.

Wrapping around her in a seductive, sultry way, a voice whispered, "Huntress."

A vampire. Not a wolf. A blood-seeking vampire.

A woman's voice? A man's? She couldn't tell. All she knew was she would soon be at the dance club.

Before long she would ask for Atreides's help. She fought the panic setting in.

"You will never make it before I've had my fill of you. So close, but not close enough," the voice whispered.

The threat was all too real. She started to run.

A hand seized her neck from behind. She screamed.

But no one in the noisy club would hear her.

She clawed at the hands around her neck, the strong fingers painfully tightening, bruising, attempting to subdue her, trying to force her to drop her sword. She tried to twist out of his iron grip, but she couldn't break free. In that instant, she knew she was going to die. But she wouldn't give up that easily. Make the beast fight for his meal. She stomped on his foot with the sharp heel of her sandal. He cursed in some ancient language. Then something struck her hard in the back of the head, sending streaks of light across black satin in her mind.

Her fingers loosened on her sword, and she dropped it with a clatter on the asphalt. Her senses still reeling from the blow to the head, she fell to her knees, scrambled for her sword, and grasped it with her fingertips. A hand grabbed her arm and yanked her away from the asphalt, then lifted her. Hands encircled her throat again.

The music from the club, the excruciating pain radiating through the back of her skull, the malevolent being's teeth tearing into her neck, black eyes watching her, teeth dripping with her blood...all vanished into the mist.

* * *

"My lord," Jacques said, waking Atreides from a fitful sleep. "The huntress cried out and thrashed about, but then became still as death. Her heart is still racing. You said I was to tell you if there was any change in her condition."

Atreides combed his fingers through his hair and finally focused on his loyal manservant, who looked as neat as ever in a crisp white shirt and black pants, his dark brows raised. "Jacques repeat all after you said, 'My lord.'"

Jacques cleared his throat and repeated the message.

Atreides stumbled out of bed. "She's asleep still though?" He yanked on a robe, then tied it.

"Sound asleep. Almost eerily so, my lord."

"And she has made no other sounds, or reacted in any other way?"

"I don't think the one who attacked her can control her thoughts."

Atreides gave him a disgruntled look. "We have no idea what might occur between an ancient vampire and a huntress."

Jacques coughed a little. "Your brother's mate, my lord."

"Tezra," Atreides said. "She's an anomaly in and of herself." He reached the door to the guestroom and paused. "She cried out though?"

"Aye. Maybe she had a nightmare about her assailant attacking her."

"That would be a good bet. But we believe her assailant was an ancient and is dead." Opening the door to the room, Atreides wished he could take away her nightmares like he could a human's. But he could not control a huntress's mind. And he hoped a vampire who had fed on her couldn't give her new nightmares, if by some chance her attacker was still alive—unless there had been two of them. That might explain the multiple bites on her neck.

He stared at the gown she wore, the silky material revealing rounded full-sized breasts and rosy nipples while the covers rested at her waist. He turned to Jacques who raised his brows and gave a slight shrug.

"I told you to ask Catherine to provide a gown for her. Has she nothing more modest?"

Jacques shook his head.

As much time as the man spent off-duty with Atreides's housekeeper, Atreides figured he would know. "I'll sit with her now that I'm up. Get some rest."

"As you wish, my lord." Jacques bowed, then shut the door on his way out.

Atreides took a seat next to the bed and touched the huntress's cheek. Though she'd received two units of blood, she still appeared pale, and he didn't like that she was so unresponsive. He pushed away the hair caressing her neck and considered the bite marks. They were already fading. Tomorrow, he could send her home to her hunter family and let *them* protect her. Keeping her any longer than necessary wouldn't be prudent. Even now, her family could be searching for her, worried that she hadn't returned home.

He glanced at her gown and figured he should pull the covers higher. But then again, she would probably be too hot.

Yawning, he leaned back in the chair and wondered why the hell he was sitting up on the uncomfortable piece of furniture. The bed looked much more inviting and if the huntress thrashed around, he would still be aware of it.

He slipped into bed and at one point, felt the huntress snuggling up to him. He chuckled, darkly amused, though he really shouldn't have been. She stirred his libido with her soft body pressed up against his when he shouldn't be feeling this way. Then, without another moment's hesitation, he wrapped his arm around the huntress, glad she was finally no longer having the nightmares, and he fell into a deep, peaceful sleep.

Several hours later, the huntress screamed in Atreides's ear. He opened his eyes and stared at the wild-eyed huntress who scooted back from him on the mattress and yanked the covers to her chin. She glowered at him as if he had taken advantage of her!

"Sorry," he replied, not sounding in the least bit apologetic.

He hadn't dragged her from her side of the mattress to hug her against his chest. Not like he'd wanted to. She had come to him, and what was he supposed to do? Push her away? The fact he had his arm around her was only because it was more comfortable for him that way.

He rubbed his head, trying to clear the fog from his mind. Well, maybe he did pull her against his chest later when she was having another nightmare.

Hell, he'd stretched out to rest his weary back and make sure she didn't wake alone in a strange room. He couldn't help that she'd only quieted in his arms.

She glanced at his robe that had parted, exposing a naked thigh.

He smiled at her shocked look—considering how she'd danced so hotly in his arms last night—pulled his robe closed and left the bed. Then his expression grew somber. "Do you remember what happened last night?"

"I—I asked for your help. I—I didn't expect this." A deep frown materialized.

She thought he'd brought her home to seduce her? He would have done a lot more than held the wench in his hard embrace if that had been the case.

"Despite what the situation here might appear like, you'd lost a good deal of blood last night and collapsed in a faint in the dance club's lounge, then needed blood."

"Blood," she said, reaching for the back of her head.

He pointed to her neck. "A vampire bit you."

"No," she said with a muffled grown. "He struck me on the back of the head also."

Frowning, Atreides drew close and touched her head and felt the dried blood and a lump. "Sweet Jesus." Instantly his blood burned with rage. The beast could have killed her. He examined the injury more carefully but was glad to see she wouldn't need any stitches. "None of us had seen your injury." Which had to do with how thick her hair was and that the blood had already coagulated. But he still faulted himself for not discovering that she'd been injured further. No wonder she'd been so out of it. She no doubt had suffered a mild concussion.

"We assumed he'd just drained you of too much blood." He let out his breath. "I take it you didn't see him," he said more harshly than he'd intended. He couldn't get his anger under control, seeing a red haze, wanting to kill the bastard who could bring hunters in the region down on all of them—not knowing who had done this to the huntress, and not caring. Though he thought from the pile of ashes left behind, she had killed the vampire.

Any vampire would be suspect though, who had injured her, if they couldn't prove the ashes belonged to her attacker. Any could be murdered in the name of protecting their huntresses.

"I saw a wolf."

"A wolf?" he asked.

"I-I thought I'd hit something on the road with my car. I

stopped to see if I could help. When I couldn't find anything, I turned around and found a wolf in front of my car.

"He was a wolf? The vampire was a wolf?"

"I thought at first he could be a real wolf, a wolfdog, or I don't know. Then I worried he was a vampire. He wouldn't let me get near my car, and I finally decided to walk back to the club and ask for your help."

Damnation. The vampire had been the worst kind of renegade, taunting and stalking its intended victim. But not killing—instead, he would terrorize her until he tired of the game. Then he would finish her off. Atreides had seen it before, dozens of times over the years—a vampire like any serial killer whose only reason for living was to kill again.

Like the one who had killed the huntress Tezra's parents.

He had to make sure the vampire was dead, and another hadn't been involved in the attack on her.

Atreides sat down hard on the chair next to the bed and took the huntress's hand. Rubbing her cold fingers, he asked, "Do you remember anything else about him? About his biting you?"

"The wolf followed me. Then a hand grabbed my neck. Before I blacked out, he said he was going to take his fill of me, that I wouldn't make it to safety, or something like that."

Just as Atreides expected. He would warn her what he intended to do first and follow through. It wouldn't be the last time either, Atreides was certain, if he was still alive.

"Did you see him?"

"Blue eyes that turned black. A cruel, dark smile." She took a deep breath, steadily looking into Atreides's eyes. "The attack wasn't random."

"He targeted you?"

She closed her eyes briefly, then studied Atreides. "Yes."

"Is he on your list?"

She shook her head. "But I'm on his."

He cursed under his breath. "We found clothes and ashes

where your blood was also discovered on the road where he must have attacked you. Could you have killed him?"

"I...I don't remember."

He would have to discover who he was pronto. "Would you recognize him as a wolf again, if there were two of them and one was running in the form of a wolf?" He had to stop the bastard before he put more of their kind at risk. In the meantime, he had to ensure her own people protected her.

"I think so."

"But you killed him, and his clothes were left behind." Something didn't add up.

"I killed him," she said.

"You don't remember killing him? You must have—well, I'm not sure. You didn't have wrist daggers on for close combat. You were armed only with your sword. The good thing is if you killed him, you couldn't have been turned." At least that was the good news for her.

She looked confused, like she was trying to recall anything more about what had happened, but she wasn't coming up with anything.

He patted her hand. "I'll get breakfast. After you've rested a couple of days, you can go home."

"I live at Rivercrest Apartments. I don't have to inconvenience you any further."

"Who lives with you?"

She frowned. "No one, but it doesn't matter. I feel well enough to fend for myself."

Huntresses often didn't live alone. Exceptions existed, of course, but they often shared a place together to protect themselves if a rogue learned he was on one of the huntress's terminal list.

"No. If he comes after you again, you should have hunter protection. Not only that, after being unconscious for a time, you had to have had a mild concussion. You *need* someone to watch over you."

The most disturbing look crossed her face, but her reaction quickly passed, and he wondered then what was going on with the huntress.

"I'll get hold of some hunters after you drop me off at my place and...what about my car?" Tears misted her eyes, and she lay back against the pillow.

"Gone. Colt and Renault looked for it for several hours, but they couldn't find any sign of it."

"Would the vampire have taken it?"

"Maybe. Or someone else might have who found it abandoned on the road. If they knew how to start a car without keys..."

She gave a ladylike snort. "The keys were in the ignition."

He quirked a brow.

She scowled back. "I left the door open to give me more light while I searched for a body. I didn't walk very far from the car, and there wasn't a soul on the road. I certainly didn't expect to see a wolf guarding the car when I turned around."

"Renault notified the police that your car was missing, but he didn't know your last name or your tag number." When she didn't reveal anything further about herself, he tensed. "Sorry, I know this has been a traumatic experience for you and—"

"You can take me back to my place, now. I appreciate all your concern but—"

"Damn it, woman. You're not going anywhere but home to your family. And I won't hear another word on it." He rose from the chair, expecting an outburst in response to his.

Instead, her eyes filled with fresh tears again.

"All right, listen. After you eat, you'll feel better. Then we'll talk." The woman would see it his way or else. "Eggs, hash browns, sausage links, and toast all right?"

She nodded, but her expression remained mutinous.

"I'll be right back." And he would have some more questions for the huntress. This time he would know the reason she went to the dance club, unarmed, alone, and looking for something other than a drink and to dance with a vampire. To speak with Twilight?

What the hell was that all about anyway?

CHAPTER 6

*S*elena shoved the comforter aside, intending to get dressed. She was ready to leave this place, though she had no idea where she was.

She glanced at the slinky nightgown she was wearing and wondered whose it was. One of Atreides's vampiress girlfriend's? Probably the one who got in her face at the dance club and planned to wring her neck before Atreides interceded on Selena's behalf. She wondered if the woman knew he had loaned the gown to a huntress for the night. The woman would probably rip out his heart, or Selena's, if she knew. And burn the gown afterward.

Glancing around the room, Selena looked for her dress. There was no sign of it or her sword, and she let out her breath in exasperation.

She heard someone coming and she scampered back under the covers and yanked the blue comforter under her chin.

Instead of Atreides returning with the tray of food, a kindly woman in her forties did. Cheerfully plump, she hurried in, her blond hair swept up on top of her head in an elegant fashion and her green eyes bright with intrigue. She greeted Selena. "I'm glad to see you sitting up, dear. Atreides wished me to bring you something to eat right away, and…" Her mouth twitched in a smile.

"He said you might be concerned about your clothes. I'm washing them. But I'll…I'll find something for you to throw on over my nightie. He wasn't pleased that it was so… revealing. In a pinch late last night, I didn't have anything else. I think he didn't like that Jacques was watching over you last night and saw you like that." The woman winked. "I'm Catherine. I've worked for Atreides since he was little. I'm his housekeeper, cook, you name it."

A vampiress. Selena had thought the woman was a blood bond since she hadn't shown any animosity toward her.

But then she thought back to the woman's comments. Despite that Selena was a huntress, she thought that Atreides didn't mind seeing her in something so revealing. Selena was as confused about the way he viewed her, and she suspected he felt the same way about her. "Thanks, Catherine. I appreciate everything you've done for me."

"He's a Leo, you know." Catherine set the tray up and hovered over Selena. Her eyes sparkled with effervescence. "The lion."

"My father is a Leo. He's bossy. But then most hunters are."

"Right. And interfering."

Yep. Her father wouldn't let Selena do what she wanted to do. Being a huntress was in her blood. That was the only role she was supposed to play.

"Intolerant." Catherine gave another winsome smile and folded her arms.

Yeah, that was her father too. He couldn't tolerate her for seeing things differently from the League views.

"Pompous."

That described most hunters.

"Patronizing." Catherine glanced back at the doorway, and Selena wondered if she sensed Atreides was coming.

Selena hadn't sensed anything, but then she was too busy scarfing down the spicy cheese omelet. "This is really good."

"Thank you." Catherine studied Selena again and said, "But that's just the dark side of a Leo's personality. He's also extremely faithful and loving."

Yeah, her dad was that with her mother. And if Selena had been normal, he probably would have been more loving toward her too. As it was, her sister Rosa was the light of his eye.

"And enthusiastic. Once he gets an idea in mind, he's hell bent on seeing it through with great enthusiasm."

Selena nodded.

"And warmhearted."

Her father was with her mother, yes. But not with Selena.

"Oh, and generous. He's always helping others in need."

Selena looked up at the woman. The woman was talking about Atreides, not her father. Yes, she could see that he was like that, taking care of a huntress he wanted no part of.

"And broadminded."

"That's the opposite of intolerant."

"Ah, yes, true. But at times he's extremely broadminded and at others, extremely intolerant." Catherine sighed deeply. "So what sign are you, dear?"

"An Aquarius."

"Honest and loyal. Good." Catherine glanced over her shoulder, then again faced Selena. "I'll be right back with a T-shirt."

Then she vanished.

The woman's sudden disappearing act reminded her of the shapeshifting vampire who'd bitten her, making her skin crawl.

Just as Selena finished a glass of milk, Catherine was standing beside the bed again. "Here we are, dear. Are you ready to slip this on?"

Catherine's face wavered and Selena shut her eyes to still the wave of dizziness sweeping through her brain. Selena had experienced the same thing when she'd been bitten.

"Here, I'll take the tray."

Selena opened her eyes, but only halfway, and she felt horribly groggy. She tried to touch the back of her head but reached only to her forehead.

"She's not properly covered yet," Atreides said, his voice dark and disturbing.

The room seemed to grow dim, and she heard his voice and thought he stood near, but she couldn't see him for the lack of light. Hadn't it been daylight? Morning?

"Help me, will you, my lord? The huntress's arms have become like lead. It's like dressing the rubbery arms of a babe. And I should know. I used to dress you."

He snorted.

Selena felt her arms lifted in the air, but she couldn't see what was happening, only felt the T-shirt slide down her arms, the soft, spring-fresh material brushing over her nose and cheeks, then slipping over her breasts. She felt warmer, but she wasn't sure if it was the T-shirt or something else, because the warmth seemed to radiate from inside out.

"Why did you go to the club?" Atreides asked.

Selena stared at the darkness where his face should have been.

"Dear, you went to the club to…find someone?" Catherine asked, her voice softness to Atreides's hardness.

"Twilight?" Atreides asked. "Who is your sister?"

"What's your name, dear?" Catherine's hand touched Selena's and stroked softly.

Selena knew it wasn't Atreides's. His hands were big, strong, gripped like a vice, and there was nothing gentle about them. Compelling, sexy, yes, but not soothing.

"Selena, what's your last name, dear?"

Selena could feel the tension in the air. She sensed her father glowered at her while her mother pitied her.

"I—I'm sorry I can't be like what you want me to be. I—I tried. You know I did."

Everyone was silent and she laid her head back against the pillow, craving sleep, desiring to lock away the pain of her existence. No hunter would ever take her as a mate. Not unless she could learn to be more like the rest of them. Not have a mind of her own. Hunters were family oriented. The desire to be part of a family was in their blood. Wouldn't you know that part of her was perfectly normal?

"What can't you be like?" her father asked.

Selena frowned. *Rub it in. Make me tell you a hundred times why I can't do it. And explain the reasoning when I don't know myself!*

"Selena, tell us your last name."

She turned her head toward the female voice. Why wouldn't her mother know her name?

"Why?"

"You've hit your head and you—we want to make sure you remember it."

Oh. *The darkness swept through her, and she smelled the cool mist. He was coming for her, the vampire in the shape of a wolf, his amber eyes glowing in the dark, cold, detached, predatory. His growl was low and menacing and forced her skin to tingle with dread.*

"Selena..."

"How much did you give her? It's not working. Her mind's too muddled," the man growled.

"Dear, who's on your terminal list?"

Selena looked in the direction of the woman. "Terminal list," she whispered. She didn't have a terminal list. Her mother would know that. Who was questioning her?

His hot breath was at her neck, his hand gripping her with determination. "I will have my fill of you."

She shuddered, but she wanted to strike back. She'd been taught to fight the rogues, and she was damned good at her job—with or without hunter backup. She'd fought her fellow hunters in mock battles. But something had stirred in her other than panic when the creature had seized her neck. As soon as he'd grabbed her throat, she wished she'd had a wrist knife, not her sword, any better weapon to fight back. But still, she'd managed to cut the bastard. He'd cried out. She smiled.

Then some vague memory stirred. Something of the dark and distant past. Something buried in her memories for all time.

"Her heart is racing twice as fast, my lord," the woman whispered.

"What frightens you?" the man asked.

Selena pushed away the cover that confined her. *He wouldn't hold her down. He wouldn't take her blood. She would kill him first. She wanted to. If...if she could reach her sword. She'd... she'd dropped it.*

Reaching for her waist, she tried to get hold of the hilt of her sword, not the blade this time.

"What is she doing?" the woman again whispered.

"Trying to draw her sword."

"To kill us?"

"The vampire who attacked her, I imagine." The man moved closer and touched her neck.

Selena struck out with her fist and connected with flesh. Pain coursed through her knuckles with the impact of bone against her curled-up fist, and she cried out.

The man cursed under his breath and grabbed her wrists. She knew it was his and not the woman's because they were large and vice-like and kept her hands pinned beside her head. Trying to kick, she discovered her feet were tangled in something, and she couldn't get them free.

"This is useless," the man said, his voice angered. "I want to discover who her family is and send her home immediately."

"What if you drop her off at a hunter club tonight? Someone's bound to know her, and they can take her home with them."

Selena waited for the man to say something. Why didn't he say something? She relaxed and quit struggling.

"Unless, of course, you want to keep her." The woman sounded like she was teasing.

He released Selena and stalked away from her. "You, of all people, know how I feel about her kind."

The door slammed. But a knock followed immediately afterward.

"Yes?" the woman asked, her hand stroking Selena's.

"It's me, Twilight. I wanted to see how the huntress was doing."

Twilight. Selena struggled to open her eyes. Twilight. Who was she and what did the name mean to her? The man had mentioned her too. Twilight.

She thought a man had bitten her, but maybe...maybe it was Twilight. She...she wasn't sure, and again she reached for her sword.

* * *

ATREIDES POURED a glass of brandy and joined Basil, Renault, and Colt in the great room. Why meet in a stuffy board room? Sitting on the black leather sofas, Atreides believed in comfort instead of rigidity when he made plans in the city.

Although usually Daemon made the decisions concerning the vampire clans in this region. Atreides was glad he'd taken Voltan, his bodyguard, and Maison, his loyal friend, with him so Atreides could have free rein. As twin brothers, they were both princes, but having been born second, Atreides was Daemon's right-hand man, not the man totally in charge. Which meant he often lived his own life doing his own thing, sometimes to Daemon's consternation.

"Did you find out anything about the huntress?" Renault asked, his brows raised.

"She's an Aquarius."

Colt laughed and choked on his brandy.

Basil shook his head. "And that helps us to get her home, how?"

"She lives at Rivercrest Apartments. She wouldn't give us her last name. Catherine gave her too much of the drug, so the huntress was incapable of revealing anything. Was there still no sign of her car?"

"Nope. We have all the blood bonds and hosts searching for it though too," Renault said. "Something about her doesn't add up."

Basil chuckled. "Yeah, she entered my club and danced with Atreides."

"More than that. She was unarmed the first time she came to the club," Renault said.

"Well, she would have to be to enter a vampire club," Colt said, giving Renault a look as though he thought the observation absurdly obvious. "Or any club for that matter."

"Okay, so she armed herself when she thought she'd hit something," Renault said.

"Yes." Atreides downed the rest of his brandy. He was just glad no one had attacked her for bringing a sword into the club the second time. "She searched for something that she thought she'd hit, and so she must have left the rest of her weapons in the car."

"Since when does a huntress not wear weapons at all times? I concede she wouldn't have worn a sword to the club, but why not a concealed dagger underneath that gown, strapped to her leg?"

Atreides stared at his friend, then nodded. He knew there'd been something wrong about the situation too, when she'd described it.

"Would she have been banned from carrying weapons?" Basil asked. "Maybe she injured someone in a fit of temper, and she can't wear her weapons for a time as punishment."

"If so, she wouldn't be allowed to be out running around on her own. Her family would want her protected. Unless… hell and damnation. That's why she didn't want to return to her family. She kept saying she would be safe on her own. She has been banished; I would bet anything. Another damned borderline renegade huntress." Atreides rose from the couch and stared out the patio doors.

"Hell," Basil said. "That means we can't use her to lure the hunters to us. I mean, if she has been banished from hunting, they won't care what happens to her."

Atreides turned and frowned at Basil. "I have no intention of keeping her. I already have the huntress lure who will work with us."

"Oh, well, why didn't you say so?" Renault said. "So who is she?"

"It's best if we keep the number down who know about it to the bare minimum." At least for now. Daemon and Tezra would kill Atreides if they learned of it. They would have wanted to know if Atreides was having trouble of any kind with hunters killing vampires, but he wanted to handle this on his own.

"All right." Colt rose from the couch. "So what do we do with the huntress upstairs? You can't let her loose if a rogue's still after her, and the ashes were of another."

"Maybe it's a one-time occurrence," Basil offered. "Maybe he won't bother her again. If he'd wanted to kill her, he would have. If he wanted to keep her..." He shrugged. "He would have."

"He nearly killed her." Atreides couldn't contain the anger in his voice. If a rogue began killing huntresses, all the vampires would be in danger of retribution.

"He took her blood but only enough to make her weak," Colt said.

"He nearly killed her," Atreides growled again. "He hit her on the back of the head so hard she blacked out. That's why she didn't remember that she'd even been bitten."

His friends all stared at him and didn't say a word. He knew what they were thinking. Only a really twisted vampire would resort to that kind of violence before taking his victim's blood.

"Did he think she would die before she reached us?" Basil asked.

"He waited until she was close to the club. That makes me think he wants us involved somehow. To make it look like one of the patrons was the renegade? Maybe he has got a grudge against Basil. Or against one of the regulars of the club. The huntress believes he targeted her specifically. What if the hunters won't protect her from the rogue if he still lives and should he go after her again?"

"Ahem," Renault said, a slow smile appearing, "I've got plenty of room at my place."

Basil waved his hand in the direction of the club. "There's enough room at my house next to the club."

Colt shoved his hands in his pockets. "I have plenty of room at the ranch. And more than enough cowhands who could offer additional protection."

Atreides wasn't ready for any of them to keep her. She belonged with her hunter kind. *They* needed to protect her. "We need to find her family."

"And if we can't do that?" Renault asked.

"I'll take her to a hunter club and drop her off."

"I'll go with you. It wouldn't be a good idea for one vampire to be seen with a huntress like that," Renault warned.

"I'll go too," Basil said.

Colt nodded. "The four musketeers. Though I didn't live that long ago."

"All right, it's settled. We locate her family, try to find out which apartment she lives in, and if that doesn't work, we'll find a hunter club and someone there can take care of her."

Atreides knew that was the best plan he could come up with, but he couldn't shake the uneasiness he felt. He was certain it was the controlling aspect of his personality, that only *he* would be able to provide her with the utmost protection, no other. Which was ludicrous. She belonged in the hunters' care.

* * *

By THE TIME night had fallen, and they had exhausted all avenues of searching for Selena's identity, having found there was no such place as Rivercrest Apartments, Atreides had no other choice, but to take her to a hunter club.

Vampires escorting a huntress to a hunters' dance club wasn't the smartest thing to do, but he wouldn't trust the job to blood bonds, who could easily be manipulated by the renegade vampire, should he show up.

With the beat of the music blaring into the parking lot, Atreides and his friends parked before Selena got out of the van and walked to the hunter club. The drug still seemed to be affecting her as she was quiet and reserved, having not spoken a word all the rest of the day and on the drive over. He wondered then if she had been ostracized because she'd been banned from wearing weapons and had isolated herself from her kind. Although she'd had her unsheathed sword in hand when she'd reached their club.

Then she straightened her shoulders and gave Atreides a tight smile and shared the same strained expression with his friends. "Thank you," she said. "And…Basil, maybe some day I'll take you up on that dance."

Over Atreides's dead body.

Basil gave her a toothy grin, not caring about the dagger of a look Atreides gave him.

She left the van, walked across the parking lot, and slipped inside the brick building, disappearing from their sight. Atreides couldn't account for the strange feeling of foreboding that surged through him.

"Are we ready to go?" Basil asked, since Atreides didn't make a move to drive them away from the establishment.

Atreides stared at the door of the club, waiting for her to reappear in the event she wasn't intending to stay and thought he and his friends had left. When she didn't leave, he nodded.

"Yeah, she'll be all right. She's with her kind." And he had no business feeling anything but relief. So why did he cast another look back at the club?

Because he hoped to see that she did not leave the club without some protection this time. On the other hand, he hoped to see her standing there, smiling at him like she had done when she'd danced with him, the damned bewitching vixen.

Basil looked back at the door. "She's not coming out. If you're worried, we can sit here and watch for a while."

"Sure, we can observe the place and see who she leaves with and find out where she ends up," Colt offered, "just as a precaution."

As if Atreides wanted to see her end up at some hunter's place. Yet, he planned to do just what Colt suggested.

Atreides started the engine, then turned the van around and parked where they had a better view of the main door. And waited, hating that she might be in there all night—dancing with a bunch of damned hunters—like she'd danced with him last night.

CHAPTER 7

Selena hadn't looked back to see if Atreides had remained watching the door, ensuring she didn't slip out into the cool dark night alone. Since he was a vampire and eager to get rid of his "charge," he probably wasn't still there. Even so, she didn't want to look back in the event he was observing her, and make him suspicious, as guilty as she was feeling.

But this was such a bad idea—entering a hunter club. Nearly worse than entering the vampire club last night. Plus, here she was carrying a sword, really not cool and not legal.

The hunters were so busy drinking or dancing or conversing, she halfway thought she might be able to slip by them and make her way out the side door without anyone noticing. *Dream on.*

Gazes shifted in her direction—at first interested to see who the new huntress was who'd arrived at the crystalline joint—crystal chandeliers dripping from above, flashy colorful lights reflecting off the black-mirrored walls, the place appearing even larger than it was because of the mirrors.

Many had been watching the half-dressed huntresses and hunters shimmying to the beat on clear platforms high above.

Several hunters glanced her way, and disdain etched across expressions and the hard looks and dagger-like stares sent a chill racing across her skin. Then gazes shifted to the unsheathed sword clutched in her fist. She imagined she looked a bit danger-ous, maybe even a little unstable.

At first, no one spoke, and then the whispers began, which turned into taunts.

Hell, she hated that she'd had to kill the hunter, but he hadn't given her a choice. He had been in the wrong, a rogue, and would have killed an innocent vampiress.

Some of the hunters hadn't see it that way. She had murdered one of their kind while defending a vampire. Even though the League had mostly exonerated her, several hunters still felt she'd been a traitor to take the vampiress's side in the confrontation.

"This club is for hunters. Not for the likes of you," a man growled.

She didn't even know him, but it seemed everyone knew of her.

Another looked her up and down as if he'd like to have sex with her, even if he had no other use for her. She gave him a killing glower back.

Which made him smile. "Hell, I don't know what all the diffi-culty is," he said out loud. "She looks good enough to eat. Keep her unarmed and naked in bed, is my motto."

"And if you had a kid by that abomination?" another man said, shaking his head. "You would have to destroy it before it became just like her."

Then she saw Daniel. Oh hell, if he saw her, there would be hell to pay.

She'd tried to slip through the crowded club before anyone stopped her and forced her back out the front door. Although it might not matter if Atreides had already left. Surely, he wouldn't sit there any longer than had been necessary. He'd dropped her off, and then he and his friends would be gone.

But it was impossible to move about the club in the slinky red dress with her reputation and remain unnoticed. Still, she'd almost succeeded to reach the side door until one of the women—superior huntress Candy Kline—caught sight of Selena and instantly leaned over and spoke to Selena's brother. Daniel's head whipped around as if he'd just been told a vampire was coming in for the kill, and he'd better prepare himself.

Selena turned her head away and reached for the knob to the side door, not about to put up with Daniel's hateful words, if he thought she intended to stay, and he was going to ensure she didn't.

As soon as she twisted the handle, his hand grabbed hers, and he jerked the door open, then shoved her outside. As if, damn him, he was trying to prove to the hunters in the club that he would show her who was boss.

She whipped around and growled, "Go to hell, Daniel. I wasn't planning to stay."

He fisted his hands, his face reddened with anger. "What the hell do you think you're doing here? Carrying an unsheathed hunter's sword into a hunter club? And you aren't even supposed to be armed. What's the matter with you? You don't belong here, damn you. Don't you *ever* show your face in here again."

"I hadn't intended to, you prick." She spun around and meant to stalk off, but he grabbed her arm and whirled her around to face him.

"I asked you what the hell you were doing in here."

"It's none of your business. Don't you dare touch me again," she growled low.

This time when she turned and stormed off, he didn't make a move to stop her. Her head was pounding, her whole body hot with anger, and she felt she could have taken him out, forget that she was supposed to take down rogue vampires—when she wasn't on restriction.

Damned hunter ego that he had to act as though he was taking out the club's trash—her.

The door squeaked open, and she thought Daniel was returning to the club, but instead she heard Mack say, "What did you go and send her away for? I wanted to dance with her."

"The hell that's all you want to do with her, Mack."

Neither spoke a word, though she knew they were watching her. Had to be because the door didn't open again so that they could return to the club.

"Where the hell is your car?" Daniel hollered.

"Go to hell, Daniel," she shouted back, still not looking in his direction. She turned down another street, hoping to get out of his sight before he decided to question her further about the fact her car was nowhere in view and ask again why she'd visited the hunter club, armed with an unsheathed sword.

* * *

ATREIDES STARED IN DISBELIEF. Not only had a hunter tossed her out of the club, but he'd manhandled her in such a violent way that Atreides had wanted to kill the bastard himself. He'd felt the tension in the van rise as his friends watched the confrontation unfold. His teeth had immediately unsheathed, and he suspected his friends' teeth had also. The others had been just as irritated as Atreides was.

What Atreides couldn't believe was that, despite the hunter recognizing she was without transportation, he'd let her go, not caring for her safety in the least. What the hell was wrong with the two hunters?

A brunette poked her head out of the club's side entrance. "Aren't you coming back inside, Daniel?"

The huntress was nearly out of sight, and the man nodded. He started back into the club, but the other named Mack stood watching the huntress still. "Coming, Mack?" Daniel asked.

"Yeah, hell, Daniel. She's not that bad." Mack joined him, and the door clunked closed.

"Damn, where the hell does the huntress think she's going, alone and on foot? Does she have a death wish after what happened to her near our dance club?" Atreides growled to his friends as they watched from his van. He started the engine, intending to follow her, to learn exactly where she was living and with whom.

"Follow her. If we have to, the three of us can take care of her if someone threatens her," Renault said.

She would only need Atreides's protection, he wanted to growl back. And he was already following her. His fangs were still fully extended, and he was gripping the steering wheel so hard, he wished they'd been around the hunter's neck. As soon as Daniel had shoved Selena, Atreides's blood had sizzled with barely controlled anger.

Atreides was torn between wanting to thrash the hunter and shake some sense into the huntress for not telling him what kind of trouble she was in. Not that it should have mattered to him, but...

"Where the hell is she going?" Colt asked, echoing Atreides's dark thoughts.

Atreides drove slowly down the street, ready to jerk the van to the curb if anyone attempted to get close to her, and he would change his mind. But he'd never expected what happened next.

* * *

FOR A COUPLE OF BLOCKS, Selena had managed her composure after her brother had torn into her. Normally, she was good at burying her feelings. But she believed her nerves were on edge, all having to do with her sister's disappearance, the note about it from her friend, and she still felt groggy from—she wasn't sure what. The vampire's attack on her, most likely. So, she attributed her inability to deal with her emotions in a rational way—to everything else going on with her.

Tears blurred her eyes and rolled down her cheeks. She cursed feeling any emotion about it any further. She was what she was. She would not allow a hunter to kill an innocent vampire. If she had to do it all over again, she would. She was certain some hunters would feel the same as her, but they didn't want to end up like her, in trouble with the League. She needed to get home where she would be safe. Then she would take care of herself.

But what if the vampire came for her again? She must have some connection to him, but she had no idea what it was. Had she killed one, and there was another? The wolf perhaps?

Cool, damp mist suddenly enveloped her, and she shivered. Then a man appeared before her, too close for comfort, his massive build stealing her breath. He was blond, had brilliant blue eyes and a gargantuan smile. She recognized him at once. "You're...you're the guy who was dancing with Atreides's girlfriend at the club."

"Ragnar," he said and bowed.

She didn't feel any animosity from this man.

Before he could say another word, a sudden flurry of flapping filled the air, and Atreides appeared, his look black. He grabbed Ragnar by the throat and pinned him against the brick building.

Selena stood dumbstruck as if Medusa had turned her to stone. Had Atreides and his friends—as they all suddenly stood around them in a semi-circle watching Atreides—intended to follow her wherever she went?

"What the hell are you doing here?" Atreides asked the hulking blond vampire, his voice low and angry.

Expecting Ragnar to break free as big as he was, Selena watched in awe as the man merely smiled. "You want the huntress, yet you let her roam the streets on her own. *Ja?*"

"You will leave here," Atreides said to Ragnar.

"If you have no intention of making the huntress your ward, I will watch over her."

Selena observed the battle of male vampire wills and shook her head, not believing that Atreides and his pals had been spying on her, nor that Atreides's enemy, Ragnar, had been also. Hell, had they seen the way her brother had treated her?

"Leave, Ragnar, now," Atreides ordered.

"What say you?" Ragnar asked Selena.

"Goodnight." She stalked off, hoping to get to her apartment without any further trouble. If she could just hail a taxi...

Atreides released Ragnar and appeared in front of Selena, blocking her path. With a gasp, she took a step back. Seizing her wrist, he pulled her to his van. "You will tell me where you live, and I will take you there. I will have no more games."

She cast him her most hostile look, but he ignored her. Nearly making her run, she tried to keep up with his long stride. She hated the way his touch heated her inside, when she was annoyed with the way he tried to control her. But for now, she had little choice.

"Where do you live?" Atreides asked, his voice annoyed.

"Riverview Apartments. I already told you."

"You said Rivercrest."

"I did?" When did she say that?

He stared at her for a moment, then shook his head as he walked her to the vehicle, then made her sit in the passenger's seat.

"I just moved in. Maybe I got it mixed up."

"She told you after she was hit," Basil said. "Maybe she had been confused."

She suspected he was right.

"Why don't you like Ragnar?" she finally asked, wondering if the man had put the moves on Atreides's vamp girlfriend before and that was the reason. She could understand that.

Atreides remained silent though, his countenance darkening, if that was possible.

An uneasy silence filled the vehicle, and she figured the vampires weren't even communicating telepathically with each other. They probably figured her to be more trouble than she was worth, so why were they bothering?

Which made her change her view of them a little more. They had been protecting her all along. Yet, she reminded herself, they probably hadn't had a good diversion like this in a long time either.

Or maybe it all had to do with worrying that someone would tie her assault directly to the members who frequented the club, and they wanted to make sure she got home safely so no connection could be made. That was more likely.

When they arrived at her small apartment complex, Atreides and his friends escorted her to her front porch. She was tired, feeling as though she could sleep nonstop for a week. Then she realized her key to her car and her apartment were still in the vehicle—that had been stolen. For a moment, she just stood there, trying to figure out what to do next. Then she remembered the crown frog prince statues under the shrubs next to her door. One of them had a hidden key.

She retrieved the key and then she unlocked the door and stepped inside. Immediately, Atreides commanded, "Call your family."

He and his friends stood at the entryway to her apartment, unable to enter, but they didn't force the issue. They were attempting to keep the status quo. Vampires out, hunters in. Even so, it appeared he wasn't going to leave her alone unless she proved to him that someone was coming to watch over her.

She was torn between acquiescing, when she knew she couldn't call her family, and coming up with a foolproof strategy to get rid of him. She took a deep breath, grabbed her portable phone off its stand, and called Tara Green, hoping she could fake a scenario with her friend without Atreides or his friends becoming suspicious. "Tell my brother to come see me. I'll explain later."

"What?"

Not good.

"Daniel's not speaking to you, unless something major has changed that," Tara said, sounding suspicious.

Avoiding looking at Atreides or his friends, Selena studied the carpet under her feet and hoped the vampires couldn't hear Tara's words. "He'll be here within the hour? Thanks! I'll talk to you..."

"You're not making any sense, Selena. What about Twilight? Did you meet with her?" Tara asked.

Selena glanced back at Atreides. His scowl had deepened. Ohmigod, he hadn't heard Tara's comments with his enhanced hearing, had he?

"Uhm, no, she wasn't there. Or at least, uhm, didn't come forth."

Suddenly, Tara blurted, "Yes, yes, come in, Atreides."

"What did you say?" Selena's gaze shot to Atreides.

Tara said, "What did I just say?"

She'd just invited the vampire in. How in the hell had he done that? He had controlled Tara's thoughts through the damned phone?

Atreides moved like a panther, sleek, sure of himself, the wicked look of satisfaction playing on his lips. He motioned to his friends with a wave of his hand, and they all entered the apartment.

Before Selena could react, Atreides tore the phone from her grasp. Immediately, her heart pounded, and Selena grabbed for the phone, but Colt intercepted her and pulled her away.

Atreides's eyes glittered with malice, and he said into the phone, "What would Selena need to see Twilight about?"

"Who is this?"

* * *

A VAMPIRE *who would know the truth from the huntress one way or another.* "A friend of Selena's. But a vampire bit her last night. She needs a hunter's protection in the event the rogue returns for her. Why wouldn't her brother do it?"

"She has...she has had a falling out with her brother."

"What about a cousin? Her father? Who else could protect her?"

"Who is this?"

"You're not a huntress, are you?" Tara Green was a human, or Atreides couldn't have so easily controlled her mind, which didn't make any sense since most hunters only associated with their own kind. Though very little about the huntress made any sense.

"No. I'm her friend. Why...why don't *you* protect her?"

"She needs a hunter's protection. Why did she need to see Twilight?"

"You're...you're a vampire, aren't you? My God, you're a vampire! You made me invite you into her apartment, didn't you? She'll kill me." Tara let out her breath. "I don't know why Twilight needed to see her. She said she had information for Selena."

"About her sister?" Atreides kept his eyes on the huntress. She jerked her wrist away from Colt and collapsed on the white leather sofa. In fact, now that he had a chance to look at the place, he noticed how it looked like a puff of cloud, from the white leather couch and loveseat and the white-washed wood end tables and wood tables, to the ceiling fan overheard, its five white blades twirling around.

"What kind of information did Twilight have for her?" he asked the human.

Selena's eyes darted to Atreides's.

"I told you I don't know."

"Who can Selena call to protect her?"

"No one. Sounds to me like you're it. That would be a real switch."

He could hear amusement in the human woman's voice, but he was not amused.

"I've gotta run. Nice talking to you. Keep her safe, will you? She's the only huntress friend I've got."

The phone clicked dead.

Atreides glanced at Selena, looking red-faced and small as she sat on the couch. He crossed the floor to join her. "You have a human friend. You were meeting with a blood bond for some kind of information, and your family won't protect you. What kind of a mess have you gotten yourself into?"

She tilted her chin up and glowered at him. "I haven't gotten myself into any mess. It's my..." She shook her head. "My business is none of your concern."

"When you walked into my jurisdiction and were attacked by one of my kind, it became my business."

"We can't let her stay here alone," Basil warned.

"She can still come to my ranch," Colt offered, looking hopeful.

Atreides rubbed his chin, realizing he had no other choice but to put her under his protection until he could discover what information she needed from Twilight and why her hunter family was ostracizing her.

"Colt, Renault, search her place for huntress weapons."

The two men bowed and vanished.

Selena's back stiffened. "I'm perfectly fine here, as long as you don't invite my attacker into the place."

His friends reappeared and shook their heads, which confirmed Atreides's suspicions. Her kind had banished her from carrying weapons. Yet she had somehow kept a sword for her defense. She was a rogue huntress. None of her kind would aid her, and without other weapons at her disposal, she was no match for a renegade vampire. Despite his misgivings, he would not leave her at the mercy of the one who had targeted her.

"Pack your bags. You'll return with me."

Selena's eyes narrowed. "You won't tell me what to do."

"You don't have a choice, huntress. Either you come with me, or I stay here with you." Though he had no intention of staying here with the huntress.

Renault grinned. "What will the neighbors think?"

"Fine." Selena stormed off down the hall.

Colt snickered. "I guess she's worried about her reputation."

"I doubt she has much of one to protect," Atreides said under his breath.

"Meaning?" Colt asked.

"She's a renegade," Basil offered. "I knew when she came to the club that she wasn't a typical huntress. Hell, first your brother Daemon gets tangled up with a huntress who was a borderline renegade, Atreides, and now you are involved with one who is a full-fledged renegade."

No, she wasn't a typical huntress at all. Which made her that much more dangerous.

"Basil, can you locate Twilight for me? I want a word with her at once. It sounds to me like she knows more of the story than she's telling us."

Basil bowed his head. "I will see to it, Atreides." He cast a glance down the hall, then looked back at Atreides, his brow furrowed. "The huntress will complicate matters."

"No doubt."

Basil gave a sardonic smile and vanished.

CHAPTER 8

"I'm proud of you, Daemon," Tezra said, stretching out on a chaise lounge in the dark beside a pool of warm water in the Virgin Islands. "Atreides needed this time to prove to you that he could run the clans without your watching over his every move. That's part of why he's so restless all the time and gets into trouble, just trying to prove his worth."

Daemon snorted, then began untying Tezra's string biking top, kissing her shoulder while he did so. "It was only because of your insistence that he couldn't do much damage while things are fairly settled down in the area for now that encouraged me to do so. Otherwise, I wouldn't have given him an inch."

"He did just fine while you were in Florida helping the hunters and other vampires take out the rogues."

"Maison and Voltan were watching over the situation."

She shook her head and slipped her hands down his bare chest, her fingernails raking the top edge of his swim trunks. "He deserves your faith in him."

"You have no idea all the shenanigans he has pulled over the centuries. But this one time…" He kissed her deeply and she moaned into his mouth.

"Daemon," she whispered against his lips.

"At least while your sister is at the hunter school," Daemon added, pulling off Tezra's bikini top and dropping it on the chaise lounge, "she'll be safe and sound." His fingers began untying Tezra's bikini bottoms.

"You could just pull them down," she said, amused.

"It's the untying and letting it slip away from your body that intrigues me more."

His fingers slid between her legs, and he smiled. "Wet already and we haven't even gotten into the pool yet."

She moved against his fingers, raking her nails over the erection pressing against his swim trunks.

He groaned and jerked off his trunks, unable to hold back. He still thought of Tezra as a borderline renegade, but all his now. He was just glad his brother had hooked up with a vampiress and seemed to be satisfied enough, although Atreides had talked of wanting a huntress just like Tezra, even though Daemon knew he jested.

One renegade huntress in the family had been problematic enough. Two would be a disaster.

Thankfully, Daemon had convinced Atreides he wouldn't want Tezra's sister for a mate. No other huntress in her right mind would hook up with another vampire—so Daemon knew in that regard, he had no worries about Atreides.

* * *

ON THE DRIVE back to Atreides's home, the vampires all began talking again about how they had room enough for the huntress at their homes.

Atreides gave them all cold looks. He was in charge now, and the huntress was his to protect.

"All right," Renault said, "so you don't want any of us to take her home with us, but you have your butler and housekeeper, and no one else to protect you. At least Daemon has Voltan to serve as his bodyguard, should the need arise. But you have no one. We could stay with you and see that she has extra protection should the rogue attempt to get to her again."

Atreides could imagine his friends all vying to win the huntress's favor. Not that they would want her as a mate or anything, but just to be able to show off to the others of their kind that they had made inroads with a huntress. They would be the talk of the clans for years to come, just as Daemon had been when he took Tezra for his own.

Still, their point was valid.

"Until we sort this out, you can stay in the guest rooms."

Everyone was grinning, but the huntress. She had fallen asleep in the farthest back seat in the van. If Atreides hadn't been concerned he might need their help in protecting the huntress while they looked into this matter, he would have said no.

"What do you think this is truly about?" Renault asked.

"It could be anything from a vampire just being a psycho with no rhyme or reason for the attack, a way to get back at the hunters who have murdered some of our vampiresses with no just cause, or a way to start a war between our people and theirs. There's just no telling."

"And Twilight's involvement?" Colt asked.

"She doesn't like hunters. Yet when she came into the room to see Selena, she seemed more than interested in her. I thought it was just because the huntress was acting so out of her element and that intrigued Twilight, but then she'd said she'd intended to rendezvous with her," Atreides said.

"I would love to hear the reason," Renault said.

"I'm sure we all would," Atreides said. "It was something to do with Selena looking for her sister, but we don't even know who she is." He realized he should have asked Tara Green if she knew who Selena's sister was.

"I found Twilight sleeping at a hotel near the club. Do you want to

have me take her to your house or the club?" Basil communicated to Atreides privately.

"My house. See you there in a few minutes," Atreides said telepathically back. To his friends, he said, "Basil found Twilight. They'll meet us at my house."

"Maybe she'll be able to shed some light on this," Renault said.

"If she knows who the rogue vampire is and didn't tell me already, she'll be banned from all vampire establishments," Atreides said.

"Amen to that," Colt said.

When they arrived at Atreides's home, lights illuminated the gardens out front of the two-story brick mansion and Atreides first noticed Iconia's yellow Mustang sitting in the long, curved driveway. *Hell.*

"More trouble," Colt said. "How about I carry the huntress into the house so Iconia won't be quite as pissed about it. The huntress is still sound asleep."

"Do so."

Atreides left the van to speak with Iconia, to tell her that he had business to take care of, and they would make time for each other later. But as soon as she saw Colt carrying the huntress out of the vehicle and heading toward the front door of his home, he swore she was going to go into a feeding frenzy and spill blood, his, the huntress's, and anyone else's who got in her way.

"What is *she* doing here?" Iconia asked, her extended canines visible.

"She was injured by a rogue vampire and—"

"The way she came into the club, she deserves everything she got. Again, I say, what is she doing *here*?"

"She didn't deserve being brutalized by a vampire. No one does."

Renault opened the front door for Colt as he cradled the huntress in his arms and entered the house.

"I have some business to take care of. We'll have to see each other later."

"If you would mate me, we wouldn't have to find time to spend with each other," Iconia said, slipping close to him, wrapping her arms around his neck, pressing her body against his.

Yet, his body craved the feel of the huntress close, the impish expression she had worn when she'd danced with him, the subtle fragrance that was all hers.

"Later," he said, kissed Iconia on the forehead, and vanished. He knew she would be even more pissed off now, but he wouldn't tell her again that he had business to take care of.

Inside, Basil waited with Twilight in the living room with Colt and Renault.

"Where is the huntress?" he asked his friends telepathically.

"Sleeping in the guest room she used before," Colt said.

"All right, let's get down to business." Atreides motioned for Twilight to take a seat on one of the velour couches.

She flopped down on one as if she didn't have a care in the world. If he said she could no longer use any of the vampire establishments, would she be so carefree? As much as she loved them, Atreides didn't think so.

"You asked to see the huntress through a human, Tara Green?"

All of the vampires were watching her, smelling her emotions, studying her reactions, subtle or not. Twilight twisted her lips in a way that said she was trying to figure out what to say that wouldn't get her into trouble with the vampires, Atreides thought.

"Okay, what did you need to speak with the huntress about?" Atreides asked, getting down to business.

"Her sister Rosa has disappeared. She has done it before. She's a huntress, wild, trying to find a hunter mate. No one believes she's missing. The other hunters assume she just doesn't want to be found because she's fooling around with another hunter."

"Rosa," Atreides said. "All right." He folded his arms as he looked down at her. "But you have word otherwise?" Twilight couldn't have. Rosa was the huntress who had agreed to work with him. No one but the vampires who were guarding her knew about her.

Basil and Renault took a seat on a couch opposite her. Colt leaned on an arm of the sofa, his arms crossed over his chest. Atreides remained standing.

"Everyone has ignored the situation but her sister, Selena. She has been looking into her disappearance. Tara Green is a friend of mine. She's a friend of Selena's. Tara asked if I could check my vampire sources, that's what she calls you all, and see if I might learn anything that would lead to a different conclusion. That the huntress is in trouble. That she had a bad run-in with a vampire or a group of vampires, and that she's not with a hunter like the others believe."

"And?"

"I didn't find her. But I learned that Selena was outed by her kind."

"Why?"

"She killed a hunter who was going to murder a vampiress who happened to be carrying his child. When he learned of it, he intended to murder her. Selena protected the vampiress, but the hunter wouldn't stand down. He planned to kill both of them, huntress and vampiress. He couldn't let a vampire-hunter child of his stain his reputation as a hunter."

"Selena killed him," Atreides said, taking a seat on a chair, surprised as hell. "And for that, she has been cut off from her kind, despite doing what was right."

"Who is the vampiress?" Basil asked.

"Charlene. But she's dead. The brother of the one who Selena killed went after Charlene, determined to finish what his brother attempted to do. Except this time, Selena wasn't there to protect her."

"The hunter's name?"

"Cliff Kellerman. He's a redhead, and he was close to his brother. Rumor is he intends to kill Selena next for murdering his brother, even though she was in the right, and he and his brother were in the wrong."

Atreides ground his teeth.

"I've heard you're looking for five hunters who have killed innocent vampiresses. Some say one was the one Selena killed. One is the brother. And I don't know who the other three are," Twilight said.

"Why didn't you tell me all this before?" Atreides couldn't believe Twilight would withhold the information from him when she was always looking for ways to be accepted by their kind.

"I...wasn't supposed to know. And I didn't learn about some of this until Tara came to me. She asked me to see if I could learn anything about Selena's sister's disappearance." Twilight shrugged. "I think they're all connected. Maybe."

"But you have no clue where the huntress is?" If Twilight or anyone else knew, he would have to move Rosa to a new location.

Twilight glanced at the entryway from the hall to the bedrooms. Selena stood there and Atreides wondered just how long she had been listening. She was wearing a T-shirt that featured an angel with black wings. An avenging angel?

"Selena, are you feeling better?" he asked.

"Did you drug me?"

Everyone turned to look at Atreides, appearing a bit taken aback. "Pain medication. The effect must have lasted longer than I predicted."

She turned her attention to Twilight. "What do you know of my sister?"

"I was looking into her disappearance because Tara asked me to. And because..." Tears welled up in Twilight's eyes. "Charlene cared for me, and I adored her. She was so happy to be having the hunter's baby, and then he tried to murder her, but you protected her. So, I was trying to help you find your sister."

Okay, that made sense, Atreides thought.

"You said Cliff Kellerman killed her? And there are at least three other rogue hunters out there?" This time she directed the questions to Atreides.

"Apparently."

"You're not planning to hunt them down, are you?" Selena sounded worried about him.

"We have gone to the League about this. But they say without proof, their hands are tied," Atreides said.

Selena turned to Twilight. "Did you learn anything about my sister?"

"I think a vampire has her. I can't say for sure. But I...well, I sensed that some of them know something about her, but they wouldn't say." Twilight glanced at Atreides.

"Which vampires?" he asked, furious that anyone who was guarding her might have leaked the information.

"No one I knew. And you know a host can't just go up to a bunch of vampires and start taking down names. But I can offer my blood and I get them to talking, when they're not sucking."

Well, that was true, Atreides had to concede.

Selena sat down next to Twilight on the couch. "Why do you do it?"

"It feels great. They love me for it. I love them for it. If I didn't, I wouldn't do it."

Selena shook her head.

"You killed a hunter defending one of our own," Atreides said to Selena, admiring her greatly for standing up for their kind and putting herself into a dark hole, where the hunters were concerned.

"It was the right thing to do. I'm...I'm sorry that the other hunter murdered her. If I had known he intended to, I would have stopped him also."

Twilight nodded and brushed away tears.

"Are the hunters angry enough to kill you over this?" Atreides asked, already knowing he wasn't allowing her to leave his house. Not only would the hunters not have her back, but some rogue wanted her dead.

"The brother, Cliff, I guess. The others? I think they would have already done so if they had wanted to. Unless they want to make it look like a vampire did it so they're trying to figure out how to do that."

"They wouldn't hire a vampire to murder you, would they? One that is already rogue, and he has no qualms about killing a huntress?" Atreides asked.

"The one who tore into me? He didn't kill me. He injured me, but only when I was close enough to reach the club. Like he wanted to involve you somehow. Or Basil. The club or those who go there. I even was wondering if he'd done it to say that huntresses weren't safe while hunters were killing vampiresses."

Atreides nodded.

"I need to borrow a phone. I need to call for a loaner car until I can get mine back," Selena said.

Everyone looked to Atreides to see his take on it and he knew they would all say no to her if any one of them had been in charge.

He shook his head. "You're staying with us until we catch this rogue vampire, if he still exists, and ensure he doesn't hurt you again."

"Fine," she said, and headed for the front door.

Atreides stared after her retreating backside in disbelief. What part of she wasn't going anywhere did she not understand?

His friends were smiling at him. Hell, he knew the huntress was a lot more trouble than she was…well, he guessed she was worth the trouble after what she had done for Charlene, but Selena was going to be loads of trouble. Guaranteed.

Atreides appeared in front of her, making her slam her sweet, soft, and very delectable body into his. "You have no hunter protection. You are not going anywhere. If the vampire kills you, all of our necks would be stretched for the hunters' chopping block."

"I'm going after Cliff Kellerman."

"You didn't see him kill Charlene. You don't have anyone from the community who will vouch that Charlene didn't intend to hurt anyone," Atreides said, wanting to hold the huntress close, to kiss her pursed mouth as she glowered up at him. "And if Twilight is right, the man wants to kill you, so give him a reason. You attack him without provocation, he'll cut you down and say he was justified. That the vampiress had been *your* lover and that's why you killed the hunter who made her pregnant. Not that he was going to kill her but that you were angry about it."

Selena folded her arms and smiled up at him.

"Well? Couldn't the hunters say that?"

"Two others witnessed the event. I was afraid they would protect him, but thankfully they didn't. And they spoke to the board on my behalf, even though no one appreciated what I had done. Hunters kill their own when they go rogue and begin to kill vampires, humans, and hunters without provocation or authority. But in his case, he'd never done anything wrong in his whole hunter career."

"That anyone knows of."

"True. And no one was willing to dig up dirt on him. If he and his brother and three others have some kind of vampire death squad they're in charge of, someone must know something," Selena said.

"They're targeting our women. And we have already told the League. They're not doing anything about it."

"Your women." Selena pondered that, then frowned. "Because they can have your offspring."

"Rather than turn a person." Atreides's brows pinched together as if he was deep in thought.

"What?" she asked.

"Do you feel any...differently?" he asked.

"Tired, but that's to be expected. I had nightmares all night."

"About the attack?"

"Yes."

"Anything else?"

"Nothing that I can remember."

"All right, listen. We'll do this together. You'll have us as backup when you don't have your own hunters to aid you. We'll help you to learn who the rogue vampire is, if he's still alive, and take him down. And we'll keep you safe from Cliff Kellerman or any other hunter that might give you problems."

"They won't like it if they learn I'm working with you."

"What do you care if they've left you to fend for yourself?" he asked.

"If I stay here, I won't have any unwelcome bed guests, will I?"

Atreides smiled. "Only welcome."

CHAPTER 9

*A*treides didn't know why he said what he did to the huntress. The only way he would return to Selena's guest room was if she were fighting off a vampire. Or hunter. "Twilight, you'll stay here under our protection."

"But I thought I could hang around and hear more stuff, and let you know what I find out," Twilight said, and he knew she desperately wanted to help his kind to prove to them she was truly on their side after having hidden what she had known from them so far.

"No. If the vampire or the hunters involved have any inkling that you're helping us, you'll be dead. In the meantime, I need to take care of some business."

"Do you need any of us to go with you?" Colt asked. "Renault can go."

Atreides shook his head. "I'll return as soon as I can. If you have any trouble, let me know at once."

Then Atreides took off in the way of the vampire, needing to speak with Selena's sister, figuring they didn't need two huntresses taking the risk, when it seemed those involved in the killings were already after the one—Selena. No one had been looking for Rosa, at least that they'd known of until they learned about Selena. Rosa hadn't been at risk, and she hadn't been cut off from her hunter kind like Selena had been.

When he arrived at Colt's ranch house, Atreides figured Colt would learn of the huntress staying there before long, and the number of vampires who were also there, protecting her. Colt hadn't been home in a while, visiting with other vampires in the area, which had given Atreides the idea of sequestering Rosa there.

He knocked at the guest house door, and Basil answered, to Atreides's surprise. "Who's minding the shop?"

"I've got help. I wanted to see how Rosa was doing," Basil said.

Four vampires immediately rose from the sofas in the living room of the ranch-style guest house and inclined their heads to Atreides.

"Where is she?" Atreides expected her to come out of the bedroom and ask when she was supposed to do something, *again*. She'd hounded him for days about it, but despite wanting her help, he didn't want to endanger her before they were ready to do this right, then Selena had popped into his life and everything just sort of unraveled from there.

Rosa came out of the bedroom and he heard the TV on in there then.

"We have another huntress to do the job," he said.

"Who?" Rosa narrowed her eyes and folded her arms. "Don't tell me after you've had me here doing nothing all this time you want to swap out huntresses. You know very well that I can do this."

"Your sister, Selena. She has been searching for you and nearly got herself killed because of it."

Rosa sank into a chair, looking sufficiently shocked and upset to satisfy him. "Hunters?" she asked, her voice strained.

"A vampire."

"What? How is she? What happened?"

"She suffered a couple of bad bite wounds and a mild concussion. Tell me again why you want to help us."

"But she's okay now?"

"She's under my protection because her own kind won't offer it. She killed a hunter who was attempting to kill a vampiress. Did you know about that?" He couldn't have been angrier about it.

"Uh, yes. Okay, listen, my sister and I don't see eye to eye on a lot of issues—first and foremost—my dating habits."

Atreides raised a brow.

"But when it comes to hunters killing innocent vampires, I'm just like my sister and wanting to deal with them in the harshest way possible. So if hunters are targeting vampiresses, I want it stopped before we have a full-fledged war. I want in on this and I'm going to hunt the hunters down with or without your support." Then Rosa frowned. "Why would a vampire try to kill Selena when she had protected one of your own?"

"That's one of the things I have to discover. Do you know any vampire who would have a grudge against her?"

"As many rogue vampires as she has terminated? A few family members, friends, associates, possibly."

"What about the brother of the hunter Selena killed while protecting the vampiress?" Atreides wondered why no one had mentioned this to him, that a pregnant vampire had needed protection. Maybe because it had happened so quickly and no one had known about it, or maybe she had worried he would find fault with her for carrying a hunter's child. "Cliff now vows revenge and intends to kill Selena."

Rosa's eyes widened. "He wouldn't dare. She might be a borderline rogue hunter, but no way would he incur the League's wrath if he killed her out of revenge. He would have to have their sanction, or his own death would be ordered. Even though she has been ostracized for what she did, enough of our people stood by her, because when she protected the vampiress, the hunter had attempted to kill Selena. It wasn't right. And what the hunter had planned to do to the vampiress wasn't right."

"Why hasn't the League declared Cliff a rogue?" Atreides asked.

"No hunter witnessed him killing an innocent vampire. At least none that would tell on him," Rosa said. "And the same if Cliff vows revenge. It might be hearsay, but unless anyone has real proof he intends to? No one can do anything about it."

"What if Cliff hired a vampire to kill Selena?" Atreides asked.

"I wouldn't think one would work for a hunter. Even so, how is she alive if one of them had attacked her?" Rosa asked.

"We're not sure why either. He was dead, at least we think so, by her own sword. I'm certain he was trying to send us a message. Who does Cliff run with? What about the other hunters who might be involved in this?" Atreides wanted her to verify who else might be in on this.

"Perry Rochester, Harry Canton, and Lonnie Wilson? All of them are great hunters, as far as their kill ratio. Those who believed Selena was protecting the vampiress—still couldn't believe a hunter would kill a vampiress unprovoked. Not all hunters agree with what she did. She had turned on one of our own kind—even though he was in the wrong and wouldn't capitulate. It was kind of a wakeup call for some. Kill innocents and you could be put down for it by one of your own kind. But there are some who feel killing any vampire is justified. And Cliff and his brother and their friends are just arrogant enough to feel they can pull something like that off and get away with it. If they're responsible for the other vampiresses' deaths, they've done just that. I've heard the lies they've told about Selena or the others who vouched for her. The bullying, rallying of other hunters to bully and threaten her, only caring about making money off the venture, and not giving a damn about who it could hurt.

"I've heard they've even threatened to take over the League and run it right, unless the League changes its way of doing business. More money, fewer vampires, and anyone who stands in their way is coerced to change their thinking or else. I would like to believe I would have stood up to Cliff's brother and done what Selena had, but I wasn't there. I can help your cause now, doing whatever you need me to do in regard to ferreting out the murderer or murderers of the vampiresses."

"You didn't believe your sister could be in serious trouble after she killed a hunter?" Atreides would have been there for his brother in a heartbeat every step of the way if something like that had happened to him. He couldn't believe Selena's sister would be so insensitive about her sister's current plight just because Selena did what she knew was right. Hell, Selena wasn't even supposed to be wearing weapons and anyone who had wanted to take revenge against her meant she'd been at real risk.

Rosa cleared her throat. "Once her actions were backed by the League, I didn't worry about her. I guess I should have. But I *did* approve of what she did and that's why I offered to help your people learn who the murderer of the vampire women is or are." She let out her breath in a huff. "I want to see my sister."

"Now?" Atreides still was perturbed with Rosa for not watching her sister's back.

"Yes, now."

"What about your brother? He threw Selena out of a club."

"I told you, a lot of hunters aren't happy with her. She shouldn't have gone to a club, not right now. She should have waited a bit."

Atreides shook his head. "She could have been seriously hurt when he kicked her out of the club when she was on her own. Her car had been stolen even." He wasn't going to mention about the fact she was armed with a sword when she went to the hunter club.

"Her car was stolen also?"

"Yes. When she was attacked. So she was walking back to her apartment alone." He wasn't going into all the details because he felt guilty enough about just dropping her off at the hunter club. Yet, he had felt she needed to be with her kind. What a mistake that was!

"Oh, I didn't know. You didn't tell me!"

"I didn't know that she was your sister, or I would have had you take care of her! I didn't know who her family was. She wouldn't tell me."

"Oh." Rosa frowned. "Well, as to our brother, he only cares about how this affects his standing with the rest of the hunters. He has an image to keep up. He's one of the good guys, and I would hope that if he had witnessed something like Selena had, he would have stood up for the vampiress and defended her against the hunter. I would think he would have. But since he hadn't been there, he doesn't want the backlash to taint his good name within the hunter community."

"So he doesn't care about your sister being in the right and being on her own—subject to humiliation and threats to her life?"

"I'm sure he's conflicted. I don't believe he thought she would be in danger. But it's easier to be angry with Selena than face his friends' ridicule."

"Then he's an ass."

Rosa smiled, then she frowned. "You don't have any designs on my sister, do you?"

"I saved her three times. I never thought I would be put in that position because hunters would want to throw her to the wolves."

"Or a sadistic vampire?"

"Yes. She nearly got herself killed looking for *you*."

"I'm sorry." Tears glimmered in Rosa's eyes.

It wasn't enough, he felt. "I'll be back soon."

Rosa was up on her feet at once, looking hopeful. "I have to tell her how sorry I am. Are you returning with my sister?"

"Yes." Atreides disappeared and returned to his house. He found Selena sitting with his friends in the living room having coffee.

Colt jumped up from his seat where he was sitting too close to Selena, for Atreides's comfort, and smiled broadly as if he'd been caught with his hand in the cookie jar.

Atreides gave him a growly look. "Selena, you need to come with me."

"To go where?" She rose from her seat.

"Yeah, where are we going?" Colt asked, eager to go with her too.

"To see her sister, Rosa."

Everyone gasped.

"You have her sister?" Colt asked.

"Yes, she's the huntress who was supposed to help us lure the hunter or hunters who are out to take down our female vampires," Atreides said.

"My sister? And you didn't tell me that she was safe?" Selena asked, her voice angry.

Now Selena was upset with *him*!

"You hadn't told us who you were, or who your family was when I wanted them to protect you. Rosa actually came to me to offer her services after you killed the hunter who tried to kill you and Charlene, though she hadn't said why. I had to talk with her before I told you what was going on. Since you were already involved in this, I was going to tell her that she was being replaced. She hadn't told me anything about you or the trouble you were in with the hunters. She should have been there to protect you. I didn't even know the two of you were related. I only learned of it when Twilight mentioned it at the house."

"But Rosa is still going to help you?" Selena sounded hopeful that her sister would be on her side in this.

"Yeah, but she should have been there for you all along."

Selena frowned at him. "You could have told me that she was helping you before you went to see her and taken me with you then."

"I didn't want anyone knowing she was helping us. It could

have gotten her killed. Since you are already being targeted, I had the idea you could swap places with her and she could return home, but she still wants to help, and she wants to see you. I'll take you there to see her now."

"Where?" Colt asked.

Atreides smiled at him. "You never go home. She's staying at one of your guest houses." Then Atreides took Selena into his arms and transported her to the guest house at Colt's ranch.

His friends soon followed, since they were not done protecting Selena and now they wanted to meet with Rosa too and learn what Atreides had in mind to do.

When they all arrived at the guest house, they went inside to speak with Rosa. Selena and Rosa hugged each other, tears in their eyes. He was glad the sisters showed real affection toward each other, but he still couldn't let go of his annoyance that Rosa hadn't been there for her sister.

"I can't believe you've been with the vampires all this time. Why didn't you tell me you had planned to do this?" Selena asked her sister, sounding annoyed.

"I couldn't tell anyone, without jeopardizing what we were trying to do. Any of the hunters could be suspect as far as being involved in the vampiress killings."

"You think I could have been?" Selena asked.

"No, of course not you."

Selena let out her breath. "You didn't think I would search for you?"

Rosa sighed. "I'm sorry, Selena. No, I didn't realize you would. I guess I was so busy wanting to help the vampires after what you had done for them, I didn't think of it. I certainly never thought you would be hurt. But a vampire hurt you. Not a hunter."

Selena scoffed. "What if, in trying to locate you, Cliff and his friends tried to eliminate me? Or they were involved in hiring a vampire to hurt me?"

Rosa glanced at Atreides to get his input.

He shrugged. "We don't have any idea why he would have hurt her and not killed her then."

"Okay, fine. My sister and I will do this together," Rosa said, determination in her voice.

"Then Cliff and his friends will have a target on your back too." Selena sounded worried.

"I should have been there for you all along. So should our brother have been. I'm sure the word will get out before long that I'm working with the vampires to take down the rogue hunters." Rosa gave her another hug.

"So I'll stay here with my sister then?" Selena asked Atreides.

"I think it would be better if you are separated in case anyone learns about one of you. Then you both won't come under attack." Atreides didn't want the women together. If hunters, or vampires, were out to get one of them, they would have both of them in the same location and could try to kill them then.

Rosa agreed, but Selena looked like she wanted to object.

Rosa said, "He's right, Selena. Atreides is in charge. I think his plan is the best."

Selena folded her arms and looked crossly at Atreides. He gave her a small smile. He suspected she was still annoyed he'd been in her bed last night, but he wouldn't go there again. Now he knew just who she was and what she'd done to anger the hunters in her League. Unless she needed his protection, he was staying out of her room.

"We'll go tonight, both huntresses stationed at different locations, armed, ready, a couple of vampiresses walking down the street to a vampire pub, talking, not paying attention to their surroundings, male vampires on the rooftops ready to swoop down, but we want the huntresses to initiate the fight, or the hunters can say rogue vampires attacked them. We need to record that vampiresses are being attacked for no reason," Atreides said.

Then Atreides had a telepathic communication and he wondered what had gone wrong now.

"A hunter and a couple of his hunter friends are here at the vampire club looking for Selena. The one is named Daniel and he said a hunter had arrived at the hunter club when Selena was just going inside while carrying a sword. The newly arrived hunter saw Daniel throw her out of the club and then a vampire showed up and then others came to speak with her, took her in a van and drove off. He recognized you, Atreides. Daniel is Selena's brother, and he wants to see Selena at once or he'll bring the whole League down on you."

"He didn't care anything about her when he threw her out of the club," Atreides said, annoyed.

"She was armed and shouldn't have been in the club. She knew better, the brother said."

"That still doesn't excuse him for abandoning her. At the very least, he should have taken her home." Atreides paused. *"Put him on the phone."*

"Yes, sir."

"This is Daniel Townsend. Who am I speaking to?" The hunter sounded arrogant and pissed off!

"Atreides. I find it odd that you would kick your sister out of the club after she looked like she'd been hurt, and you realized her car wasn't even there so she had no safe way to transport herself back home, yet you did nothing for her. What did you think would become of her?"

"A vampire like you would take advantage of her?"

Atreides hadn't changed his opinion of the hunter. He was still an ass. "Take care of her, you mean, when your own kind won't watch her back. She's here with us, under our protection for now."

"Put her on the phone."

"Since you ask so nicely"—Atreides didn't want to make a worse situation out of this than it already was—"here she is."

"You have some nerve hassling the vampires who protected

me when you didn't give a damn about me. I was injured! And they took me in. So get lost. I don't need your 'help,'" Selena said, putting the phone on speaker, to Atreides's surprise.

"You know what Mom and Dad would say about this?"

"They've already said enough. Besides, do you know where Rosa is?" Selena glanced at Rosa who arched a brow.

"Off with a hunter friend, I imagine, like usual."

"That's who I was looking for, if you even gave a damn about that. Family is supposed to mean something. Family is supposed to take care of family, but that doesn't work in your book." Selena was angry and Atreides was glad she was letting it all out and not trying to hide how she felt. With a sibling treating her like a pariah, it had to hurt.

"I can't believe you're putting all the blame on me." Either Daniel just didn't get it, or he was in denial that he'd done anything wrong.

"Did you know Cliff plans to kill me?"

Daniel didn't say anything. Which bothered Atreides. Did he know or not?

"Well, he does. So just think on that. You have a hit out on your own sister for doing what was right and it's coming from your own hunter friends."

"I'll look into it, but you can't stay with a vampire." Daniel acted like he was still fully in charge of the situation, like he was her second dad, and she would have to do what he expected of her or else. Atreides hoped she didn't cave.

"Why? Will it hurt my reputation?" She scoffed. "And what do you care about it anyway?"

"You're my sister."

"You should have thought of that when you threw me out of the club and didn't make sure I got home all right. Atreides not only wanted to make sure I got home safely, he realized I didn't have any hunters to watch my back and wouldn't leave me alone." Good. Selena was standing her ground.

"I'll...I'll be in touch." Daniel hung up on her.

"I'm so sorry," Rosa said to Selena. "Hearing more of the story, I am really angry with Daniel."

"I was carrying a sword," Selena conceded.

"But you'd been injured, and you didn't have your car to leave it in. You couldn't have just parked the sword outside the club. I would have taken you out of the hunter club and talked to you and learned what had happened, and then I would have called Mom and Dad and taken you home to stay with them. I never would have thrown you out of the club and made you fend for yourself like that. I'm glad Atreides and his friends protected you when your own family should have. For that, I'll forever be grateful. But you shouldn't have felt you couldn't give out your name or solicited our parents' help either. You could have died!" Rosa said.

Finally, the gravity of the situation was sinking in!

It didn't take long before Daniel called back. "I'm helping you to find the hunters and turn them over to the League for disposition."

Atreides was really surprised, but glad her brother was finally willing to help them out. He still felt Daniel needed to make amends to Selena. Still, it was better if more of the hunters sided with them in this effort than if they did it alone. As long as the word didn't reach the hunters' ears who were killing the vampiresses. Then what? They would lay low until everyone got complacent again?

He explained the plan to Daniel and the others who volunteered to help and then it was time to set up the traps.

Set up strategically around town, they would start searching for the rogue hunters who would attempt to kill the vampiresses. The women would be in pairs, for the most part. A hunter, or two, would be waiting in the wings, watching for trouble, stepping out to protect the vampiresses. The vampiresses would telepathically communicate they were in trouble, the hunters helping

Atreides would identify the rogue hunters, while others were transported to the scene of the battle if there was a fight and to apprehend the rogues. The hunters couldn't move easily like the vampires, and that meant they would have to aid the hunters, so the killers couldn't easily escape.

At least that was the plan, and Atreides prayed it would work out to everyone's benefit—the rogue hunters taken into custody and no other hunters or vampires injured or killed in the process.

Daniel and his friends were helping in a cause that neither Selena nor Rosa thought they would.

Selena said to her sister before they parted company, "Be safe, Rosa."

Renault and Colt were taking care of her while she did her part.

"Be safe, Rosa," Atreides said.

"You be safe, Selena. You're the one some of the hunters want to take down, and there could still be a vicious vampire after you," Rosa said.

"I know. But maybe the wolf was there to help me, to guide me, not to hurt me. And besides, you put yourself in harm's way all the time."

"When it comes to a broken heart, yes, but when it comes to real danger, the kind you put yourself in, no. But you have a good heart and I'm proud to be your sister." Rosa gave her a hug and she hugged her back, then Atreides whisked Selena away to her place in the city to watch for the rogue hunters who were in this game.

CHAPTER 10

Glad Daniel and his friends were now helping them to catch the hunter rogues before they killed again, Selena was watching for the vampiresses to arrive, Atreides at her side. And she was glad he was here for her. But she wasn't feeling quite herself and she didn't know what was wrong.

Sometimes hunters came down with common colds or the flu, but they healed twice as fast as humans, so it was no big deal. But she was just feeling off as she and Atreides moved again, making their way to where they would monitor the vampiresses and ensure they would be safe. They couldn't always do this or be everywhere either. And the vampiresses would feel they could just take down the hunters if they so much as threatened them, instead of calling on Atreides and leaving the area in the vampire way. It was ludicrous, but they were as arrogant as the vampires when it came to fleeing in the sight of danger.

She took a deep breath and saw the three vampiresses they were supposed to watch, including Iconia. Selena sighed. She wished they were protecting another vampiress other than Iconia, but she should have realized Atreides would have wanted to protect his girlfriend and yet he still wanted to take care of Selena.

Selena suspected Iconia would *not* be happy with the arrangement, and worried Iconia might even take her on when she learned she was here with Atreides instead of helping with the mission.

About half hour into the night while the ladies walked the streets headed for a different vampire club, they saw nothing but buildings and sidewalks glistening with raindrops from an earlier rainstorm and shops with their security lights on, the shops having closed four hours earlier.

Selena was feeling tired, like she could sleep for weeks. She thought it was from the blood loss after the vampire had bitten her. Or maybe the concussion she might have suffered. Or the trauma from the whole experience. She was definitely off her game.

The women's pointed heels clicked on the pavement as the vampiresses chatted about what vampire bash they were attending next. Iconia had been quiet the whole while as if she hadn't been interested in vampire bashes or anything else the women had to talk about. But then Iconia said, "If that huntress stays with Atreides for very much longer, she's dead meat."

Amused at Iconia's comment, Selena smiled. The vampiress could try and kill her, but Selena was really good at taking down vampires. Then she sighed. Maybe not tonight. Maybe not the way she was feeling. She realized she really should say something to Atreides about it. If she couldn't fight hunters well enough, she couldn't protect the vampiresses and she could get herself killed. And for what? For not being honest about the way she was feeling so under-the-weather?

Then they saw a couple of hunters on the prowl and immediately, whatever strangeness she was feeling subsided and all her senses were attuned to the potential crisis in front of them. Selena and Atreides stiffened. Atreides immediately wrapped his arm around her waist and she knew he was going to grab her up and deposit her in between the vampiresses and the hunters, should they attack the women. But all they did was stop to talk to them.

That surprised Selena. Unless they were after a particular vampire and they thought the female vampires might know who he was or where he was. They had an uneasy peace between the vampires and hunters at times. If a rogue vampire was killing innocents, the hunters would deal with it and usually the vampires would turn the rogue over to the hunters if they knew who and where they were. They didn't need a war between both groups just because the vampires were protecting one of their own. Just like the hunters shouldn't have been protecting those who had murdered the vampiresses.

Atreides still had a hold of Selena though, ready to transport her so she could protect the vampiresses. But if he did transport her there, would he then have to protect Selena from Iconia's wrath to see her there with him? Selena suspected so.

The vampiresses had all folded their arms and looked at the hunters with disdain. But then they shook their heads and moved around the hunters.

The hunters watched them for a moment but didn't make a move to attack and continued on their way.

"If we don't find the rogue vampire soon, the League will give the mission to someone else," one of the hunters said.

The blond shook his head. "We've had good leads, supposedly, from vampires and humans alike and every time it has turned out to be dead ends. We'll keep looking, even if the League assigns someone else to the mission."

"All right by me."

The men were two of Selena's brother's friends. She was glad they hadn't acted threatening in any way toward the vampiresses. But she and Atreides had to keep after the women and ensure their safety. They sure didn't want the vampires to kill hunters, if

Selena could intervene. Though she figured if she killed another hunter, the League would believe she was in with the vampires. Particularly since she was staying with Atreides for a time.

Though she was glad her brother was helping her and their sister now, she really did wish her sister hadn't gotten involved. What if all three of them perished in this fight? Her brother and her sister and Selena? Their parents would be devastated.

"They killed her," a voice said in Selena's head and she thought she was hearing things, that her head was giving her issues. That she needed to lie down for a while. That fighting rogue anythings wasn't in the cards for her tonight. *"You shouldn't have lived,"* another voice said to her.

Okay, so she really was losing it.

She rubbed her temple and Atreides looked down at her. "Are you all right?" He looked more than a little concerned.

"I'm tired."

Atreides was studying her when he should have been worried about the women, especially his girlfriend. "You don't look well. Your skin is flushed. Is your head hurting again?"

"I'm just tired. And...." She frowned. "I thought I heard someone say, 'They killed her.'" She took a deep breath. "And someone else said I shouldn't have lived." She shook her head. "I'm just tired is all."

Atreides was frowning. "Did you hear the women talking?"

"Of course. My hunter hearing is as good as a vampire's, you know. Anyway, Iconia said she plans to kill me if I stay with you much longer. She could try. She wouldn't be successful."

"Can you hear what I'm saying?"

"Of course. I'm not deaf. I'm just tired."

"Hell. I'm not speaking openly to you but telepathically."

She frowned at him. "No way." She didn't believe it, one iota.

He looked really concerned about it. *"Yeah. I wouldn't lie to you about it."*

Wait, that meant she'd been turned? She was a vampiress? Oh, just great! She couldn't believe it. She wouldn't believe it. "You think I'm one of you?"

"Yeah, that's about the gist of it." He rubbed her back consolingly.

"No way. I can't be." Wouldn't she be able to do all the things Atreides could do? She didn't want to think of all the ramifications of that. Or how it would affect her standing with her family. Or the League!

"The vampire who bit you could have shared his blood with you after he took your blood. You were unconscious for a while, you said. That's possibly why he knocked you out." Atreides sounded sympathetic, but a little worried too.

She shook her head. "You said he was dead. That I had killed him. I couldn't have killed him if he had turned me."

"Hell, maybe the rogue vampire dumped ashes and clothes there to cover that he was still alive," he said, "so we wouldn't hunt him down."

"And then the rogue just told me I should have died. That he meant to kill me. So it wasn't as we thought, that he was trying to direct me to the vampire club and get help." Telepathically. Ohmigod, she couldn't have heard the two vampires any other way. Unless...unless she just imagined she'd heard them.

"But you heard two voices? Two distinct voices? Both male?" Atreides asked, his attention focused on the vampiresses again. Where it should have been all along.

"Yes, they were distinctive. The one who said they killed her— did it mean one of the vampiresses? That the hunters killed his mate?" Selena glanced around the area, looking for anyone else who might be in the area watching them.

"Now that could be." Atreides didn't say anything more for a moment as the vampiresses continued to walk along the street talking to each other while Selena was lost in her thoughts.

She kept trying to think of any other time she had heard anyone talking like that—in her head, but she didn't recall any voices like that. Unless someone had talked to her in her sleep and she didn't remember it.

"Maybe, you're naturally telepathic, Selena. Like Tezra is."

Tezra was a borderline rogue and she'd had the odd gift of being able to read vampire's minds. They hadn't known it either and that meant they didn't hide their thoughts from her. Fatal mistake on their part. But no way was Selena telepathic. If she had been, she would have heard everything that the vampires were saying in the club that night she went inside looking for Twilight.

"No."

"Maybe your concussion has something to do with it."

"But...if a rogue had turned me and he was still alive, he could control me then, right? Nothing like that has happened," she said.

Atreides was grinding his teeth.

"What are you doing?" she whispered to him.

"Controlling my fangs."

Her lips parted. He immediately looked at her mouth as if checking out the size of her teeth. She ran her tongue over them. "I don't have teeth like yours. Let me see yours."

Usually, a hunter would not ask to see a vampire's extended teeth. A vampire only showed them to a hunter when he was angry and ready for a fight.

Okay, so they were darned wicked looking, she thought. "Why are they out?" Because of the hunters talking to the vampiresses?

"Because I'm furious that the rogue vampire might have turned you."

"You think he did for sure." There was no "might" about it. At least she thought he felt that way. "All right," she said, "I'm damned angry, ready to bite the bastard and no vampire teeth are coming out." She ran her tongue over them again, just in case she might not feel them unsheathe until she had more experience at this.

He smiled at her and because of his extended canines, he looked a lot predatory.

She frowned at him. She was serious about this! If she was angry, why wouldn't the vampire teeth just—appear? "I tell you that nothing is happening. And I am angry. So if I had been turned, they would extend, right?"

"You're not angry *enough*. If you were, there's a good chance you would have no control over your fangs."

Suddenly, Iconia was in their space, realizing Selena and Atreides were nearby and together. "What the hell do you think you're doing here?" Iconia said to Selena, then sliced Atreides a glower. "And with Atreides?" But she was in Selena's face, too close for comfort and *her* fangs were fully extended!

"We're protecting you," Selena said, matter-of-factly.

Iconia sneered at her. "As if one of your kind could actually do that."

"Well, I did before." Selena wasn't going to allow Iconia to intimidate her.

"See how well that worked out for her," Iconia said, her tone biting.

"You're right. I couldn't watch her twenty-four seven. But had I been there when they came for her again, I would have fought any rogue hunter to protect her."

"Believe me when I say I wouldn't fight a vampire for you to save you," Iconia said.

Well, that was a given.

But if Selena were one of them now, why didn't some saber tooth fangs appear? Iconia was in her space, baring her teeth, giving her grief, and when Selena ran her tongue over her teeth again, there were still no vampire-size teeth anywhere.

"She's here to fight hunters on your behalf, believe it or not," Atreides said, sounding highly annoyed with Iconia. His teeth were still fully extended.

"Why are you growling at me?" Iconia asked, undoubtedly incensed that Atreides would take a huntress's side over hers.

Which couldn't help but amuse Selena. Still, she was worried about this other issue though, that she could truly be a vampire. What if she pushed Iconia, and the vampire made a threatening move toward her? Then would fangs finally erupt? Selena was halfway tempted to force the issue, but she didn't want to have to have Atreides break up the fight when they were supposed to be watching out for the vampiresses.

Selena started thinking more of the consequences of what could have happened to her. Could she fly? Vanish? Transport herself to somewhere else? Would she crave drinking blood? She couldn't do any of those things. Atreides had to be wrong about Selena hearing vampiric conversation in a telepathic way. Iconia had to have been talking aloud to her friends and with her superior hunter hearing, Selena had heard. That was all. And the other? She was tired. The two male voices she'd heard had just been a figment of her imagination.

Yet Atreides seemed to have believed he had talked to her through telepathic conversation. None of it made any sense.

Then she realized Atreides and Iconia were having a stare down. Which meant? They were telepathically communicating. Okay, so then why couldn't Selena hear any of it? That proved Atreides was wrong!

Then she saw trouble ahead. Two hunters were approaching the two vampiresses who had been with Iconia while she was having her meltdown with Atreides. One was Cliff, the brother of the one Selena had killed. She hurried to get into place so that she was close enough to protect the two women, should the hunters threaten them. Atreides had made sure that all the women who were taking part in this manhunt were not rogues and shouldn't be on any hunter's target list.

That was all the vampires needed was to kill a hunter who was legally hunting a rogue. The two hunters were respectfully asking the vampiresses questions, not hassling them or acting threateningly in any manner.

Atreides had quickly joined Selena, while Iconia had appeared next to her friends, which she wasn't supposed to do because she could have spooked the hunters and made them believe she was coming in for the attack. But they just eyed her warily, hands on the hilts of their swords, naturally, but no one fought anyone, thankfully.

Selena heard her name mentioned, which surprised her. "We're looking for Selena Townsend," Cliff said. "We know she has been hanging around vampiresses to protect them."

Oh, great, so they already knew what she was up to, or maybe, because she'd tried to protect Charlene, they had just assumed it.

"What do you want with *her?*" Iconia asked, as if she was protecting her, but Selena suspected if they had a beef with Selena, Iconia would happily just point behind them where Selena and Atreides were lying in wait in case there was any trouble. Which would blow their whole operation.

"She has gone missing and a human reported that she might have been...abducted by a vampire. Then her sister has gone missing too." Cliff acted as though he cared about her safety, when in truth Selena knew he wanted her head on a platter for killing his brother.

"I've heard she and her sister are together and they're having a great time. I'll be sure to let them know you want to hear on their status should I ever run into them somewhere, though I highly doubt I will. You might know that hunters and vampires don't generally socialize. I'm sure they'll get in touch with you and let you know they're fine." Iconia sounded arrogant, her arms folded across her chest, looking like she had no intention of "finding" said huntresses or of telling them a hunter wanted to hear about them. Not that Selena blamed her. Under normal circumstances, it would probably never happen.

Cliff nodded. "Then we'll be on our way."

"Wait," Iconia said. "Aren't you glad they're together, having a great time?"

How did Iconia know she and her sister had seen each other and were working together on this? Unless she'd just made it up.

"Yeah, sure, but I'll really be certain when I find...them. Like you said, you probably won't be seeing them, but I still need to know for sure that they're...fine."

Cliff didn't care anything about finding her sister, unless it led him to Selena, she bet. Then the hunters wandered off into the thickening mist. The fog had started out light, but it was getting to the point where they couldn't see anything very far away. That gave the vampires the advantage because they could still hear the hunters' footfalls even if they were trying to sneak around in the dark. All of them could see well in the dark. But the vampires could move with their vanishing act and keep ahead of the hunters.

As soon as the hunters left, the vampiresses watched them until they disappeared into the foggy night, and Iconia and her friends continued to walk.

"Do you often see this many hunters about near the vampire clubs?" Selena asked Atreides. She didn't think this was usual.

"No. I don't know whether it's because the hunters that we just saw want you dead, or if some of the others are looking into who might be hunting vampiresses. If the hunters truly don't want a war on their hands because of whoever is killing our people, then it would behoove them to help us with this. Or at least help themselves by taking down the rogue hunters."

"I agree." But about this other business—Selena being a vampire—she knew Atreides was wrong. "I'm not one of you, you know. You are mistaken."

a treides knew he wasn't mistaken about Selena having been turned. He just didn't want to upset her further about what she'd become while they were trying to safeguard the vampiresses. Unless a huntress had the rare telepathic gift, she couldn't hear vampires' thoughts when they communicated that way with each other. And Iconia had been telepathically speaking to her friends. She hadn't spoken to just them, but for any vampire in the area to hear, which meant she'd been highly perturbed with both him and Selena to air her grievances like that.

"Your friend is going to get herself killed if she's trying to protect our kind," Iconia said to Atreides in her telepathic way, but she was channeling her thoughts directly to him and no other vampires could hear her, just like she had done earlier with him.

"She has risked her life already for some of us. She's one of us now."

Iconia looked sharply back in the direction Atreides and Selena were hidden from their sight. *"What? A huntress who is now claiming to be one of our clan?"* She scoffed. *"That would never happen unless she was bitten and turned. And you better not even think of doing that to her."*

"Unless I'm wildly mistaken, she has already been turned."

Dead silence. Atreides knew that wouldn't go over well with Iconia. Then yeah, Selena would be a member of their clan, just like the huntress turned vampire Tezra was. It also meant Iconia might have some competition because Selena had already said she wanted to dance with him again. Never in a millennium would he have figured this would come about. His brother would have a fit when he heard all that had happened. Atreides's only solution was to resolve the issue between the hunters who were out to kill their vampiresses and turn them over to the League for their disposition. He did not want, under any circumstance, for his people to attack the hunters, even if the hunters were in the wrong.

Forever, their people would stand up and fight and not back down. He'd tried repeatedly—and unsuccessfully—to convince them that they needed to just vanish if confronted by hunters. The problem was the vampires, as a whole, felt they were vastly superior to the hunters and humans. And that was ingrained in them from the time they could vanish and flee a fight, and the hunters taunted them for being cowards and not facing them in battle.

"You've got to be kidding. If not by you, then by whom? Ohmigod, the vampire who brutalized her?" Iconia asked, sounding shocked.

In a way, Atreides hoped she was one of them, but he knew Selena would be upset about it and the League and her family could have real issues with it. *"Yeah, if what I believe is true."*

"So why do you even think it's true? When I was aggravating her, she didn't expose fangs, not even baby ones," Iconia said.

"You were telepathically communicating to your friends on an open broadcast about wanting to kill her if she saw me any further."

Again, Iconia was silent for a prolonged period, then she laughed. *"That's precious."* Then she grew serious. *"You heard too."* She didn't sound contrite about it or unsettled, just surprised.

"Yeah, I heard too. You know she's my ward and—"

"Hell, if she's one of us there's nothing to be done about it. All right. Damn it. But you're not dating her. We're together and you'd better let her know it," Iconia said.

He smiled. He would date whomever he wanted when he wanted and if Selena was a vampiress, albeit a huntress too, she was fair game. He knew if he didn't date her all his friends would be interested, and maybe others also. She was unique like Tezra had been unique. Since she'd been turned by a rogue and because she'd tried to protect one of their own, it was different than in Tezra's situation. Most of the males would accept her. Some of the females, like Iconia, would feel they had lost the chance to mate with one of the vampire princes ruling the clan. Others, who had some hope of gaining his support if Iconia had slipped from his favor, would lose out.

Someone would have to take Selena under his wing, and he was already doing that. The thing about a huntress turned, from what they'd learned of cases like that, the hunter could still walk the streets in broad daylight, lay out in the sun, and be a vampire all in one. That meant their offspring would be able to do what? That was the question right now. He knew a huntress turned in Florida was due to have her baby soon and everyone was awaiting the outcome.

He hoped it would turn out well. He hoped the baby would have the same qualities that the hunter and vampires possessed and would not turn rogue. Then they would all be in for a world of hurt. Daylight vampires, some had called them. But they didn't really know for sure what would happen to them.

When he didn't agree with Iconia about dating Selena, Iconia broadcasted to any vampire around. *"I mean it. If she's a vampire, you're not dating her."*

Her friends both looked at her in astonishment. Atreides immediately glanced at Selena to see her take on it—had she heard Iconia's threat or not?"

Selena scoffed. "As if I planned to date a vampire."

* * *

SELENA THOUGHT tonight would be a bust, or maybe the hunters were being more careful to target vampiresses because of the recent attacks and they were afraid of retaliation both by vampires and hunters who had a moral code of ethics. She worried it might take some time before the hunters tried this again, waiting for the vampires and hunters to get complacent and then the rogue hunters would strike again.

She couldn't believe Iconia would even think that Atreides would "date" her. He must have told her that Selena was a vampire. He was so wrong about that.

He'd been quiet though while he walked beside her, and she figured he was listening for sounds everywhere, just like she was. The fog couldn't get any thicker, she didn't think and then she thought she heard someone running toward them. Just a human? A hunter with his sword raised? She didn't think it would be a vampire. They could just vanish and reappear where they wanted to.

Then she saw Twilight. Oh, God, she didn't need to be out here in the gloomy night. What if a rogue hunter thought to dispatch her because she was a blood bond and they might think she would learn what she could about the hunters, acting as a spy for the vampires?

"There you are!" Twilight said, sounding like she was out of breath.

"What's wrong?" Selena asked.

"There's a fight on First Street between—" Twilight didn't get anything more out.

Atreides swooped Selena up, startling her, and carried her to the fight. But it wasn't between hunters and vampires. Three humans were beating up a single man and Selena pulled out her sword and ran into the fray, putting herself in the middle of the fight, serving as a shield to the single man. At least he appeared to be the underdog in the fight, but maybe he deserved to be just where he was at. Who knew?

Atreides and the vampiresses were off to the side, not interfering. It was better for a hunter to quell the violence between humans instead of vampires getting involved. It could look like they were ready to turn a bunch of humans or dine on them tonight otherwise.

"Who started the fight?" Selena asked.

"He did," the one man said, the others agreeing. "He stole my money at the club. Damn pickpocket."

"Do you have his money?" she asked the accused man.

"And mine. He took our wallets," the second man said.

"And yours?" she asked the third man.

"No, he didn't manage to get mine. But I caught him trying. That's how we knew he had taken my friends' wallets."

She pointed her sword at the man she'd been protecting. "Give them their wallets back, now, or I'll leave them to take them from you in their own way. Make it easy on yourself."

He seemed reluctant to do so, but finally went ahead and pulled out the wallets and handed them to her.

"Now get out of here before these guys want to beat you up some more."

He tore off and the men took their wallets from her.

"Thanks," one of them said.

"Yeah, thanks. He wouldn't tell us the truth when we tried to get him to tell us that he had the wallets. But we knew he had them because he went for mine and the other guys' wallets were missing."

"Well, you're good now."

Then the men left, and she returned to speak with Atreides. "Will we find anyone do you think? Any rogue hunters?"

"If that one wants to kill you," Iconia said. "Why didn't you do something about him when he talked to us. You saw him, didn't you?"

Selena had wanted to, but she couldn't until she had proof that he'd actually murdered Charlene. "I would have if he had threatened any of you." Iconia included.

Selena's phone vibrated in her pocked and she pulled it out to see she had a call from her brother. "Hey, Selena, I just checked with Rosa and she's calling it a night. Have you seen anything suspicious?"

She still couldn't believe her brother and his two best friends were helping them. "Just some humans fighting. And Cliff was out here with his friends looking for Rosa and me—to make sure I'm fine."

"Hell, you should have run him through."

"Yeah, well, you know that would make me a rogue hunter then. He questioned a couple of vampiresses, but then they continued on their way."

"Okay, so you're good."

"What about you? Are you going home for the night?" she asked.

"In a while. I'm afraid whoever did it, if it isn't Cliff and his friends, they realize we're watching for them and they're going to be on their best behavior—for a while."

"I agree. And we won't be there when it happens. Daniel, I need to tell you that I was bitten by a vampire." She hated to tell him about it.

He didn't say anything at first.

"A rogue. Not someone looking to hook up."

"A vampire bit you?"

"Tore into me. It wasn't a love bite. Yet he didn't kill me. He wanted me to reach the vampire club and get Atreides and his people involved, somehow, we figured, but now I'm not so sure. I'd been bitten and then ended up at the vampire club and they had to take care of me. After that, they dropped me off at the hunter club to get help."

"How do you feel?" Daniel sounded really concerned, more than he'd ever sounded. "Hell, and I threw you out of the club."

"I had a sword on me." Giving him sort of an out.

"You had been bitten by a bloody vampire."

"Yes."

"How do you feel, Selena? Honestly?" Daniel asked.

"Tired. Atreides told me I heard vampire communication."

"Damn it."

"Yeah. I have to tell you if it's true, I might be one of them."

"Hell."

She needed to let him process the information, good or bad. "Good night, Daniel. I'll talk to you later."

She felt the same way as her brother did, but she couldn't do anything about it. It really truly was becoming a hazard of being a hunter of vampires now. In the past, they killed hunters, period. Now they were turning some of the hunters, to try and get them to work for them. A hunter couldn't kill the vampire who turned him. And they had to do their bidding. The rogue vampire wanted to control a hunter, the ultimate treasure.

No hunter wanted to be controlled in that way. It was worse than death. And they had no way to kill themselves. They could only fight the vampires to the death and hope to die in a good fight. But she didn't feel that way. Some of her hunter friends: Tezra Campbell, Rachael Bremerton, Crystal Anderson, and Alena MacLeod had all been turned and they had been great huntresses. Now they were a combination of hunters and vampires. Selena would never have wished it on herself, or on them, but she wouldn't regret it. Not when she knew she would have friends all over the States who were just like her. Not that many, but enough to know she wasn't the only one.

She would somehow learn to live with it. She wondered, facetiously, if she could dance any better with Atreides with new moves as a vampire, if she were one.

"Let's go back to the house," Atreides said.

"She can stay with me," Iconia said. "I can take care of her."

Yeah, like get rid of her! She would much rather stay with Atreides. He was a much safer bet.

"She's my ward, she stays with me."

"You know what Daemon's going to say about all this?" Iconia asked.

Selena assumed Atreides was hoping no one told Daemon about what was going on here while he and Tezra were away.

"Well, don't you have anything to say about it?" Iconia asked Selena.

"I might as well stay with Atreides. He set me up in the guest room already." Selena hoped he would be fine with her staying there until she could figure out what she was going to do. She could return to her apartment, she figured.

What if the rogue hunters come after her there though? She guessed she could stay with Colt at his ranch too. He seemed to have a bunch of vampires living there to guard her sister. Well, in truth she should stay with her sister, so why did she want to stay with Atreides?

Thankfully, she wasn't feeling thirsty for blood and she couldn't do anything else the vampires did, so she still wasn't sure about what was going on.

Then she said to Atreides, "If the women are all going to their places safely, then I'm ready to stay at your home. I'm going to need my clothes though, unless you think I can return to my place and will be safe enough. I'm sure my sister or brother wouldn't mind staying with me or watching out for me now."

"No, you stay with me. I don't want to worry about you being there alone if they should leave." He wrapped his arms around her. "I'll talk to you later, Iconia." Then he transported Selena back to the house. Basil, Colt, and Renault were there and Atreides said, "Go get Selena's clothes and bring them here."

"I should go with them," Selena said, "so that I can get everything I need."

"Okay, then we all will go," Atreides said.

"How long is Rosa going to stay with you?" she asked.

"Until we catch the rogue hunters. She's all in on this. She admires you greatly and wants to do what you did for the vampiress—to prove that the hunters are rogues and not all hunters are like that. I just hope that we can get them quickly."

"All right. I feel the same way."

Atreides contacted the other guys and they all arrived to ride in the van to her place so she could pack. Thankfully, when they arrived there, they could see no one had been in her apartment. She was halfway expecting someone to have trashed her place— hunters, mainly, angry she got away with killing the rogue hunter. But no one had touched. She packed her bags in the bedroom and her toiletries in the bathroom. Then she got her perishable food out of the fridge. She was glad the vampires still ate food. She wouldn't want to give up that hunter or human aspect.

"Are you hungry for anything other than food?" Atreides asked. "I'll feed you when you need something to eat."

"Blood, you mean? I don't feel any urge to have blood." She wrinkled her nose at the thought.

"You don't mean the rogue vampire turned her," Colt said, looking shocked, but then he smiled. "That could be good news."

"No one's dating her," Atreides said.

"As if I wanted to be with a vampire." Selena didn't want them taking it for granted that she just wanted to throw out her hunter sensibilities and start dating vampires.

"If you're one of us, would you be interested in dating a hunter? I'm not sure a hunter would be interested in dating a vampiress even if she's a hunter too," Renault said.

"I doubt a hunter would be interested in a vampiress. I would probably be stuck with having to date a vampire," Selena conceded.

"I love the way she says that. She would be stuck with one of us. I believe she would be happy to have one of us after she got used to this," Colt said.

Then they carried all her stuff to the van and drove back toward Atreides's place. Near her apartment, they saw a wolf on the side of the road, and she stared at it. "That's it."

The guys all looked out the van windows and Atreides jerked the van to the side of the road, but when they got out of the van, the wolf was gone.

"Are you sure that was the same wolf?" Atreides asked.

"Yes, the same one. Exactly. And he's following us—me."

They all piled back into the van.

"I would kill him if I could," Renault said.

"I would beat you to it," Colt said.

Atreides shook his head. "We have to know what this is all about. His showing himself to us like that has to have a purpose. He knew she would recognize him, and then we would know him if we saw him again. But I don't recognize him in wolf form."

Selena knew they could turn into bats or wolves or ravens. "Maybe he's the one who said to me that they killed her. I heard him whisper it in my ear."

"He could talk to you because he knew you had been turned, maybe because he had turned you," Atreides said. "You were with me when you heard him speak. He was talking to you telepathically, privately, so I didn't hear his conversation with you."

"Privately? You can talk with someone privately?" She was surprised, though she thought it was cool.

"Yes."

"Wait! When you were with Iconia, you were talking to her telepathically, weren't you? I thought you two were having a staring contest, but that wasn't what was going on, was it? You were talking secretly to each other." Now Selena was getting it.

"Yes. When Iconia was speaking at first, she was broadcasting her telepathic conversation, not caring if anyone heard her. She had no idea a huntress could hear her."

"Broadcasting. I can't do any of that."

"You'll learn to. But you need to be with us, to learn about us. You'll do it. We'll help you," Atreides said.

"So do you want to date me?" Yeah, yeah, so she said she didn't want to date a vampire, but… She sighed. He was a hot dancer and there was a lot more to him that she really liked—his protectiveness when no one else wanted to protect her. His taking care of her when she was injured. His willingness to have her help the vampires to take down the rogue hunters. Even having his friends search for her car.

Atreides laughed.

She smiled. "I know, crazy notion, right? Especially when you already have a girlfriend who wants to kill me."

"We'll see."

"Nah, I'm just joking. I might date the owner of your club. He wanted to dance with me in the worst way."

"You're not dancing with Basil," Atreides said.

She laughed this time. "Who's stopping me?"

"Me. No one who dances like you do can dance with anyone other than me." His voice was firm about that.

She smiled. "You were hot."

"I *am* hot. You are too. I know there was more than one vampire who would have switched with me in a heartbeat to dance with you," Atreides said, smiling at her.

"The vampiresses were ready to terminate me."

"Right. And some probably still feel that way about you."

She sighed. She knew that. "Yeah, I'm totally popular, aren't I? Well, thanks for all the help with bringing my things here. But I'll have to return to my own place at some point in time." She really had no intention of staying at Atreides's place forever. What would his brother, Daemon, think when he returned home from his vacation? He probably wouldn't like it one bit.

CHAPTER 12

$\mathcal{N}$ ot if Atreides could help it was he allowing Selena to return to her apartment. He could see why Daemon was so intrigued with Tezra that he didn't want to give her up. Atreides already felt the same way about Selena when he shouldn't be feeling that way at all.

"I'm going to bed, and I don't expect to find you in it again," Selena said.

He smiled. "Not unless you invite me in it."

"I won't. Night." She left him then and his friends were smiling, shaking their heads at him.

"You know your brother is going to be upset if he returns to find that you mated a huntress turned vampire in his absence," Colt said.

"Well, he really has nothing to say about it. Not that it's going to come to that anyway."

"You still have Iconia to deal with," Renault said.

"Yeah, I do. And she's going to be unbearable to live with."

"Maybe Basil can date her," Colt said.

"I'm not in the least bit interested in Iconia," Basil said. "Selena, yes."

Atreides went to have a drink with his friends.

"You're really going to date her?" Renault asked. "It's one thing to take care of her, to protect her after she did the same for our kind, but to date her? Leave her to us to date."

"No, she only danced with me." Atreides took a sip of his brandy.

"He's not giving her up. Don't you remember the way he chased after us when we were trying to talk to the huntress in the parking lot at the club, and he was in vampire rage mode? I've never seen him act that way over any woman he has ever dated. And he wasn't even dating her," Colt said.

"I worried you were hassling her."

"You were worried she would take one of us up on an offer of a dance," Colt said.

"She would not have danced with you, just like she wouldn't with Basil." Atreides was sure of it. Something about him had drawn the huntress to him, just as he had been drawn to her. No way did she want to be with any of the other vampires. Even when she'd been injured, she'd come to the club asking for him, seeking him out, wanting his help.

"Will you join the huntress in bed tonight?" Renault asked.

Atreides smiled. He couldn't help himself. But he would not join her unless she invited him into her bed, just as he had told her. Though the notion was tempting. More than tempting. He wanted to hold her tight, kiss her until tomorrow, and make love to the vixen. Yet, he would hold back the inclination to show her how much he wanted her—this early on—when she was so newly turned.

He heard the shower shut off down the hall, imagined her wearing just a towel, her hair dripping wet, and water droplets trailing down her cheeks and throat, begging him to kiss her there. He wanted to join her in the worst way when Colt cleared his throat and Atreides glanced at his friends.

All of them were smiling at him.

Colt said, "Like I said, I can just imagine where your mind has wandered to."

"He'll end up in bed with her," Renault said.

"I agree. If only I could be there instead, but I will dream of it," Basil said.

"Iconia will be rabid," Colt said.

"Sweet dreams," Atreides said to Selena, channeling the telepathic words just to her.

Colt shook his head. "He's speaking to her."

"You think? I would be too if she would listen to me," Renault said.

Atreides glanced at Renault. "Don't *even* try."

Colt laughed. "I bet Iconia had a word or two to say to her once she heard you thought Selena had been turned."

"Yeah, no dating the huntress turned," Renault said.

Atreides poured everyone another sniffer of brandy. "You know I will do as I please."

"Oh, for sure. What will Daemon and Tezra say?" Colt asked.

"Under the circumstances, I believe they will be accepting. What else can we do about it? And the League has to respect that we are taking care of their huntress when their own kind would most likely reject her." Atreides finally sat on one of the chairs. He couldn't get his mind off her, but he needed to. "I believe the one who bit her had a mate or someone he cared about, and the hunters killed her. We need to learn more about the vampiresses who died. We need to make sure all of them are accounted for."

"Some live at the fringes of our society. They don't really follow Daemon's rules, or partake in our social functions," Basil said.

"I agree. I suspect it might be someone like that. And the vampire who hurt Selena was one also. A nonconformist." They weren't rogues, per se, in that they didn't kill people for the fun of it. They followed some rules, but they wouldn't bow down to Daemon's rules, and when Atreides was in charge, his rules.

Daemon's vampires allowed the fringe vampires to exist, but they didn't support them either. If the vampires played by the prince's rules—he was a good leader and well-thought of by most—he would back them in any way he could. If vampires wanted to live by their own rules, they could move out of the territory, and that's what some did. It was a dangerous thing to do because they didn't have backup should hunters wrongly target them.

Atreides had reached out to them on a regular basis, one of his jobs under Daemon, as a sub-leader, but none of them had shown any interest in becoming part of the "establishment" as they called the prince's reign.

It did worry Atreides and his brother, because there was always the chance that the fringe vampires would gather under an emergent leader and try to force the current leadership out. There could be chaos, a civil war between vampire clans. They needed to stay strong, to ensure that they weren't persecuted by the hunters, and work together.

But there were always those who couldn't abide by rules. And it was like that before the Black Death had turned them. He'd heard there was some dissent in the way the League of Hunters operated also, and that they had a fringe group of hunters too. Atreides wondered if they ever got the upper hand, would it be better or worse for the vampires?

Order came at a price, but chaos, a bigger one and he knew if either of the fringe groups were to gain a decisive foothold into the ruling powers, chaos would ensue.

Right now, they had peace between the hunters and vampires —of a sort—and they tried to keep it that way.

"Who's volunteering to check out the fringe groups?" Atreides asked.

None of his friends volunteered.

Atreides shook his head.

"Hey, I had a fight on my hands, the one time I went there to speak with some of them on your behalf," Renault said. "I didn't think I would come out of that alive."

"Your brother counts on you to deal with them because you have such a magnetic power about you," Colt said to Atreides.

"You ought to go and take Selena with you," Basil said.

"You don't think they would see her as a threat?" Though Atreides had another thought. What if she could identify the vampire who stalked her? He would have to be a wolf, but maybe she could smell his scent, or maybe he would act nervous if she turned up. Maybe he told others what he had done and one of them would out him.

"I think she might figure out who he is," Basil said.

"Let's retire then to bed." The day was going to be stormy tomorrow and Atreides figured they could be out and about during the day. Though he would sleep some midday and go out again at night when the rogue hunters might be on the prowl. He wanted to know who was on the hunters' terminal lists also, and he thought to ask either Rosa or her brother to see if they knew. He wasn't sure if Selena would know that or not.

Everyone went to their respective bedrooms and he want to his suite. After showering, he climbed into bed and telepathically communicated to Selena in a whispered voice, just in case she was sound asleep, *"I'm taking you to the fringe groups in the morning, if you are up to it."*

She didn't respond. He assumed she was asleep.

"Fringe vampires?" she finally asked, her voice sleepy.

He knew it. She was one of his kind! That was the first time she'd actually communicated telepathically with them. He was over the moon. He smiled, closed his eyes, and said, *"Yeah. Vampires."*

She sighed and then he left her alone so she and he could sleep. They would have a busy morning and evening tomorrow so he needed some sleep tonight.

He was just drifting off when she appeared in his bedroom, touching his shoulder, stirring him awake.

"You think the vampire who bit me was a fringe vampire?"

"Possibly." He pulled her into his bed with him. "And the vampiress he might have been talking about could have been a fringe vampire also. We don't have very good records of who they all are. I try to, but they move around so much, it's hard to know who and where they are at all times."

"I never would have thought that. What if the hunters who killed the vampiresses were on the fringe also?"

"Hell. Well, if that's the case, it exonerates the rule-abiding hunters and vampires."

"Except for Cliff and his brother and their friends. They worked directly for the League," she said.

"He just had a hidden agenda. The vampiress was carrying Cliff's brother's child and he had to hide the fact, probably using the other murderer's technique so that the League and the vampire clan would believe it was the work of another group of hunters. If that is the case."

"Fringe. I never think of them because the hunters that are on the fringe really never cause any trouble. They might not live by League rules, but that doesn't mean they're rogues. Now I wonder though."

All he cared about was that the huntress had joined him in bed.

CHAPTER 13

$\mathcal{S}$elena didn't believe she would be staying with Atreides in his bed tonight, but when he'd spoken to her and she realized he wasn't in the bed with her as close as he seemed, she went looking for him. And found him in his own room, nearly asleep. That was when she realized he had communicated with her telepathically and she'd heard him! No way could she do that unless she had become one of them. She still didn't seem to have any other symptoms of being a vampire except for the telepathic communication. Which was pretty cool, really. She could listen in on vampires talking to each other and for a while, they might not know that she could.

She thought the moving from place to place like they did could be a neat way to deal with rogue vampires and hunters also. She realized she would be able to do a lot of things that she couldn't do before. Good things. So it wasn't all bad. And from what she knew of Tezra's new condition, she wasn't limited to moving around in daylight only on cloudy days. Which worked for her. She wasn't a night owl normally, though taking down rogue vampires did often mean doing some night work.

She sighed as she planned to stay on the other side of the bed, but Atreides seemed to want her close and after they had danced so close, she was feeling the same way about him. She couldn't figure out why she felt a connection with the vampire, when she had figured her genetics would preclude it. But she was really glad to be working with him.

And learning from him how to deal with all the changes she would be experiencing. She really didn't want to drink blood, but she suspected once it came to that she would feel differently.

She snuggled against him, loving the feel of his hot body and muscular form. She knew he got it from all the sword fighting they did. Not against rogues all the time, but she knew they practiced sword fighting with each other, just like the hunters did so when they took on the vampires, they would be in shape to win against their enemy.

"Sleep," Atreides said. "Tomorrow will come soon enough." His voice was soothing, and she closed her eyes.

But her mind wouldn't shut down. She kept wondering if she could transport somewhere, how would she make it happen? She thought of being in the kitchen and getting a glass of water. And then she was in the kitchen, standing beside the sink, amazed. Was she dreaming?

Suddenly, Atreides was standing next to her and she blinked at him.

"Did you need something," he asked.

"Water. But I wanted to see if I could really...I can't believe I can...or that I'm...one of you."

He wrapped his arms around her and kissed her lightly on the lips. "It will all come as a surprise to you, all your new abilities, I'm sure. I would have a celebration, welcoming you to our clan, but I need to wait until Daemon returns. Even though I'm in charge while he's away, it still would only be right if I do this when he's here."

She sighed and kissed him back. "I guess now I really won't be welcome in hunter clubs. And I'm still not sure about vampire clubs."

"The vampire clubs will welcome you. I won't lie and tell you all vampires will welcome you to the clan. There will always be those who want to keep with the old ways and aren't happy about change. And there will be those who will be jealous of your abilities to be a daylight vampire. I think if we could have that ability, we would all want that." He released her then and got her a glass of water. "Ice?"

"Yeah, thanks."

Then he handed her the iced water and she sipped from the glass. He wrapped his arm around her waist and carried her to his room. "This doesn't bother you? The transporting business? Some who are newly turned find it hard to stomach."

"No, I feel fine. Thanks. I'm…I'm just glad I can do it."

She liked the togetherness when here she never thought that would have happened. With a hunter, yes. Man, had her life been turned upside down.

"What will Iconia think of all this?"

"She won't like it, but she and I haven't really enjoyed each other's company in a long time. And hopefully this will make her move on," Atreides said.

"My family's not going to like this."

"It's inevitable. You can't help that you were turned and unless a hunter is interested in a huntress turned vampire, you could be unmated for all eternity. But with me, that's not happening."

She laughed. "We just met. What if I don't care for you after I've gotten to know you for a while?"

"I'll take you back to the club and we can dance together again and prove just how good we are for each other. That wasn't in the least bit faked."

She sighed. "Yeah, that was good. Hot. Unbelievable. You rocked my world."

He smiled and kissed her temple.

* * *

"WHEN WE DANCED on the dance floor at the club, all I thought of was bringing you back to my house and making love to you." Atreides kissed her mouth and ran his hands over her bare shoulders.

"I had never seen dancing that was so erotic in my life. Hunters just don't get that wild at their clubs. And I really didn't think I could dance with you like the others were dancing. I was burning up. And knowing it was crazy, but I would have gone home with you—uh, just to talk, but if we'd danced like that somewhere more private, you never know."

He smiled down at her. "We would have been right here, just like we are now."

"But so much has changed. I've changed."

"And I'm ready to dance with you at the club again. I doubt you could make your dance moves any sexier, even as a huntress turned."

Then they kissed again, their tongues doing a duet, their bodies rubbing against each other's in a way that said they were hot for each other. Their hearts were beating hard and she ran her hands all over his body.

He was trying to keep his teeth sheathed, but she was too sexy, too desirable and they extended right away. He wasn't going to bite her, her own teeth still small, though when he speared her mouth with his tongue, he felt they had extended like his had and were sharper and longer than before. She touched his long canines with her tongue, the change in their relationship evident.

As a huntress, would she have done so? Maybe. They seemed to have been attracted to each other from the first time they'd met. From the time he'd caught her eye and she had seen him. The challenge to him to join her had been in her gaze even then. At least to his way of thinking. She'd been an enigma, and now she was his. And he couldn't have been more thrilled.

Daemon would have to live with the way things were now, if he was at all disappointed in the outcome of Atreides's relationship with Selena. She was everything he'd ever wanted in a mate and more. He couldn't believe how the stars had aligned to allow this to happen either.

She slid her hands down his back and cupped his buttocks, just like she'd done on the dance floor, sending his blood to lower regions, preparing him for the next phase of the seduction. His cock was full blown already, eager to join the huntress. She was rubbing her sweet body against it as if ensuring that he stayed rock hard before she made love to him.

He cupped her breasts and kissed her mouth again and she cupped his face, her lust-filled gaze on his. "Don't bite me," she said.

He smiled. "I wouldn't dream of it. If you ever want to, we can do it, but it's totally up to you." Then he kissed her reverently, and he swept her up and set her on the bed. "I will do whatever you want."

She smiled wickedly at him. He gave her an evil smile back. Maybe he was being a bit hasty.

"Make love to me. All the way."

"That I am glad to do." Then he was kissing her mouth pressing his body against her nakedness and moving his mouth to her throat. Her heart was beating like crazy. He couldn't help the natural instinct a vampire had to follow the path to the neck and the need to bite for the sexual fulfillment it gave them both. He hoped someday she would agree to it. He heard the whoosh of her blood pounding wildly through her veins, just like he knew she could hear his. Did it give her the same draw now that she was a vampiress too?

A smile settled on her lips, but he didn't bite her, no matter how much he wanted to, no matter how much he thought she would enjoy it when they first tried it.

"Me first," she said, surprising him. Unless that wasn't what she had in mind.

She pushed him onto his back with a huntress's strength, or a vampiress's. And then she was straddling him, bearing her small vampire teeth that could certainly do the trick even though they weren't full size yet.

She licked his neck and his cock jumped.

Then she bit gently into his neck and his groin tightened with need. Her soft touch mixed with her tentative exploration nearly sent him over the edge. Then she sucked a little, licked the tiny wound, and sealed it. She smiled at him.

He ran his hands over her thighs, glad she wasn't revolted by the experience, though he hadn't thought she would be. Not when that was part of their nature. Then he flipped her over and tasted her neck, scraping his teeth against her skin in a tickling way, no injury, just the foreplay before the bite. He would do as she did, a soft bite, slow, suck a little so she could experience the pleasure, and then seal the wound. It would be healed before they finished making love. His was nearly healed.

He pressed his teeth against her skin, heard her pulse racing to the moon and back, heard the rapid beat of her heart, and wanted to tell her to relax, it would be good. Then he recalled what had happened the last time she was bitten. This wasn't the same, but he was afraid she was feeling *déjà vu*.

"Relax," he telepathically told her. *"It won't hurt, and you can shove at me or scream at me, anything to get me to stop."*

"Do it," she softly said back, her words showing she wanted to do it, but she couldn't help feeling apprehensive.

He realized she would probably have felt that way no matter what she'd gone through. She was still half huntress, not full vampire. She hadn't lived like this as long as he had.

He sank his teeth in gently, and then sucked. He meant to lick the wound sealed, her blood like an aphrodisiac to him. He had full control of his senses, so he could stop anytime, and would never harm her intentionally or accidentally.

She held his head in place, wanting the pleasure from his sucking from her, the cosmic connection they felt, and she cried out. He thought he'd hurt her, though he couldn't believe he would be able to, but then he realized his sucking at her had made her come.

He smiled, realizing she was really getting into their ways and he sealed the wound, then moved over her and she spread her legs, welcoming him in. He didn't ask if she was ready. Everything she did told him she was ready and willing.

And then he was surging into her, slowing down the pace, and thrusting again, their mouths seeking each other's out, kissing, licking, her tongue running over his teeth in a seductive caress and then he did the same with hers.

He couldn't get enough of her and wanted to spend the rest of the time with her wrapped in her arms. He was still pumping into her when she sighed and lifted her pelvis to make a deeper connection, wanting to participate in pleasuring him. He leaned down and licked her neck on the other side and she cupped his head, arching her neck so she could bite him again. Now she got it.

Then she was biting him, but he had to turn his head so she could do it, and he stilled his cock in her, wanting to thrust, but not wanting to mess up her concentration and end up with a torn neck. Though her teeth were small so she wouldn't be able to make too bad a wound. But he didn't want to upset her either, should she make a mistake. He could imagine what a setback that would be.

She sucked a little harder and this time, it was as though he were thrusting, the sucking motion creating a surge of need through his blood. He was ready to come when she licked his wound, and he began to push deeply into her again. He lifted her legs around his hips and surged deeper.

She groaned with pleasure, her hands on his shoulders, rubbing, kneading, and then before he could delay the inevitable any further, he exploded deep inside her. He thrust until he was finished, feeling satiated and ready to sleep with the huntress, but he wanted to do more. He moved beside her and with a leg propped over hers, he kissed her again. He moved his hand down to reach her clit and he began to stroke, wanting to bring her to fruition once more.

* * *

SELENA HAD NEVER IMAGINED what it would be like with a vampire making love and she'd always wondered what the draw was for blood bonds and hosts. Now she knew. It was amazing, and having an orgasm from Atreides sucking off her neck? Instant orgasm. Remarkable, wonderful. Now he was pleasuring her again and she couldn't love him more.

Love. Yeah, she loved him. She'd been in lust with him before, but she felt an even deeper connection with him now.

He was so eager to please her, and she felt the same way about him as she fell under his trance, not the vampiric gaze like he could do with humans, but just the way he mesmerized her with his need and love and want. She dug her heels into his buttocks, feeling like the end was coming soon as she licked his cheek, and then he thrust his tongue into her mouth. She sucked on it and kissed him again, nibbling on his lower lip in a gentle way, then kissing his mouth again when she felt the leap into the solar system and cried out, not meaning to.

Not with a whole house of vampires who could hear their lovemaking. Oh, she hadn't thought of that either. Certainly, if they didn't hear the rest of it, they had to have heard her cry of pleasure as she sank into the mattress, feeling like she'd touched a bit of heaven. She'd been so lucky to capture Atreides's eye. He was the maker of dreams when it came to pleasuring her.

He smiled at her and moved his hand from her clit to her breast, stroking her nipple before pulling her into his arms and covering them with the light comforter.

For a long time, they just rested in each other's arms like that, and then she did what she hadn't planned to do for a while, at least. "I love you, Atreides."

"I hoped you would. There's no getting rid of me. I love you too."

"Well, you're stuck with me too. You're just too hot to let get away. The other vampiresses lost out."

He snorted. "None of them ever felt the way you do about me. And I've never made a long-term commitment to any of them for the same reason. When you came along, I was lost."

She laughed. "I'm glad I found you and claimed you. Even though I was fighting the inclination."

"So was I, but it was a losing battle. Even if I'd managed to leave you off at your apartment, I wouldn't have left you alone."

"You worried about my safety."

"It was more than that. I wanted to be with you in the worst way. Now I know how Daemon felt about Tezra."

"She wanted to be turned so she could fight the rogue vampire who was trying to claim her, and she knew she would have more of a chance against him that way."

"She did. We were all worried about it because Daemon was so reluctant to turn her and she was going behind his back to ask the rest of us to turn her instead."

Selena smiled. "I bet that didn't go over well with Daemon."

"No. He was incensed. He told us if any of us turned her, we would be dead by his hand. And we knew he was serious. I hated what had happened to you, but I have to admit I was glad I didn't have to turn you."

"I'm glad it was taken off your shoulders too. We might never have gotten to this point otherwise." Though Selena suspected if she'd gotten to know Atreides better, she might have been ensnared by his charm and given in. They would never know. It didn't matter. She was happier than she'd ever been.

"We won't tell the others we're together as a couple," Atreides said.

She scoffed. "As if anyone would think otherwise." But she hoped he didn't feel he would be ostracized for taking her as his mate.

"I just want to let Daemon know before anyone else tells him."

So tell him already!

"I'm afraid if I explain what has happened to you, to us, he will return with Tezra to straighten things out," Atreides said.

"Oh, sure." She understood how he felt about that. He wanted to prove he could handle managing the clan. So it wasn't that he was afraid to tell the rest of the clan what was going on between him and her. She still figured they would all assume it. Yet, it wasn't the same as just coming out and saying it. She just hoped Daemon wouldn't cause Atreides too much grief when he returned home. She assumed he wouldn't with her because she couldn't help what she'd become. "Well, I can't be happier to be with you."

Atreides stroked her arm with a soft caress. "You are the light of my life, Selena. Since the moment you walked into it, I knew my world had changed. I think that's why Iconia was all over your case. I'm sure she realizes this isn't just some wild infatuation I have for you and it will end soon."

"It better not be," Selena said. "I don't often declare my love for another person."

Smiling, Atreides raised a brow.

"I did twice, but the hunters weren't ready to settle down and felt I was a little too borderline rogue to deal with. Most hunters stay with the same mate for life, but I could see getting dumped by a mate if the heat was on me and he ended up in a negative spotlight."

He kissed her cheek. "Many vampires mate for life and if you end up getting yourself in trouble, I'll back you all the way."

"Okay, it's a deal." She cast him a devilish smile. "If you turn rogue, I promise you a quick and painless death—the huntress in me coming to bear."

He laughed. "It's a deal."

But she didn't really know what would happen in a case like that. All she knew was she didn't want to lose Atreides for any reason.

She snuggled against him and tried to get her mind off the business with the wolf, the murdered vampiresses, Cliff and his buddies gunning for her, and Daemon's take on what his brother had done in declaring to her that he wanted her forever. She breathed in Atreides's scent and licked his chest. "Night, Atreides."

"Night, Selena." He smiled at her. "I love you."

* * *

AFTER MAKING LOVE TO ATREIDES, Selena finally managed to doze off, heard what she thought was a whispered thought in her head, but she couldn't catch the words, and saw the wolf in her mind's eye again. *The same wolf she saw when they were coming back from her apartment. The vampire knew she was staying with Atreides. Did he know she could even be staying with him for good if it worked out between them? Had he thought he could tempt fate in this way to make it happen?*

The fog surrounded her, swallowed her up, made her see beings in the mist, not anything she thought she could recognize, then one form came to her out of the fog. Iconia, her simpering smile telling her that all was not well with Selena's conquest of her boyfriend. Then Iconia's fangs were exposed, and she hissed at Selena.

Selena thought she was above that. She thought she could control her anger better. But as soon as Iconia hissed at her, Selena hissed back, extending her canines, furious with the vampiress. Selena hadn't intended to. She had planned to keep her cool, look superior, that she wouldn't resort to scare tactics, but she couldn't help herself. The fangs extended and the hiss followed.

And then she woke. Atreides was smiling at her.

"What?"

"You were fighting with someone in your sleep."

Selena ran her fingers through her hair. "Iconia. She bared her fangs first."

"Let me see." He looked at Selena's small fangs. "Baby fangs. They'll get longer in a few days. But when you're newly turned, they have to work their way out and then they'll come out with ease. Practice a while before you bare them at another vampire. They're bound to just laugh when they see them if you're angry with any vampire."

She smiled. But then she leapt out of bed and raced to the bathroom. She wanted to see them before they disappeared. Atreides was with her in the next instant as she peered at her enhanced canines.

He ran his hand over her back as if in trying to reassure her, and she suspected then he thought she was going to be upset, but she thought this was the coolest thing ever.

"Baby teeth. But I can't just extend them unless I'm angry?"

"Or hungry. We have sustenance in the fridge. You don't ever have to suck on somebody unless it's for the pleasure and they're mutually interested in it."

They heard a noise in the kitchen, and he said, "I'll meet you in the kitchen. Catherine is preparing breakfast but might not realize we still have a whole houseful of guests right now." Then he vanished.

It was so different now for her. Before when a vampire appeared and vanished, it would fill her with momentary alarm, worried the vampire would reappear somewhere else and attack.

Now *she* could do that. But she wouldn't be as arrogant with rogue hunters or rogue vampires. If she was in a confrontation with one and she was losing, she would vanish in retreat.

She dressed, transported herself and ended up in the kitchen nearly on top of Colt.

He stepped back in alarm, then realizing it was just her, he smiled. "You'll get the hang of transporting so that you can feel objects close to you, like the sonar in bats."

"What about shifting into other animals?"

"That takes more time," Atreides said. "Coffee?"

"Tea."

"I've got it, and everyone get out of my kitchen, please," Catherine said, shooing them out. "I'm glad you joined the clan," she said to Selena.

"Thanks. I guess I didn't have much of a choice."

"You could join the fringe groups," Catherine said.

There was a resounding "no" from Atreides and his friends.

"I'm really not a rule breaker so I think I'll be fine with the clan, but I'll have to learn the rules first."

"He's in charge," Catherine said, "when Daemon and Tezra are away. Tezra is still learning the ropes and there are still some who are having trouble accepting a huntress turned as our co-leader."

The same would happen if they learned Selena had mated Atreides, she figured. If she had ended up with a vampire who didn't have such a high status in the clan, she probably wouldn't have as much difficulty being accepted.

"I still say things might be different for Selena," Atreides said, ushering everyone into the dining room. "Since she was turned against her will by a rogue vampire. Some will sympathize with her cause, and she did try to protect one of our own before that happened."

"I totally accept her," Colt said.

"Me too," Catherine said.

"And me. Basil says he does too," Renault said.

"But it's all the others who would have to," Selena said as Catherine served up the food, then left the dining room. Selena's stomach was grumbling, and she couldn't believe she was just as hungry as she normally would be when she hadn't eaten in some time in her pre-vampiric state. She served up some of the hash browns, passed the platter to Atreides, forked up several slices of bacon, three servings full of scrambled eggs and two slices of toast.

"I think we ought to go with you to the border towns," Colt said to Atreides.

"No, they're used to seeing me going into the border towns. If a bunch of clan vampires arrived in their towns, they would be sure to think we were coming for a fight," Atreides said. "If one of you went, it would have been fine."

After breakfast, Atreides and Selena went to the first of the fringe towns to see if they could learn anything about the vampire who had turned her. She was afraid that they wouldn't talk to them and give up one of their own. But Atreides knew a lot of them and greeted several vampire men and women and no one seemed to have any animosity for him. At least with the ones who came out to talk to him. Those who wouldn't? Who knew? Maybe they couldn't be bothered with the prince when they didn't care about the rules of the clan. Or maybe they didn't like him interfering.

She thought he was mostly going to ask about the vampire who might have bitten her, but instead he asked, "We're looking to determine if anyone living outside the clan has lost anyone due to rogue hunters killing their loved ones."

That was a good in. Rather than focus on a rogue vampire, concentrate on someone they might have lost.

A vampire suddenly appeared, and she thought she'd seen him watching them from a second-story shop window. He was black-haired and eyed, and his anger was directed at Atreides. She was glad the man was leaving her out of it for the moment. But she realized if he took an angry step toward Atreides, she would be showing her baby fangs to him. When here she thought she would flee in the face of imminent danger that she knew she couldn't win at.

"What do you care about those of us in the border towns?" the man asked.

They didn't call themselves fringe vampires, but border town vamps. The hunters who didn't live by League rules weren't allowed to hunt, and they considered themselves free hunters. But if they hunted a vampire down, they were considered rogues by the League.

"We've had word that possibly a vampiress living in a border region was murdered by a rogue hunter. Some of ours have been too. We're searching for the hunters who have done this," Atreides said.

"And what does the League say about his?" the man asked, motioning to Selena.

"She's a huntress and protected one of our own."

The man finally turned his attention to Selena. "The one who killed the hunter?"

"Yeah, and one of our kind turned Selena, and in a vicious way," Atreides said. "It would have been one thing if she hadn't protected one of our own and was even in alliance with the rogue hunters who are killing our people. But what the rogue vampire did to her was unconscionable."

"Maybe she asked for it," a vampiress said, that Selena hadn't seen until now.

"Maybe you know who did it and are in collusion with him," Selena said, when she hadn't planned on speaking a word! What was wrong with her? But both her huntress and vampiress strengths were influencing her and she wouldn't be cowed by some snip of a vampiress.

The vampiress smiled, her canines on full display, but Selena didn't advance on her. Now wasn't the time.

"So why do you want to know if we have lost any vampiresses to the rogue hunter threat?" the man asked.

"Like I said," Atreides reiterated, "they have already killed some that we know of. Selena and her sister and brother and his friends are helping us to locate the hunters. We'll—"

"Kill them?" the man asked. "A rogue hunter should be dead at our hands if he murdered our kind without provocation."

"I agree," Selena said. "And if I can't turn them over to the League for their disposition, because believe me, they don't want to have a civil war between our people and yours—"

"She's still a huntress," the one woman sneered.

"I am both. But I've been a huntress for a lot longer than I've been a vampire so it's hard for me to think in terms of being one of you. But rest assured, I would never allow a hunter to kill a vampire who isn't a rogue," Selena said.

"What about the one who bit you?"

"I could have died. I made it to the club where Atreides and his friends saved my life, no thanks to the vampire who savagely tore into me. There was a wolf at first. I thought I'd hit him with my car. Well, I wasn't sure what I had hit. But I couldn't leave a wounded animal, or person, on the side of the road. He stalked me. And then I was attacked. That's not right in any way you want to think of it."

The other vampires seemed to agree, a few nodding, no one speaking for a moment.

"Atreides, you have always been welcome. You've always cared about our welfare. We know you have always wanted us to join you, but you've reported back to Daemon, letting him know we're fine as we are and living in a peaceful existence. Selena, you are right. No vampire would be considered anything other than a rogue who had bitten you and left you to die. There's no call for it. If we determine he is one of us, we'll deal with him ourselves. We will speak among ourselves and learn if any of our women are missing. No one has reported anything about it, so I'm not sure if any of them are," one of the men said.

"The one who bit me said, 'She was killed by them.' It made me believe a vampiress close to him died at the hands of the rogue hunters, but I can't be certain. And what have I got to do with any of it, except that I want to take down the hunters who have done this as soon as I can," Selena said.

"Are you welcome to return to the League?" the man asked.

"I would have been. I was given hunting restrictions after killing the hunter instead of handing him over for trial, but I didn't have a choice. Now that I'm a vampire also, I'm not sure that my saying anything will have much weight at a Counsel trial. They might even believe I asked to be turned, to be one of you so that I could fight the hunters as a vampire. I would hope they wouldn't believe that. But this is all new to me and there's not much I can do but find the rogue hunters and turn them in."

The vampiress said, "Not women? What if the hunters are huntresses?"

"Then they'll get the same deal. It doesn't matter if they are male or female. All that matters is that we stop them before they kill any further," Selena said.

A few of the vampires gathered agreed among themselves. The crowd had already grown to twice its size, about forty people there now. That was the thing about vampires. They didn't have to use cell phones to get in touch with each other. All they had to do was telepathically broadcast the news, alerting the others they had an issue, and the vampires could just magically appear. But they had to be shielding their communication with her because she hadn't heard any of it.

She wondered if they would let Atreides's in on the secret. He didn't seem ruffled by the appearance of so many vampires, and she hoped she could keep her cool. How would that look if she got angry or scared? She had to tell herself this was important for all their kind and just like when she had gone into the vampire club looking for Twilight, she was standing her ground on this.

"We'll start canvassing our people right away," a giant of a vampire said in the back, towering over everyone. "If we discover any vampiress is missing that we can't account for, we'll let you know, Atreides."

"Is she replacing Iconia?" the vampiress asked Atreides.

Atreides didn't answer her. Selena suspected he felt it was none of the vampiress's business, but Selena wanted to tell the vamp she was. Iconia was out of the picture, as far as she was concerned. She just hoped it wouldn't lead to a fight between her and Iconia.

"And the wolf?" the black-haired, male vampire asked.

Now this was where it got tricky, Selena figured. They wouldn't want to hand over one of their own to the League. But they had to know it wasn't good business to shield a rogue either. She did know that the vampires did hide the rogues on the fringe, if they felt they hadn't done that much wrong. Some were dealt with though, in their own way. If they would do evil in one place, they would do evil in another. Let the fringe vampires take care of them then.

CHAPTER 14

*T*hat was the best they could hope for, Atreides thought. He was glad Selena didn't draw her sword. He worried she might be intimidated by the numbers of vampires that had suddenly appeared.

"We'll await your word on the vampiresses and in the meantime continue to bait the rogue hunters to try and draw them out." Then Atreides took Selena's hand and transported her home.

"You didn't answer the woman about you dating me."

"I didn't want to give some fringe vampiress the word before I talked to Iconia about it. She deserves to hear it from me, not from someone living on the fringe."

"I want to go to the hunter fringe to try to learn if the rogue hunters are living there. But I think it would be better if I go with my sister and brother and maybe his friends."

"I don't want to leave you alone but—"

"I will be well protected, and you could cause more trouble than it's worth. If you got hurt or killed, I would never forgive myself."

"We will transport you there. I don't want you to take too long while I'm not protecting you."

"*You* just worry about speaking to Iconia about *us*. That will be your duty."

He smiled. "I think I will have the harder task."

"I think it's best done while you're alone."

Next, they took the hunters via the way of the vampires to see the fringe hunters, both her brother and one of his friends getting sick from the vampire way of transportation. At least they were only somewhat disoriented and didn't throw up.

Then the vampires left, and the hunters went together as a group to speak with the hunter in charge of the rabble. They hadn't established a rapport with them like Atreides had with the fringe vampires.

She thought it was a good idea if the League would reach out to try and develop one though. But she assumed they were too high and mighty to think the hunters who wouldn't be part of the "establishment" were worthy of working with at all. Who knew if some of them might change their mind and leave the fringe and become legitimate hunters working for the League?

She thought it was a mistake that they wouldn't even consider working with them, especially after she saw how well Atreides worked with the fringe vampires.

* * *

ATREIDES KNEW he would have a fight on his hand when he told Iconia he was seeing Selena. When he arrived at Iconia's place, she was having a tea party with a couple of her woman friends and Ragnar was there. Atreides would have been mad if he'd been interested in continuing to date her and she'd taken up with the Viking warrior.

Ragnar smiled at him as if knew Atreides was ending the relationship with Iconia and he was there to take his place. That would help to take the edge off. Atreides said, "Can I speak with you alone, Iconia?"

"No, tell me what you have to without all the secretiveness."

"I'm dating Selena. She needs someone to teach her our ways and I'm the one to do it."

Iconia snorted. "You don't think I know that? After the way the two of you danced at the club, and she returned to seek your help? And then we learn she's one of us? Save your breath. I'm with Ragnar now. I think you and I both have known it was over between us for some time."

Which was why she was late coming to the club that night. She was always late for events, when he was always early, and it frustrated him to no end. He was glad that she wasn't angry about it. He had been afraid she would try to take it out on Selena. She already had enough to deal with after having been turned. Ragnar was a good enough guy so he knew Iconia couldn't do much worse by him.

"You know, I might not care that you've taken up with the huntress, but others won't like it," Iconia said.

"She's one of us, Iconia."

Iconia let out her breath. "I won't disparage her name any further."

"I appreciate that. She's going to be going through a lot with the transition, and she still wants to do everything in her power to help our people. Even now, she's going with her brother and sister and some hunters to speak with the hunters on the fringe of society."

"Alone? Without you?"

"Yeah. We figured the hunters would object more if a vampire showed up with them."

Iconia narrowed her eyes at him. "A vampire *has* shown up with them."

"If they can help it, they're not going to let on that Selena is one of us now," Atreides said.

"How did your trip to the vampire border towns go?" Iconia asked.

"They are going to provide a list of the women's names who are missing from their areas." Atreides was greatly relieved about Iconia and her decision to not cause trouble for Selena. He inclined his head to Ragnar, who smiled and inclined his head also in acknowledgement. Atreides said, "Ladies," and then he vanished and returned to the house.

He wanted to check on Selena and was amused at her last night when she came to join him in bed. And he knew when she was telepathically communicating back to him, she was becoming more vampiric. That was another reason he was staying with her. He and Iconia had separate places to live. With Selena, he already wanted to stay with her always.

"How are things going with you?" Atreides asked Selena telepathically, while he paced across the living room. The other men were off looking for leads as to who the wolf might be and who the rogue hunters could be.

"We haven't found any hunters willing to talk to us. And we haven't found any hunter name for someone who might be in charge of the riffraff in the border towns. We're hoping that if we hang around long enough, we might learn something. What about you and Iconia?" Selena asked.

"Surprisingly, she is supporting my decision to date you and ditch her. She's already dating Ragnar."

"Well, I'm glad for that at least."

"I agree. She even said she wouldn't spread any more bad words about you."

"That's good. I figure I'll be having to deal with enough vampires who don't like me. What about your brother? What will he say?"

"He'll be glad I'm settling down." At least Atreides figured he would be after he got over the initial shock. In fact, he had no intention of telling Dameon about all the issues he'd had. Just that the huntress had been turned and he had taken her under his

wing, fell in love with her… He had fallen in love with her! He couldn't believe it. With all the years they lived, he had dated countless vampiresses, but Selena was the only one he had such deep feelings for. He felt totally connected to her and ultra-protective of her. If Daemon was angry about him being with her, he would leave the clan to go with her anywhere that she wanted to live. He had never felt that way about any woman, that he would leave his brother and their clan behind to live with a huntress turned vampiress somewhere else.

"I love you," Atreides said to Selena.

"We found a hunter who's in charge. Hold that thought."

He was glad they had found someone who might help them discover who the hunters were who were killing vampiresses, but he'd declared his love to her, and he felt a little bereft that she hadn't declared the same back to him, even though she'd done so before. He couldn't believe how needy he could be when it came to Selena. He had work to do, but he casually asked his manservant, Jacque. "You love Catherine, don't you?"

Jacque smiled at him.

"Have you ever told her so?"

"Not in so many words."

"Tell her. If you really feel that way, you need to spell it out."

"Are you projecting?" Jacques asked.

"What?"

"Catherine and I have discussed that you and Selena seem like a good…fit. In truth, we've never seen you act like this around any other vampiress you've been around. So we know she's the one for you. Don't listen to what Daemon has to say about it. If he's angry, remind him about Tezra. You didn't turn Selena, you've protected her. So it's not the same thing," Jacque said.

"He turned Tezra to give her more power against the vampire who was targeting her."

"Yes. But Daemon only has to realize how you feel about

Selena to recognize that it was the same as he felt for Tezra. So what are you going to do now?" Jacques asked.

"No one is to tell Daemon about all the issues we're having. Not even after they're resolved, and he returns home."

"And about Selena?"

"She is mine."

Jacques smiled. "As I said."

CHAPTER 15

*S*elena was still so newly turned, she couldn't wrap her mind around the business of being a huntress and a vampiress all in one. She needed to talk to Tezra about how she'd felt about being turned, the emotions, her feelings for Daemon, and everything else. But Selena knew Atreides didn't want his brother to know what was going on here while they were trying to hunt down rogue hunters.

Still, she felt she needed to have someone to talk to—another woman who had gone through what she had, to an extent. A huntress who would understand what she was going through.

But right now, her brother was talking to a man who called himself King. Not as in he was king of the fringe hunters, but that was his last name, and he didn't go by any other.

"Okay, look, I know that the border towns where hunters hang out govern themselves, and though we would want to take in the rogue hunters who have wantonly killed vampiresses without provocation to be tried by the League and be dealt with, we also understand that you might want to deal with the rogues on your own, as you see fit. The vampires might not like it, if they don't know if the rogues are terminated or not. The League won't either, but we don't care, as long as the rogues get their just rewards and they're prohibited from killing any more innocents," Daniel said.

King tilted his chin up in a condescending way. "It would be fine with you?" As if he didn't give a damn about how Daniel and this group of League hunters felt.

"I would hope you wouldn't want a civil war between hunters and vampires. This is a powder-keg situation. One little spark could set the whole thing off. Your people won't be any safer than anyone else as the conflict spreads. None of us will be safe. And lots of innocents will die. And for what?" Selena was desperately trying to keep her fangs sheathed, but it wasn't working. Still, her brother didn't seem to be getting through to this guy. "So that you can wield power over your little dominion?" She didn't mean to sound condescending about how many people he might actually be in charge of, but she didn't think being nice about this was going to work.

King was frowning at her, and studying her damn mouth, as if he'd glimpsed something that wasn't quite huntress about her. "You're not a huntress. What the hell? You bring one of them into our border towns?" King switched his attention to Daniel with accusation in his expression.

Her brother looked exasperated with Selena.

She was ready to bare her teeth at him. She touched them with her tongue, and they seemed a little longer than they had been before.

"She's our sister," Rosa said. "And she killed a hunter who tried to murder a vampiress for carrying his child. We don't know if they are the same hunters involved in the other vampiress killings or not."

"You could already have the right ones who, what? Work for the League?" King snorted. "And you come here seeking them? Typical. If you want to blame someone, do it with those who aren't members of your own League." He studied Selena again.

Their talk with the fringe hunter leader wasn't going half as well as the talk Atreides had with the fringe vampires.

"Yes, I'm a vampire too. I was turned by a rogue. All right?" Selena guessed it was time to let the world know what she had become. Truthfully, even though some vampires would still hate her because she was a huntress by birth, she'd felt more nervous about revealing the truth to hunters, even the ones on the fringe. Maybe more so because they lived by their own rules.

King shook his head.

"It wasn't by choice," she said again, even though she'd said the vampire was a rogue, which indicated it wasn't her choice to become turned.

"All right. Well, we have two other huntresses turned vampires who live among us. If you want to join us, you're welcome."

Selena and her companions all looked shocked. She couldn't believe that it had happened to a couple more huntresses.

"They weren't from this area," King explained. "They planned to join the League, then decided they would rather be with us. They were in the League's territory, though, when they were attacked."

"Both at the same time?" At first, Selena thought it was the same rogue vampire that had bitten her.

"Separately. He seemed to target huntresses who were alone."

Like what had happened to Selena. "How long ago?" It had to be before she was bitten since she had killed the vampire, if Atreides was right about it. All except for the vampire who had telepathically told her she should have died, and that made her doubt the vampire who had bitten her was dead.

"A month ago for one, two weeks ago for the other."

"Every two weeks," Selena said. "If it was the same one who tore into me."

"Viciously?"

"Yeah. But he didn't kill me. I killed him though."

King looked skeptically at her. "You couldn't have killed him if he'd turned you."

"His body—ashes—and clothes were left behind. The vampires who took care of me told me they had found what was left of him." Except nothing added up. Like Atreides said, she couldn't have killed him while he was biting her. And if she'd stabbed him with her sword, he would have disintegrated before he could have bitten her. The only other thing was that if he had been a wolf, and if she'd killed the wolf, no clothes, just ashes would have been found.

"Unless his blood mixed with yours hadn't turned you fast enough?" King shook his head. "It doesn't make sense."

"I agree. But I thank you for your offer. Can I speak with the women?" She hoped she could learn if it might have been the same one, yet she'd never seen his vampire face, just as a wolf. Unless there had been two of them. Or...three?

"Let me set up a meeting with you and them."

"Are they okay?" Selena asked, genuinely concerned.

"Yes. We don't treat them like the League hunters would." King got on his phone and texted the women.

Selena thought of broadcasting a telepathic message to them, but she figured it would probably be better if she just let King arrange the meeting since they would trust him.

"They're on their—"

The women appeared in the hall. And looked the hunters over. "Which one of you is—"

"I am," Selena said. "Selena Townsend."

"Brittany Hollingsworth," the one blond said.

The other's hair was a darker blond and she smiled at Selena, showing off her wicked canines. "I just had to show them off. I'm Eliza Broom. So what did the guy look like who attacked you?"

"I only saw a wolf."

"A wolf?" Brittany said. "The one who turned me was black haired and had nearly black eyes. He was tall, maybe six-foot, and he was sadistic, savage, but he fought me for a while. It was my fault. I shouldn't have been alone. I had parked my car and was some distance from a vampire club, near a drugstore. I was going to go into the drugstore to ask directions. I was looking for one of the border towns, deciding I didn't want to work for the League. I'd worked for one back home in New Jersey, and then lived with a border town there and was much happier. Anyway, I didn't make it to the drugstore. He nearly killed me, but it was like he didn't want to finish the job."

"Like he hated huntresses with a passion but wanted to turn us and leave us as one of them. Maybe he thought our own people would shun us and so would the vampires," Eliza said. "I was out late, making a run to the grocery store. I was already a member of the border town here, but the closest grocery store was in League territory and near a vampire club. I was supposed to make a cake for an event the next day. As soon as I left my car, I was attacked."

"But you were both near a vampire club, by yourself." Selena explained what had happened to her. "Did you have any indication why he would go after you?" Selena figured he had to have some motivation. Or maybe not. He just wanted to build a huntress army for himself. "Did he ever tell you to do something?"

"He just said he'd tell us what to do when he was ready, otherwise, just go about our business. I suspect he wanted us to be part of a community before he had us doing his dirty work for him and giving huntresses a bad name," Brittany said.

"We killed his triplet sister, Feather," Eliza said. "She wore black feathers on the collars of her outfits, black feathers in her hair and when she was strolling down the street, five young men, early twenties, we guessed, taunted her, ridiculed her. We were just coming into the area, looking for a hunter club when we saw the scene begin to unfold before our eyes. We raced to stop her— wishing we had vampiric movement like the vampires do because we couldn't get there soon enough before she had killed all the humans. We reached her and killed her. She was the worst sort of rogue. She was on the League's list to terminate, but we weren't League hunters. We were also in League territory when it happened."

"I remember Feather being on a list of rogue vampires to take down. No one could ever locate her, and she'd killed humans before. She'd always left her signature black feather behind to mark the kill. So you didn't report it," Selena guessed.

"No, since we weren't members of the League and sanctioned to put her down, but we'd actually witnessed her murdering the humans, so we knew, as huntresses, we had to do it. She had two brothers. The one bit us and turned us, two weeks apart, like we had told you," Brittany said. "We figured it was payback for killing their sister."

"And the other brother?" Selena asked.

"He wanted to kill us, but the one who turned us was in charge. If the other could have, he would have killed us," Brittany said.

"But you killed the bastard who bit you?" Eliza asked Selena.

"It doesn't sound right to me," King said.

"What if someone else killed the rogue vampire?" Brittany asked.

"Like who?" Selena asked.

"The wolf. What if he, shifted, grabbed up your sword when you were passed out, and killed the vampire for what he had done to you?" her brother asked.

"That could be. The wolf didn't attack me when I was trying to make my way to the vampire club. He was steering me that way. Maybe he had killed the rogue vampire." Selena hoped that was what had happened. That the rogue was truly dead and the other one? Hadn't been a rogue at all. But if that was the case, there had to be another—the one who had said she should have died. "How are you feeling about what has happened?"

Eliza sighed. "I never thought that this would happen to me in a million years. Die at the hands of a vampire during battle, sure. But be turned? Never. I've found acceptance. It has been a learning curve for me. The teeth extending, hearing telepathic conversations when I shouldn't be able to when I'm near vampires. At least when I'm with hunters, I don't hear any of that."

Brittany agreed. "Same for me. I've been turned a little longer than Eliza, but I was so glad when we were able to commiserate with each other about it. I had known her as a huntress first, so it was a shock to learn she'd been bitten also. And we were certain it was the same vampire who had bitten both of us. The problem was we couldn't report it to the League. They wouldn't help us when we live in the border towns. It didn't matter that it happened in *their* territory. Idiots."

"I agree with you there," Selena said. "And it's wrong."

"But you're not with a border town, are you? You're with the League," Eliza said.

"I was. We don't have any hunters turned working for the League, so I don't know how effective that will be." Selena figured she would be teamed up with the vampires not the League anyway.

"You can join us," King said again.

Selena smiled. "I'm with the vampires."

The women looked shocked. King shook his head.

"They took me in, protected me, cared for me when I was so badly injured. My own kind wouldn't help me."

King glanced at her brother as if accusing him of being worse than a rogue. But her sister hadn't helped her either. Still, her brother should have been there for her, and she still was irritated with him for kicking her out of the hunter club when she hadn't had her car and she was still recovering from her injuries. Then again, if he hadn't kicked her out of the club, she might not have seen Atreides again. So she had to give her brother that.

"I love one of them," Selena said.

That surprised all of them. They were hunters and that still probably didn't sit well with them.

"If that makes you both happy," Rosa said, "then I'm happy for you. It's Atreides, isn't it?"

"The prince of the vampires? Brother to the leader of the clan?" King asked, still looking astonished to hear the news.

"Yes."

The turned huntresses looked astounded.

Selena wasn't surprised at their response. If anyone had told her she would have fallen in love with a vampire? No way. And for him to be the sub-leader of the vampire clans in their area? Really, no way.

King sat back on his chair. "Well, his brother does have a huntress turned mate also. So I guess it runs in the family."

Except his brother didn't know anything about it.

"Wow," Eliza said. "I don't know how I would feel about being with the vampires after one nearly killed me and because of all the training I've had in hunting down the rogues."

"I feel the same way," Brittany said.

"We're looking for hunters who have been killing vampiresses indiscriminately," Selena telepathically told them, realizing that she had the advantage here. That she could connect with the women on some level because they'd been hurt by the same vampire. She believed. Maybe the hunters on the fringe wouldn't care anything about the murdered vampiresses, but maybe Eliza and Brittany could help her convince them that it was a just cause and to turn over hunter rogues if they knew anything about them.

King was asking her brother about why he hadn't helped his sister, berating him for being with the League and not being there for family in the meantime.

Which helped Selena conceal that she was speaking telepathically with the women. She noticed Rosa watching her and she smiled a little. Her sister knew what she was up to.

"You want us to learn what we can from the hunters living in the border towns?" Eliza asked Selena.

"If the rogues are here." Selena explained about the one she killed and that the rogues might be League members, but if they weren't, they needed to cover all bases.

"We'll try to," Eliza said. *"We don't want to be kicked out of our home here."*

"Are you seeing hunters?"

"Not right now. Brittany and I moved in together. We just felt more comfortable doing that after all the changes we've been facing."

"I know what you mean."

Rosa touched Selena's shoulder, to bring her back to the current discussion. She said to her, "I'm sorry for not telling you where I was going to be. And I'm sorry for not being there for you when you had to kill the hunter."

"I know. That's why you're here with me now, helping me." And Selena was grateful that her sister was aware enough of what was going on that Rosa helped her to hide the fact she was having a private conversation with fellow huntresses who had been turned.

"We can't broadcast what we're doing," King finally said. "If the hunters are hiding among my people, we don't want them to know we're looking for them. Brittany and Eliza will be my eyes and ears and report anything to me that they learn. Everyone respects them and they haven't been members of the community long enough to be part of the problem. And since they're also vampiresses, they have a stake in this should these rogues decide to kill huntresses turned."

Selena wondered if the women, or one of them, had compelled King to capitulate. She hadn't thought he would.

"Thank you and we'll continue to look for the hunters in League territory," her brother said. "We'll let you know if we find them."

"Same here," Brittany said.

Selena was glad they were working together on this, probably the first time the fringe hunters had worked with League hunters.

"Keep in touch with us," Eliza said.

"Yes, do," Brittany agreed.

Selena was glad she had two new friends that were like her to visit with. "I will. We'll have to get together and visit."

The ladies agreed and Selena realized she had been feeling a little on the outs. Not all vampire, not all hunter. These ladies, and Tezra, would be the same. All of them would have to visit with each other socially.

Jacque brought the van around to the border town to take them to Atreides's house, and Selena telepathically communicated to Atreides, *"I've made a couple of new friends in the fringes."* Then she explained about the women being bitten, probably by the same vampire who had bitten her, and she told Atreides about what her brother had come up with concerning the wolf.

"That would make more sense," Atreides told Selena.

"So why not just tell you—forget it. You wouldn't have listened to him, figuring he was a rogue or something. But if the wolf did kill the vampire, I want to know this and thank him."

"Then a vampiress he was close to was murdered. Why wouldn't he come out and just tell you? Doesn't he believe you would want to know about it? Everyone knows you've been to the League about the ones you know of," Atreides asked.

"Unless he's in trouble with us for something he's done and doesn't believe we would do anything for him. Maybe he's on a vampire's hit list."

"So he could still be a rogue."

"Yes."

"Okay." That wasn't good. If he was, then he couldn't really get help from the vampires or hunters, unless— *"What if he's on a hunter's hit list because he killed a hunter involved in the killings?"*

"*Then we would have to clear him of the crime. Why not come to me then with the problem?*"

"*Because the League wouldn't believe him. That's why a hunter needs to deal with these hunters. Vampires who kill them will just be seen as rogues. We still have the issue of the other vampire's voice you heard.*"

"*Right.*"

Basil telepathically communicated to Atreides, "*We found Selena's car. It was at a mall. Tara Green came through for us. She saw it and immediately knew it was Selena's. Selena had a little stuffed baby Yoda hanging from the rearview mirror, and of course it's a red Firebird.*"

Atreides shared the information with Selena.

"*I'm going to get it,*" Selena said.

"*We've got some of our hosts watching it now. If someone comes out for it, the hosts will stop him,*" Basil said.

"*Don't show your fangs,*" Atreides warned Selena.

"*I'll try not to. I'm suddenly really tired.*"

"*You need blood.*"

"*I want my car back and my brother and sister and his friends are going with us. I'll let someone else drive it home for me, I mean to your house—*"

"*Our home, you're right.*"

"*I love you,*" she said. "*Unequivocally. I should have said so before I had to meet with King.*"

"*The fringe hunter calls himself a king?*"

"*No, that's his last name. Don't worry. He's not about to try to take over the League and usurp the princes' powers with the vampires.*" She was glad she'd told Atreides she loved him back, despite having said it to him before. She'd meant to, but so much had been going on she couldn't say it at the time. She hadn't wanted to leave him hanging.

"*I know.*"

She chuckled. *"I just hope this doesn't get you into trouble with your brother."*

"It better not. I'm serious about us leaving the area if he doesn't want me in the clan for what I've done."

But she didn't want to leave her family behind. She dreaded telling her parents she'd fallen in love with a vampire though. She wasn't sure if they would be okay with it or not. She was sure Tezra would back them though.

"You have me to work with the women who are living in the border towns though. Maybe I can help us with fringe hunters in the future if we have trouble with them since the League won't help." And maybe she would have more influence with the League since she wasn't just a vampire explaining what was going on with the hunters who were rogues. She had been and still was one of them, in part. She, or someone like her, needed to represent her kind on the League Council.

CHAPTER 16

*W*hen they reached the mall, the hosts directed them to her car, and Selena saw it. She was thrilled. It looked just like she had left it the night the wolf stalked her, and she'd been attacked, except that the people who had used it had smoked joints in the car, which irritated her to the max. Because of her hunter's heightened sense of smell, smoke irritated her. And they'd left hamburger wrappers, french fries, and empty beer cans all over the floor.

Even so, she was thrilled to have her car back, no dents or broken windows or anything.

"We wait for whoever stole it to return, right?" her brother asked.

"Yes, they have my car keys." She had the spare keys at home, she realized, but she didn't want them to have the other set of keys any further. And she wanted them arrested for stealing her car.

Daniel shook his head. "I can't believe you left your key in the ignition."

"Tell me about it." But at least by doing that, they hadn't broken a window to get into it and hotwired it to steal it anyway.

They hung around the parking area for about an hour, the sun out, clearing away the clouds and she was glad only hosts and hunters were here, waiting for the car thieves. The vampires would have had to leave, like Jacque had to do.

"You're feeling all right?" Rosa asked.

"Tired. But I'm fine." Selena wondered if that meant she needed to drink some blood. Ugh.

They kept seeing people headed toward their cars near hers and thought they were the ones, though none of them had looked like beer-guzzling, pot-smoking, hamburger-eating car thieves.

There were families, a couple of young women, three older teens, more families, but nobody who approached her car. Maybe the thieves had figured her stolen car was too "hot" and left it at a crowded mall so no one would find it soon.

Then three males and two females in their late twenties headed in their direction. They set off a car alarm, walking too close to another vehicle and one of the men slammed his fist down on the car hood in irritation. Which made her think these were the right people. She had smelled that three males had been in her car, so maybe because the women were with them, they weren't the right people after all. But she suspected they were, and they'd just picked up the two girls at the mall. Wouldn't they be surprised when they learned they weren't going to drive the car they had stolen anywhere, if these were the people who had done so.

Selena couldn't help glower at them. They were so busy cursing and laughing about stealing stuff from a couple of stores, one of the girls bringing out a necklace from her purse, the price tag still attached to it, another slipped a pair of earrings out of her pocket, still attached to the display card—they didn't notice the hunters or vampire hosts hanging around the cars, texting people, trying to look unobtrusive. But to anyone who was observant, Selena thought she and the others looked like danger —for them.

Selena hadn't planned to extend her canines. So far, she had kept them sheathed the whole time, trying not to get angry.

She was moving closer to her car though. She didn't want them jumping into it and driving off and losing them.

They were almost to her car, three of the people splitting off to the right of it, the guy bringing out Selena's car keys and the other girl heading to the driver's side. The hosts and hunters ran toward the thieves then, but Selena just vanished and reappeared in front of the would-be driver. "Hand over the keys." She held out her hand.

The guy's mouth gaped. He glanced up at the sun, which was spilling all over her car, nearby cars, and the parking lot in general, only a smattering of clouds blocking it for seconds as the clouds continued to move along.

"Do you want to see the fangs?" she asked. "Hand over the keys and take your trash out of my car."

"You...you're dead. You were supposed to be dead."

The two girls with them started to back away, but Rosa and a couple of hosts stopped them. Even though they weren't usually in the business of dealing with human crime, if they had the opportunity present itself, they helped the police out.

Rosa was on her phone already, her sword out, the girls staying put.

"Hunters?" the man with her keys said, sounding just as shocked.

Rosa called in the theft of Selena's car and of the girls stealing at the mall.

"We didn't help steal the car," one of the girls said.

"No, we don't even know these guys," the other said.

Her brother was standing beside her, his sword out in case the driver had a weapon. His friends were on the other side of the car apprehending the other men.

"I don't look dead. Why do you think I should be dead? Because the car was abandoned, and I wasn't anywhere in sight?

Ohmigod, you saw the vampire attack me?" Selena couldn't believe her luck if that was the case.

"Uh, yeah. We saw the car first, and it was just sitting there with its headlights on and the engine running, keys in the ignition." *Ripe for the taking.*

"And?"

"We saw, uh, you, walking away from the car and some vampire suddenly—"

"Wait, wasn't there a wolf?"

"Uh, yeah," one of the other guys said. "A wolf was following you."

"And you didn't try to protect her?" her brother asked.

They didn't respond to that. Of course not. All they cared about was that the car was there, begging them to steal it.

"Then?" she prompted.

"A vampire appeared, and he grabbed you by the throat. What could we do? We were scared. We're only human. We can't deal with vampires."

"And you thought I was human and only thought to steal my car." She was afraid they would say they just took off in her car because they were afraid of the vampire coming after them and they hadn't seen what else had happened.

"Another vampire appeared. I mean, it was like a damn vampire convention," the guy with her keys said.

"The one bit you and the other tossed him aside, then bit you and hit you and then the two vampires were glowering at each other like they were telepathically communicating to each other. What do we know?" the other man said.

The driver said, "When the one hit you, you fell to the pavement and we thought you were dead."

"So you thought you had inherited *my* car. You must have driven in a different vehicle. You didn't have to steal the car. It would have gone to my family. What happened to the wolf?"

"He, uh, turned into a vampire and he picked up the sword you'd dropped on the ground—"

"Then you knew I was a huntress."

"Uh, yeah, and he stabbed the vampire twice—the one who had bitten you and struck you—before the ancient collapsed in a pile of ashes and clothes. And the other vampire—the one who the dead vampire had pushed aside—vanished before the wolf guy could take care of him. We quickly jumped into the car and took off."

So there *had* been three vampires, the one who had bitten her and the one who had followed her as a wolf and killed the other, and the one who had first bitten her and told her telepathically that he should have killed her. She suspected the wolf had wanted her to return to the club, and then out of nowhere, the rogue vampires had appeared, waiting for a lone huntress to make her appearance so the vampire could turn her. But the other had wanted her dead. Did the wolf know who the rogue vampires were?

"What did they look like? The ones who had bitten me?" she asked.

"Both of them had black hair and they were tall, about three inches taller than me," the driver said.

That made him about six feet tall.

Two police cars pulled up and her brother explained to the police about the two girls and the stuff they had heisted at the store. When a female officer searched them and their bags, they found other jewelry they'd stolen. They read them their rights and placed them in one of the patrol cars.

"What else did you see about the one who attacked me?" Selena asked.

"Nothing else. Just that they were tall. And they were vicious. I mean, we knew they were vampires—maybe even brothers."

Brothers.

"And you did nothing to help," Rosa said.

"She was done for," the driver said. "What could we do? She was a huntress and couldn't fight back. How could we have helped? Besides, the other vampire killed the one and the other vanished, so it was done."

"She wasn't dead. She had to stumble her way to the vampire club," Rosa said.

"The vampire could have taken her there," the driver said. "He shifted back into the wolf and waited for her to reach the club, and then go in. What were we supposed to do? What if we'd tried to do something for her and the wolf had attacked us? No way were we getting involved in that."

"She protects humans, you know," Rosa said. "Maybe if she sees you're in trouble the next time, she won't be bothered. I know I wouldn't."

Selena figured she wasn't going to get anything more out of the car thieves. "You can arrest them for stealing my car." She told the officer when and where it had been stolen while her brother retrieved her car keys for her, since the thief still hadn't handed them back to her, and then the officers took the men into custody.

The hosts hurried to clean up her car for her, which she hadn't expected and thought it was nice of them. She didn't want to drive in the vehicle until it was aired out, but she put down the top and figured that would do the trick. Her brother and sister rode with her back to Atreides's house.

"I'm so glad I got the car back, but I'm equally thrilled we learned that at least one of the rogue vampires who bit me is truly dead. And I'm hoping the one that had been a wolf was only there to solicit my help in the hunter murdered vampiress's cases," Selena told her siblings. "As to the other, we're going to have to find him."

"I agree," her brother said. "Not to change the subject, but you need to talk to Mom and Dad about all this."

"You haven't told them already?" Selena was surprised. She figured her brother would have told them right away.

"No. Rosa and I discussed it and we felt it was your call when you felt ready to talk to them about having been turned."

"Okay, I guess maybe we could have a family dinner and discuss it then. Should I invite Atreides?" Selena wanted to but she wasn't sure if that was the best way to handle this. They had been upset with her for killing a hunter, even though she was in the right. What would they have done in her situation? She wanted to think only good of her parents, but everyone dealt with a situation differently. Side with the hunters, even if they were wrong, but keep their standing with the hunter community, or side with the vampires who had been wronged, and face the consequences, like she'd done?

She'd liked to think her parents would have done what was right and protected the vampiress, but she'd gotten mixed messages from them, so she wasn't sure.

"No on Atreides," her brother said, and her sister agreed.

"It's going to be enough of a shock to them to learn that you were turned. And yes, I'll tell them what I had done to you when I kicked you out of the hunter club. I was taught better than that," Daniel said.

"And I'm mending my ways," Rosa said. "From now on, I'm letting everyone in the family know where I am so that no one has to risk their neck looking for me because I disappear for a while."

Maybe this had all been for the good then, bringing her family closer together and aligning themselves with right instead of just keeping the peace with the hunters in the League.

"But about Atreides, once you have told our parents you have been turned, then we can set another family gathering date to welcome him into the family if you think you are going to stay with him," Daniel said.

"I am."

"I'm sorry, not that you ended up with the prince of the vampire clans out here, but that we weren't the ones who protected you in your time of need," Daniel said.

"It's done. We're a family again. I think we are better off now for what had happened." Selena telepathically communicated to Atreides, *"I have my car! It needs detail work, but it looks good otherwise."*

Atreides didn't respond and she sighed. He was probably asleep. It was going to be something they would have to work out because she still wanted to sleep at night, except when she went on rogue vampire hunts, and he needed to sleep during the day, especially on sunny days like today when he couldn't be out and about anyway.

She wanted to be with him, but they would have to just work out their own schedules and do the best they could.

"Do you truly love him?" Rosa asked.

"I do."

"I heard he dumped a rabid vampiress for you. I would watch your back, if I were you. We will too, but we won't be running in the same circles as you," Daniel said.

"She conceded, graciously, from what Atreides had told me. So we're good. She's dating another vampire already. One that she had been dancing with at the club even, so it appears she has moved on."

"That's good," Rosa said. "We were worried about that."

Then they arrived at Atreides's home and Selena said, "I'm going to get some sleep."

Rosa lifted her brows.

"A nap."

Rosa shook her head. "I could never get used to trying to be up half the night and half the day to be with a vampire."

"You would do it if you loved one of them. See you tonight to hunt for the rogue hunters." Selena gave her sister and brother hugs.

"See you tonight, but don't put off telling our parents about what's happened. They'll learn about it before long when you should be the one to tell them, not the rumor mill," Rosa said.

"I will." Though she wanted to take down the rogue hunters first. "Maybe we can do lunch instead of dinner, then we can continue to try and entrap the rogue hunters at night."

"That will work," her brother said.

"Let's do it. This afternoon," Rosa said.

Then Twilight came out to greet them and said, "Do you all need a ride back to the ranch or somewhere else right now?"

"Yes, to the ranch," Rosa said. "Daniel, you're staying with me too."

CHAPTER 17

Selena was thinking of having lunch tomorrow with her parents and telling them the news. She agreed with her sister and brother. She didn't want any other hunters to learn of what she'd become before she told her parents herself, and she needed to go before the League Council and tell them also and see what they wanted to do with her. She wanted to continue to do both—work to protect the vampires who were not rogues and fight the ones who were, with the League's sanction. She was still a huntress after all.

She called her mother before she went to bed with Atreides. "Mom, Rosa and Daniel and I want to have lunch with you this afternoon, if you can swing it." She had to be mindful that her parents weren't just sitting around the house waiting for her to show up at her leisure.

"Yes, that would be great. I'll make, uhm, your favorite meal if you would like."

Selena thought her mom sounded a little choked up, and making her favorite when it wasn't her birthday? She suspected her mom knew what had become of her and she was upset. Tears pricked Selena's eyes. She didn't want to upset her mom, and she had really thought they would be mad at her, not saddened and she had come to terms with it. She had to remind herself if they did know, this all had to be a shock to them. But she was what she was, and she couldn't do anything differently now. Who had let it slip? Maybe one of Daniel's friends.

"Sure, that would be great. Everyone loves your Italian sausage spaghetti."

"Would noon be all right?"

"Is that Selena?" her father asked in the background.

"Yes, the kids are all coming home today for lunch," her mom called back to him.

"Noon would be fine, Mom. I've got to go," Selena said.

"We'll look forward to seeing you all then."

They ended the call and now Selena was all choked up. Her sister and brother hadn't been, so she just figured her parents wouldn't be. It was just something that had happened, and they had to deal with it. Then she texted her brother and sister about the lunch date and when she finished, Atreides swooped in, swept her into his arms, and transported her to his bed.

Now that was the way she liked to be welcomed home by her mate.

"I'm having lunch with my family at noon. But I'm taking a nap with you for now."

"To tell your mother and father you were turned?"

"Yeah." She curled up in Atreides's arms, but he was removing her clothes and he was already naked, just like she liked him. "I think my parents already know."

"I wouldn't be surprised if they had heard the news via the grapevine. Word spreads fast when things go wrong."

"I think things turned out right for us. Even though some of the stuff I'm dealing with is disorienting, being with you and making new friends, even with the huntress turned vampires on the fringe, is a good thing. I love you, Atreides."

"I love you, my huntress and vampiress in one beautiful, sexy package." Then she was naked, and he leaned her back and his fingers sought her nubbin, but she really loved it when he sucked on her neck and made her come.

She didn't know if the feeling would always be that intense and would give her an insta-orgasm practically, or if it was just because he'd worked her up so much before that and then the experience was so new that it crashed over her before she was even ready for it. And she'd felt wonderful, like a million bucks.

"You are insatiable." But he didn't start biting and sucking right away, as if he knew he had to work her up to it. He was a consummate lover and she adored him for it.

He began to kiss her lips, running his hand over her breast with gusto, and moving his arousal against her leg in a way that showed her he had been ready to make love to her for some time. Here she'd been talking and talking, making him wait. His heart rate was kicking up and so was hers. Maybe that was what he needed. To hear her heartbeat thumping in her chest, to make him crave her blood to such a degree he couldn't hold back. Or not.

Still, it made her own blood pulse like crazy and she could hear his too as he continued to assault her mouth with punishing kisses, alternating with gentle kisses. Their tongues were at it again, long strokes, invasions, touching teeth, and she felt his had already descended, and hers had too, and now she was thinking hers were even a little longer than before. But she might be mistaken. She realized she wanted adult vampire teeth, if she was going to have them at all. They might as well be just as long and wicked as the other vampires' fangs were.

Then he was sweeping his hand down her belly, but she was baring her throat, ready for him to bite her neck first. To give her the orgasm that way. Was she boring or what?

But she couldn't knock a good thing. Then she reached down to stroke his cock, but he wouldn't let her and moved so he could continue to glide along her leg, his fingers working their magic on her feminine nub. She concentrated on that, until he leaned down and suckled a nipple. Oh, yes, that was good too. Everything was good. Just. Keep. Doing. It.

He seemed to be able to read her mind and kept up the friction between his cock and her, and the strokes to her nub that were undoing her. His mouth moved to her neck and he licked it, kissing it afterward as if he were feeling the pulse against his mouth and was as eager to penetrate her with his teeth and suck on her as she was to feel him doing it.

She even had the momentary hope that he would bring her to orgasm while he was stroking her to madness at the same time he sucked on her neck. Would that put her over the edge?

She moaned with the way he was working her, but he wasn't biting her yet and she had to stop thinking of that as she stroked his arms and back, loving the things he did to her body, loving the feel of him beneath her fingertips. She just hoped she could be quieter this time when she came.

She hadn't planned to do it, but suddenly, she just had the greatest urge to bite him, unable to control it, the bloodlust rising, and she bit into his shoulder. Not hard, gently enough that she penetrated the skin, surprising him as he turned his face to hers and his eyes were wide.

She sucked then, not letting go of his shoulder. She'd done it, she wasn't letting this moment go to waste, and to her astonishment, she came. Atreides smiled as she cried out, releasing him— that she hadn't planned to do, and then latching back on. She wasn't finished.

But he quickly thrust inside her, and she realized by feeding on him, he had the same sexual pleasure and couldn't hold on. He pumped into her with wild enthusiasm, and she quickly had to release his shoulder and seal the wound.

"You are perfect for me, Selena," he whispered and kissed her breast, but he didn't let up on his thrusts, driving in and nearly pulling out, his hand slipping under her leg to raise it over his hip so he was penetrating her more deeply. Then he was kissing her mouth and she was turning her head, begging him silently to bite her.

He did, gently like she'd done with him, and sucked, just as gently. The pleasure it gave her was driving her insane. She didn't think she could come again after having come so quickly the first time. But then he groaned against her neck and she felt he'd climaxed, but she was nearly there, just…a…little…bit…more, and then she came, crying out, not meaning to a second time.

He sealed the wound on her neck and kissed her lips, running a hand through her hair.

He moved off her and pulled her close, stroking her hair as she rested her body against his side and chest. "I'm so glad I danced with you that day."

"I never thought it would lead to this."

He smiled at her. "I wanted it to, but I felt the same way. It was just a very pleasurable experience I would relive the rest of my life in my thoughts, but nothing more would come of it. Not until you were so savagely bitten."

"Do you think, if I hadn't been, and I had returned home after the incident, you would have ever tried to locate me and see me again?"

"I know we would have seen each other again. You were still looking for your sister, and I had her. I have no doubts that you would have eventually discovered she was working with us, and then? You would have joined our ranks to help."

"Because you were in charge?"

"Because you had saved Charlene and it's in your nature to protect those who are innocent of any crime."

She sighed and ran her hand over his chest. "You're pretty sexy for a vampire."

He smiled. "You're damned hot for a huntress, even before you were turned. I knew, once I had danced with you, I was lost, no matter how much I had told myself otherwise. And when I smelled your blood? I would never have forgotten its magnetic draw."

"Then to put us out of our misery, it was a good thing that things had worked out the way they did." Selena sighed, knowing this was the best choice she had ever made in her life.

"I agree."

Yet Daemon still didn't know what had gone on between her and his brother. Would he feel that it was the best choice his brother could have made? Two princes in charge of the clan moving forward, both hooking up with huntresses turned? She wasn't sure the whole of the vampire clans would be happy with that, especially when the vampiresses themselves might have had a chance to mate with the princes instead.

Still, she was happy with the way things had turned out and she wasn't giving Atreides up for anyone or anything.

She closed her eyes, the happiest she'd ever been…for now.

* * *

WHEN SELENA WOKE, she realized it was time to go to her parents' home for lunch. She kissed Atreides. "I'm off to my parents' place."

"You'll have an escort there."

"I'll be fine. I'll just drive. Your people can't go with me. It's too sunny out."

He ground his teeth. "Then have your brother or sister join you here and pick you up for lunch. With Cliff out for your blood, I don't trust you being alone."

She sighed. "All right." She got out of bed and dressed, then left the bedroom so Atreides could sleep further. He needed to be at the top of his game to fight whatever he needed to also.

"Hey, Daniel," Selena said, calling him on her cell phone.

"We're already on our way over to Atreides's place. You're not safe with Cliff wanting to take you down. He could do it at any time, night or day," Daniel said.

"All right. I'll be waiting here for you." She was glad he was taking the threat to her seriously.

Within half an hour, Daniel drove up in his Jeep and Selena climbed into the vehicle and saw Rosa sitting in the back seat.

"I think Mom and Dad might know already," Selena warned them.

"We were hoping not, but thinking the same thing," Rosa said.

"Mom sounded upset and she asked if I wanted my favorite dish for lunch."

"Italian sausage spaghetti? She only fixes that for you for your birthday," Rosa said.

"Yeah, I think she thought it would be like comfort food for me. I don't know what I was thinking. I just thought she would react the way you two did."

"We were fine with it since you seemed to be all right with it. Mom hasn't seen you yet," Daniel said. "When she realizes you're not all broken up about it, that will be different."

"Okay, well, I hope it won't be a tearful reunion."

No one said anything, and she figured it would be.

She got on her phone and called the League Council secretary. "This is Selena Townsend. I need to make an appointment to meet with the League Council."

There was dead silence on the phone. Daniel glanced at her.

"Hello?" Selena said.

"Uh, yes, hold a minute."

Then Selena heard relaxing New Age music playing. "Apparently it's a big thing. The secretary put me on hold."

"They know then," Daniel said.

"Maybe. I wonder if they learned of it and talked to our parents about it. I doubt our parents would have learned of it and told the League Council. They would have wanted me to talk to them first, I'm sure." Or maybe not. Maybe her parents had

187

contacted them to learn what they should do. They did have a League psychologist and maybe they even met with her.

Then the secretary got back on the phone and said, "Would one this afternoon work well for you?"

Selena's jaw dropped. Never had the League Council convened that quickly for a single hunter unless they thought they had to avert a war.

"Yeah, sure, one this afternoon would be fine. I'll be there then." She ended the call.

"Holy hell, they know," Daniel said. "No way would they hurry up and convene that quickly otherwise."

When they arrived at their parents' two-story, brick home, both their Mom and Dad came out to greet them. Her mom had definitely been crying, and she looked a little hesitant to hug her, as if she was afraid of what Selena had become. She gave her mom a warm hug. "Love you, Mom, Dad." She gave him a hug, both warmly hugging her back.

And then they all went inside the house. All the surrounding neighbors were hunters, all protecting each other in the event rogue vampires threatened any of the families. Since they were in the business of killing rogues, they were always on the alert should the rogue vampires they were hunting begin hunting them.

As soon as they walked into the house, they smelled the delicious spaghetti cooking in the kitchen and all the best dishware and silverware were set out as if it were a holiday or other special occasion. Selena guessed it was. She was still alive, after all.

"We know something of what had happened," her dad said as they sat down to eat. "No sense in pretending we don't. But we only know bits and pieces."

So Selena ate some of her meal and then proceeded to tell them all that had happened. Daniel had to get a tissue box for Selena and her mother because when her mother cried, it made Selena cry. And then Rosa was crying. She'd held out the longest.

Daniel and their dad looked on sympathetically.

She was glad to get all this out in the open. She hadn't realized what a relief it was.

"When are you going to tell the League?" her dad asked.

"Right after lunch."

"You should have seen it, Dad," Daniel said. "As soon as she called them to speak with the Council, they scheduled her for one. That never happens unless there's the threat of a war going on."

That could either be good news or bad. She suspected it wouldn't be all good. And she hoped they didn't have hunter guards standing by because they were afraid of her.

Selena smiled. "It has to be good news." She wouldn't let on that she was worried it might not be.

"They can't kick her out of the League." Daniel ate a slice of bread.

"They would be foolish to do so. She can telepathically communicate with other vampires," Rosa said. "She made friends with two huntresses who had been turned and are living in one of the border towns."

"Oh, is that wise?" her mother asked.

"It's a whole different world now," Selena said. "I don't have a lot of choice. But if I can help both sides, I'm all for it."

"It's going to take some getting used to. If you get angry with someone, do you show off your canines?" her dad asked.

"Only once, and they're not very big. Not like the ancients have. I guess it will take some time to work up to that. But I have to admit the transportation and flying leaps sure are fun to use, especially when I need to get to places fast."

"Or leave places fast," her mother said. "You know how we always say the vampires would rule the world if they weren't so arrogant. If they were getting overwhelmed in battle, they need to just vanish, and gather more of their people."

"I know, Mom. I promise that I'll vanish if I get overwhelmed by the bad guys—whether they're hunters or vampires." At least in theory she would. She wasn't sure if it might just be in their genetic makeup that made them feel the need to finish a battle against the hunters. Maybe, now that she was one, she would feel the same way.

"What do you think they're going to say to Selena?" Rosa asked.

"If they know what's good for us, they'll keep her employed as a hunter and give her a special job that she's going to be well-trained for," her dad said.

As long as they didn't expect her to spy on good vampires and just learn what she could about rogues. She could see herself getting killed quickly if she was just serving as a spy for the League. Besides, she wanted to help the vampires with dealing with hunters who didn't respect that some vampires were the good guys.

They finished lunch and then they gave each other hugs. To her surprise, her whole family wanted to go to the Council meeting. They might not be permitted inside the Council chambers, but she appreciated that they wanted to give her moral support in any event.

"Thanks, I appreciate you all being there for me," Selena said, getting into the car.

"If they hassle you in any way, we'll all jump in to make sure they understand what a bad mistake that would be," her mother said.

Both her parents were excellent fighters, so were her brother and sister. She was certain the Council wouldn't want to lose all five of them as hunters in one fell swoop.

Then they drove over to the League's office building and she thought there was a little more security there than usual. Maybe she was mistaken. She knew there had been when she went to testify concerning why she had killed the hunter. Otherwise, she rarely visited the Council headquarters.

She was glad to have her family with her when here she thought she would be going it alone. Maybe Daniel would have dropped her off for the meeting and picked her up when it was done, but all of them actually coming in with her?

When they reached the third floor where the Council chambers were, the secretary rose from his seat and inclined his head to her, but he looked surprised to see all the family members there.

"Let me ask the president of the League if you can all go in or if they want just you to go in, Selena," the secretary said.

"All of us, if we can," her dad said.

She was proud of him for speaking up and not just leaving things to chance.

"Right."

"The family needs to hear what's being said, in case there's any doubt," her dad added.

"Uh, yes, sir." The secretary disappeared into an office behind him and quickly shut the door. Normally, he would have just called back to the president's office.

She figured he was afraid of how they might react if they didn't have their way.

He ought to know them better than that. They weren't going to make a scene. At least she didn't think so.

A few minutes later, the secretary reemerged. "Sorry for the delay. Yes, you can all go in." The secretary was perspiring.

She hoped that he hadn't been afraid of how she would react.

Then he said, "You may proceed."

Selena was going to lead the way since this was all about her, but her dad and mom did instead, as if they were protecting her. And her brother and sister followed her in. The conference room was huge, thirteen Council members presiding, one the president, and an uneven number so they couldn't have a tie vote. They had decided long ago, no one Council member had any power over the rest of them. The president just gathered the collective votes, made the final decisions based on the voting of each Council member, so he wasn't a president who dictated to the others.

"We understand your situation, Selena. We've gotten several reports from various groups, fringe hunters, fringe vampires, the regular clan vampires, and our own League hunters," the president said, motioning for them to take seats at the table across from them.

She couldn't believe they'd been gathering information on her all this time. At least she didn't have to explain everything that had happened to her. It seemed they already knew.

But then the president said, "Tell us in your own words what had happened."

She again explained everything that had gone on, but this time her mother didn't cry, and Selena felt better about that. She couldn't imagine what it would be like to have a daughter of her own and know she'd been brutalized by a vampire.

"Okay, well, based on your testimony and the reports we've received," the president said, "We have a proposition to make."

She was going to ask to see the reports. After all, she should have those so she knew exactly what people had reported. But she would wait until after she heard the Council members' verdict.

"We had thought of having you join the Council. One of our Council members would retire. This was acceptable to all within."

Becoming a Council member could help both sides, Selena thought, but she wanted to fight still and take down the rogues. When she was older, maybe when she was ready to retire from hunting, then she could do that.

"But then we believed you would be more useful in the field. We've never had anyone reach out to the fringe hunters before. We would like it if you would continue to do that. Maybe with your brother and sister helping you, so that you're protected should you need to be. We are prepared to pay a considerable sum to have you serve as special agents working with the fringe hunters. It doesn't mean you're required to recruit them. Just let them know we're on their side if they need our help with anything. We need the rapport like what Atreides has built with the fringe vampires.

"But we also would like you to work directly with the vampires, as their representative, with the fringe huntresses who have been turned, and anyone else who ends up like them, male or female, Selena. Also, you will get special pay for this work. It's something none of us can do, which makes you highly qualified in the scheme of things."

Wow, she couldn't believe it.

"Now, we've learned for certain that Cliff has a contract on you and intends to take you out. He is on a rogue list for termination, and so are three of his hunter friends. We can't have hunters killing vampires indiscriminately. If you need an additional bodyguard to watch your back, we'll pay for it."

"I am mating a vampire. When I have night work, he and his people will be there for me." She might as well let the truth come out about that too.

"Well," the president said, rubbing his head, "we had hoped to find an acceptable hunter mate for you, but I suppose that will work as well."

"He's Atreides, prince of the vampire clans and their sub-leader," Rosa said as if she was proud of Selena's choice of mate.

Everyone just stared at Selena, then a few of the Council members smiled at her.

"Well," the president said, "that is great. Just great. Does Daemon know?"

They'd lost Tezra to the vampire clan, though she still helped the League when she could, but she had immersed herself in vampire issues, being Daemon's mate. But Selena was different, and she had a mission to do. She hadn't been a borderline rogue, not really, and she was happy to be with the League, as long as they policed their own hunters.

But Daemon was an unknown.

"He doesn't. He has been off on a vacation with Tezra. When he returns, Atreides will tell him what has gone on."

The president gave a small smile. "Atreides is in charge and he doesn't want his brother to know about all the problems we're having because he'll return and take charge."

"His brother deserves a vacation after all the hard work he puts in while taking care of his people. And Atreides can handle things," Selena said, speaking on Atreides's behalf.

"With your help," the president said.

"Yes," Selena said.

"And with ours," her dad said, and the president looked over at him as if he'd forgotten he was sitting there with the rest of her family.

"All of ours," her mother said.

The president nodded. "If the conditions of your new employment are acceptable, we'll have the contracts written up and you can sign them. All of you. We look forward to working with you and hopefully making better choices in the future."

Selena sure hoped so. Maybe the hunters needed better training. She said, "Maybe we could have sensitivity training for the hunters—I'm not sure it would work for vampires, but the hunters might need it to understand the vampires better."

"That sounds like something you could entertain also, once we locate the rogue hunters causing all the trouble right now," the president said, glancing at the other Council members.

They all inclined their heads in agreement.

Then the president adjourned the meeting. Selena and her family left the Council chambers.

The secretary said, "I have the contract drawn up, if you'll read it over and sign it, please."

Each of Selena's family members read over the agreement and

then she said, "Do you have the reports that were filed concerning what had happened to me?"

"Uh, yes, here's a copy of all the transcripts, should you wish to see them. The president and other Council members approved it."

She and her family members signed the contract, then she looked through the signed reports from: the two huntress turned vampiresses in the border town, from King even, the vampire in charge of those on the fringe, from Atreides and all his close friends, Colt, Renault, Basil, from Tara Green and Twilight, from Iconia also, and one of Iconia's friends who Selena didn't remember meeting. And from a vampire named Quail. She didn't recognize the name as being anyone she had met.

But when she read his affidavit, it said, *You are the one who will change everything, the light in the darkness, good against evil.*

"That was the last one that came in. A young hunter boy delivered it. He said he saw a wolf and it dropped the envelope, pawed at it, barked at him, and then ran off. That's when the boy picked up the envelope, saw it was addressed to the president of the League and brought it right here," the secretary said.

"A wolf," Selena said. The wolf? She couldn't imagine it was from anyone else. "Thank you."

Then she and her family left, and they all hugged each other.

"Man, we didn't know you would be famous, and we would have special positions because of you," Daniel said.

"Just remember that if you get mad at me over something dumb," Selena said, patting his shoulder.

"What can you turn into?" Her sister sounded intrigued. "I never thought of that."

"I don't know, but I'm curious too."

Selena didn't know what vampires could shift into. Some said crows, some wolves, some bats. Maybe other creatures? She just didn't know. But a crow would be neat if she wanted to learn what was going on and be inconspicuous. Particularly during the day. A wolf at night. A bat didn't especially appeal, but at night, they could fly and could be a little stealthier. Though both the hunters and vampires could see what was going on at night, so maybe not so inconspicuous.

"A wolf, that's what I'd want to be," Daniel said.

"Yeah, me too," Selena said.

"What if you shifted and couldn't shift back?" her mother said.

Everyone was quiet in the car for a few minutes, then Rosa said, "Yeah, that would be the pits. I was thinking of a crow for daytime sleuthing, but I wouldn't want to be one always."

"I wonder if you have a choice. I've never been on friendly terms with vampires, so I don't have a clue," their father said. "You'll have to let us know what you find out, Selena."

She realized she was going to be the premier connection to the vampire world for the hunters. It did make her feel special. When they reached her parents' home, she said, "I've got to go. But I think we're all in agreement things could be better for the hunters and vampires if we could work more closely together."

"I agree," her mother said, giving her a hug. "Does he, I mean, Atreides, ever want to meet us?"

"Of course. We wanted to make sure you knew what had become of me first, and then we'll have everyone get together with him to welcome him to the family," Selena said.

"All right. Make it soon," their mother said. "I want him to feel like he's part of the family, not some outcast we don't want to meet."

"I'll make it soon."

"Are we on the hunt again for the rogue hunters tonight?" Daniel asked.

"Yes. And every night until we catch them. We can't let them get away with any more murders."

Then she gave everyone hugs and Rosa reminded her, "Remember to ask Atreides what you can be if you shift."

Selena smiled and before Daniel could ask if he could drive

her back to Atreides's home, she vanished and sometime later, appeared inside the living room in Atreides's home, startling Colt and Renault who were playing poker.

"We're here to watch over you. Imagine our surprise to learn Atreides was in bed without you," Colt said.

Atreides came out of the kitchen. "How did it go?"

"I'm a special agent. So are my brother and sister." Selena was feeling so lightheaded all of a sudden, she had to sit down at the dining table.

Atreides brought her a glass of red wine, but then she realized it was blood. She thought she couldn't drink it, but when she felt compelled to drink it, she took a sip and sighed. It was refreshing, coppery, smooth, and fed the need to have it. And she felt invigorated all at once.

Then she explained all that had happened at the Council.

"That's a tall order," Atreides said.

"*And* my mother wants you to come over for dinner soonest so they can welcome you to the family."

He slowly smiled.

"Really. Don't show your fangs though. I'm sure my parents will be the perfect hosts. Not as in vampire hosts. But they want you to know you're part of our hunter family just like I'm part of your vampire family, once Daemon knows about this."

Renault threw down his hand of cards. "I don't think you should wait on telling Daemon."

"He would return here in a heartbeat and have a major meltdown. You know how he is. We need to take care of business and when he returns with Tezra, well-rested and ready to work, everything will be just fine," Atreides said.

Selena sure hoped so.

CHAPTER 18

*A*treides was thrilled the Council had accepted Selena for what she had become and not only that but had given her special assignments. And he was glad her family wanted to meet him.

"Oh, and that's not all. So the Council received all kinds of reports on what had happened and they took those into consideration. I have to thank you, Atreides, and you also, Renault, Colt, and your friend Basil. But the most surprising report was the one from a man named Quail, who was the wolf." She read the statement he had made. "Do you know him?"

"Quail," Atreides said, trying to recall the name. He glanced at his friends, but neither of them seemed to know him. "We have vampires who are part of the clan but never participate. They're not fringe vampires as they commit their loyalty to Daemon and our family. But they just keep to themselves."

"Could he be a fringe vampire?" she asked.

"That's entirely possible too. We'll have to check with them about that."

"Oh, and I want to know what I can turn into."

Atreides raised a brow. The guys were smiling. "A crow, bat, wolf, fog."

"Fog? Oh, that would be so cool. So how do I do it?"

"It takes practice. And it can take a long time before you can shift into something else."

"What's your preferred shifter form?" she asked.

"A wolf, though I've been known to be a bat or a crow," Atreides said.

"A bat," Colt said. "It seems more...traditional, as far as fiction literature goes. But like Atreides, I've shifted into all of them. You know, it can really be great. One minute you're a wolf, a hunter comes along, and you vaporize into mist or fog. Makes it damn hard on hunters."

"Oh, I like that."

"For me, it's the wolf," Renault said. "It's much more...wild and beautiful at the same time."

"Oh, I can't wait. How do I do it?" she asked.

"Think about becoming one with the wolf, concentrate on only that thought, nothing else. Like I said, it might be a while before you can shift." Then Atreides changed the subject. "So tonight, we'll have the same plan in place, vampiresses walking along the street toward a vampire club, or even leaving one, and the rest of us will be lying in wait to protect them."

"When the two women were attacked by the rogue vampire, he waited until he found a huntress who was alone. Were the vampiresses with each other or alone?" Selena asked.

"Hell, alone," Atreides said. Selena appeared to be as astute a huntress detective as Tezra was.

"Okay, so I had another idea. What if the rogue was paying the hunters back, except he wasn't killing the huntresses like the hunters were killing the vampiresses, but turning them, making them one of his own kind, an army of huntresses at his beck and call. Because once he turned us, he could have made us do his bidding. He told the two huntresses he had turned that he would give them orders later."

"And he wouldn't have known the two other huntresses were on the fringe and not League huntresses, but you were with the League. He could have gotten you to go along with whatever he wanted, within the League. He could have done the same with the fringe huntresses, but they wouldn't have been in the League, so no access there." Atreides was so glad Quail had killed the rogue vampire. But who was he?

"But there's another rogue vampire. He bit me first," she told him. "And another appeared, tossed him aside, and then he bit me. Quail, the wolf, shifted and killed the second vampire and the other rogue vanished."

"Hell," Atreides said. "And he's the one who must have wanted you dead. He wouldn't have been the one who attacked the huntresses because he hadn't wanted them dead either. The second vampire had to be the one turning them, and you."

"The guys who stole my car said that both men looked similar. Black-haired and six feet tall. They could have been brothers."

"Okay." Atreides got a call from his brother and he took a deep breath. "Daemon," he said to Selena. "Hey, how's it going in paradise?"

"I didn't realize how badly we needed this getaway. Is everything going all right with the clans?"

"Absolutely. Minor vampire fights as usual. Nothing big. I visited the fringe groups, and everything seems to be going fine with them."

"No other problems? Nothing major?"

Atreides was afraid Daemon had heard something about what was going on. "No, I would let you know otherwise. I'm glad things are going well for you though."

"Yeah, Maison and Voltan needed this too. We'll be raring to go when we get back."

"That's good. I'm glad, though I've enjoyed the increased scope of my duties while you've been gone, I'll be ready to turn over the reins when you return." Atreides did love being second in command. But he loved taking charge of the whole of the clans too. It gave him a chance to prove to his people that he had what it took to lead should his brother ever perish or want to step down.

"Tezra said you needed this too, to lead without Maison and Voltan watching over things."

"Yeah, thanks, Daemon. We've been good."

"Okay, I'm glad to hear it. I'll check in with you later then. Keep up the good work."

"I will. Thanks! Enjoy your vacation."

Then they ended the call and Selena raised a brow.

"He doesn't seem to know what's going on."

"That's good, until he returns, and you have to tell him what happened. All of what happened, including about me."

"By then, we'll have everything resolved." He hoped. "I'm sure he will be glad to see all the changes—I mean with you working between the hunters and us. You're a valuable asset and that works in all our favor." But he was damn angry a rogue vampire was still out there who had bitten her to kill her.

"The hunter that goes by the name of Cliff is in the red-light district," a voice telepathically said to Atreides.

"Who is this?" Atreides didn't recognize the vampire's voice.

"Quail. I don't know if he killed my sister, but he's the one who killed Charlene, isn't he?"

"We believe so. I'm headed there now."

"With hunters."

"Yes, they can take him down. Did you kill the rogue who wounded Selena?"

"Yes, but his twin brother, Gorgio, got away."

"Why didn't you come to us with the information right away?"

There was silence and Atreides knew the vampire was no longer listening to him.

Then Atreides told Selena what was going on and she called her brother and Rosa. "They're meeting us over there."

"It would be faster if we take them with us."

"As vampires?" she asked for clarification.

"Yes. Otherwise, Cliff could get away before we get there." Atreides told Colt and Renault what was going on.

"We'll get the others and meet you over there," Renault said.

"No going after the hunter. Only the hunters can take him down—but he'll need to be turned over to the League. Unless he puts up too much resistance and it's a fight to the death. Then the hunters will deal with him." But if Selena or her siblings were overwhelmed, the vampires would fight—swords out, no teeth though. Even though he told his friends not to fight, if he got embroiled in it, they would follow his lead.

When they arrived at the red-light district, they saw several females soliciting passersby either walking to the human clubs or strip joints, tattoo parlors, or cars driving through looking for a pick up. At first, they didn't see any sign of Cliff.

"He won't be alone," Selena said. "He always goes with his friends."

"That will make him easier to spot," Atreides said.

Colt and Renault were scouting the area up ahead, moving as mist. It was a misty night already—which allowed the vampires to move through it without being noticed, streetlamps shedding light into the streets, lights on in all the establishments making the night seem more eerie than it would have otherwise.

"Should we split up too?" Rosa asked.

"No," Atreides said. "Since you're Selena's sister, Cliff and his buddies might believe you'll be here for his head also. And Daniel too. Any number of hunters might have leaked the word to them that we're coming after him."

A van pulled up to the curb next to where they were walking and Atreides and the hunters suddenly stopped in their tracks, wary of a potential threat.

"What do you think?" Selena said as they eyed the van.

Then the side doors opened, and the front passenger and driver's doors did, and eight hunters got out of the van.

"Daniel told us Cliff was prowling the red-light district. We're here to help track him down," Bernard said. He was Tezra's former investigative partner.

Selena smiled. "Thanks, Bernard."

"We didn't want you to get all the glory. The council has named Cliff and his buddies the League's Most Wanted. They respect you and know that Cliff and the others want your head, so they want you protected at all costs." Bernard inclined his head. "I worked with Tezra, I will work with you."

Atreides couldn't believe this turn of events. He really hadn't thought the League would be this serious about helping them out and really, making a pact with the vampires to take down rogue hunters.

"Where is he?" Bernard asked.

Atreides respected him and was glad he was here to help.

"I have a couple of my men scouting ahead. We don't know how big their force is," Atreides said.

"Okay, we're going to split into groups of four. We'll keep in touch." Bernard led one group, another man leading another as they split off and started to roam the streets, the call girls trying to solicit them while they were searching for Cliff and his cohorts in crime.

"Do you think we'll spook them with so many hunters suddenly descending on the area?" Selena asked.

"We might," Atreides said.

Selena lifted her nose and smelled the air. "I smell Cliff's scent. Over here."

"That was the car he was using," Atreides said.

Daniel pulled out his sword and sliced up the tires. "He won't be getting away in this vehicle if he gets spooked."

"Would they have come in different cars?" Atreides asked.

"I doubt it. They always rode together," Selena said. "Though they could steal a car. Why would they be down here? That's what I wonder. They're not into prostitutes. Hunters usually don't frequent these areas. Vampires either. And if they're looking for vampiresses to kill, they probably won't find them here."

"I don't know. Unless they're here because they don't think anyone would believe they would be, citing the reasons you just gave," Atreides said.

"I smell their scent down this alley," Selena said.

Everyone drew their swords and walked down the dark alley, the mist floating in the darkness. A cat scampered out of the alley and into the next street.

Then they reached the next street and looked about. He hoped they weren't being led on a wild goose chase. "Which way?" Atreides asked.

"To the left," Selena said, glancing back at her brother and sister who both agreed.

Atreides broadcast telepathically to his friends, *"We're on the scent trail of Cliff and his friends."* He told them the street they were on and the direction they were headed.

"We're on our way," Colt said.

The mist thickened into a light rain and they continued to follow the men's scents. They were fresh so Quail had been right about the men being here. Which made him wonder if Quail was here now, following them himself.

"Quail, do you know where they are?"

"I lost them. They were at a tattoo parlor when I saw them going in. I waited for them to come out, but they didn't. They'd taken so long, I finally went inside and they'd slipped out a back way."

"But they didn't know you were following them?" Atreides was afraid the men had taken off in another vehicle.

"I can't be sure."

"But they didn't ambush you when you came out of the tattoo parlor," Atreides said.

"I was mist."

Atreides told him where they were now.

"I'll meet you there," Quail said.

"Don't engage them. The hunters need to do this. We have more hunters on the scene to help take them down."

Selena got a call and said, "Bernard said they tracked down Lonnie. He fought the hunters and they had to kill him."

"Have they split up then? Cliff and his buddies?" Atreides asked. If that was the case, they would be looking for individuals and not a group of rogue hunters. It would make it easier for those hunting them down in a way, but one or two of them could slip away.

To their surprise the two huntresses turned showed up.

Eliza said, "Selena told us you needed help."

Brittany said, "We're here to offer our support."

"We're on the trail of Cliff and his men." The scent trail was leading them to an apartment complex and Atreides wondered if they had a safe house of sorts there. He was thinking if Cliff and his men had split up, with the extra help here, they could split up too. But the fringe huntresses turned weren't sanctioned by the League, so he figured they'd better stay together and if anyone of them had to resort to killing Cliff and the rest of his men, they would give the credit to Selena and her siblings.

Daniel entered the building first and invited Atreides and the others in, though the huntresses turned didn't need an invitation. They heard yelling in a couple of apartments, people fighting, a baby crying. An elevator was straight ahead, but to the left was the door to the fire stairs. Selena pointed to the door.

To keep in shape, the hunters would use the stairs.

Daniel went first, though Atreides had wanted to. Then they all headed inside.

Atreides didn't like that they were bunched up in the narrow stairs as they climbed one flight after another until they came to the fifth story of the five-story building.

Daniel opened the door, and they all went into the hall and found it clear.

"Okay, let's split up here," Daniel said quietly, when they smelled that the men had split up and moved in both directions down the hall.

The two fringe huntresses turned stayed together with Daniel, and Atreides, Selena, and Rosa went in the opposite direction.

They glanced back at Daniel and the other women. They were standing beside a door and waiting for Atreides and Daniel's sisters to be in place before they broke in the doors.

Atreides and his party were standing at the door down the hall where they smelled Cliff and the others had been. "Ready?" he whispered, though he would have telepathically spoken just to Selena, he had to let Rosa know what he intended to do. He did telepathically say the same to the others in the hall because the two huntresses turned could tell Daniel what Atreides had said.

Daniel inclined his head and then both he and Atreides slammed into their respective doors and broke them in. That was the problem with cheap doors when hunters, and vampires, used their power to break them in.

Cliff was off the couch in an instant, but instead of coming at them with a sword, he began shooting at them.

Atreides whipped Rosa out of the room's entryway using vampiric transportation. Selena vanished. Weapons were discharged in the other apartment and Atreides saw that Eliza had moved Daniel out of the apartment he'd entered.

Neither hunters nor vampires used guns. It wasn't done. These men were rogues of the worst sort.

"Hell, we've got to get out of here," one of the other men yelled to Cliff.

"Don't you think I know that, damn it?" Cliff yelled back at him.

They were in a bind, but Atreides thought Selena would reappear next to him. She didn't. What the hell had happened to her? He was worried that she had been hit. That she was dead even. He couldn't go into the room without her invitation and he didn't want Rosa to subject herself to more gunfire. Daniel was texting on his phone, supposedly for backup.

Atreides called to Colt and Renault to join them at the apartment complex. He had thought there were other hunter rogues out there, so he hadn't called to them to come before this. But he needed to get in the room.

"Where's my sister?" Rosa asked, expecting the same thing as Atreides, for her to suddenly appear next to them.

"I'm in here," Selena said telepathically to Atreides. *"I've been hit."*

CHAPTER 19

*S*elena would kill the men. Cliff and Perry Rochester had shot her because she'd moved in front of her sister and Atreides, to invite him in and to protect her sister. She'd never expected the men to be armed with guns. It was unheard of in the history of their kind.

She was in pain, bleeding, but the bullet wounds hadn't hit fatal spots. Thankfully, she managed to transport into one of the bedrooms where the men weren't at and they must not have realized it. She was afraid to invite Atreides in. The hunters needed to do this, but she also didn't want anyone else to get shot. Then she thought of her brother. What if Daniel had been hit also? And Eliza and Brittany? She invited Atreides in. *"Don't let my sister enter the apartment."*

* * *

"Are you badly hurt?" Atreides asked Selena.

"Yes. I'm in a back bedroom, first one on the left down the hall. Cliff and Perry sound like they're in the kitchen."

"I'm on my way."

"Don't get yourself killed. I would never forgive you."

Then he was in the bedroom, appearing next to her, and she was lying on the floor, holding her wounds. "Hell, Selena," he whispered. "I've got to get you out of here."

"No way. We've got to end this now. Not only for the vampiresses they've murdered but for the future ones if we don't stop them. No telling where they'll end up."

"We've got hunter reinforcements coming. Let me take you out of here." Atreides sounded desperate to move her and get help for her.

"No."

"You can't fight like this."

"Watch me. I'm healing." Not instantaneously, but she could do this. "Just give me a few minutes."

"We've got to make a break for it. We killed Selena. There are two others out there, her sister, and some other guy I didn't recognize," Cliff said.

"Yeah, the other guys want to leave too. We're hemmed in here. If they call for reinforcements, we're dead," Perry said.

"Okay, they didn't expect us to be using guns so they can't win against us. Let's do this," Cliff said.

"I still can't raise Lonnie."

"He may be dead."

Selena told the other huntresses turned to go after the men in the other room.

"Will do," Eliza said.

Selena heard Cliff and his friend running out of the kitchen and she suddenly appeared before them and thrust her sword into Cliff's heart, if he'd had one. His expression was one of shock and he dropped his gun. She couldn't pull her sword out of Cliff's body fast enough to kill Perry.

But Atreides was there for her, taking out the other hunter,

"For all the vampiresses you murdered and for attempting to kill Selena."

The men were still not dead, but they looked up at them in shock as Rosa ran into the room. She yanked Atreides's sword out of Perry's chest, handed it to Atreides who sheathed his sword, and Rosa shoved her sword into the hunter. "For being a rogue and giving hunters a bad name." Then she saw Selena barely standing, but Atreides grabbed her up before she collapsed. *She* needed a vacation after this.

Her sister retrieved her sword and they headed to the other apartment as hunters slammed the fire escape door open and rushed down the hall to the apartment where gunshots were being fired again.

"Take care of Selena. Harry Canton and Lonnie Wilson are dead," Bernard said. "We've got this."

Atreides inclined his head. "Cliff and Perry are dead."

"I'll join you as soon as I can," Rosa said.

* * *

THEN ATREIDES TOOK Selena to his home to the room where they ministered to wounded vampires who didn't have fatal injuries and called for their doctor. *"Selena's been shot twice. She's bleeding bad."* In the meantime, Atreides was binding her wounds as his housekeeper ran to get blood for her. Selena would need a transfusion, but within minutes, the doctor was there. Selena looked ghostly pale and she'd lost consciousness as soon as he'd transported her to his home.

"How is she doing?" the doctor asked.

Atreides was afraid he would lose her. But could he? Would her vampire half win out? Her huntress side could have been dead. "She has lost a lot of blood."

"Have someone available to give her blood. Drinking it won't help in this case."

Atreides began pulling up his sleeve. "I will."

"Humans did this?" the doctor asked as he put Selena under.

Only humans fired guns at each other. Sometimes at vampires, but it was rarely fatal. He hadn't heard of them trying to kill a hunter in that way, which was why these bastards had resorted to using guns.

"Rogue hunters."

The doctor shook his head. "I hope this doesn't lead to a trend among their kind and ours." He began to remove one of the bullets, his nurse showing up unexpectedly to help.

She started a blood transfusion from Atreides to Selena.

"Are these the men who killed the vampiresses?" the doctor asked, working on the second bullet.

"Yes. We got three of them for sure. Other hunters were at the scene to take down the others." Atreides was about to telepathically ask Eliza if the other men were dead, but he hadn't wanted to interfere if they were in the middle of a fight.

Then he got a call from Daniel. "How's Selena?"

"In surgery. Is everyone all right there?"

"Eliza killed one of the hunters. Bernard was going to take the credit, but she said she would go down as a martyr if she had to because she was claiming the kill of a rogue hunter. I managed to kill the other but got shot."

"How bad?"

"Not bad, but Eliza took me to a hunter facility to have a doctor remove the bullet."

"And you're still talking to me?"

"I'm just along for the ride. I'll be there shortly. Rosa is headed your way. Colt's taking her. I'll see you all as soon as I'm out of surgery."

"Take it easy, and thanks, Daniel, for helping us with this."

"Of course. Thanks for helping us and taking care of both my sisters." Then they ended the call.

Atreides saw the doctor remove the last bullet. "How is she?"

"She's beginning to heal already. She'll be fine. But I still can't believe that the rogue hunters would resort to using bullets."

They heard Colt outside of the room talking to Rosa. "I'm sure she's fine."

Rosa rushed into the room to check on her sister. "How is she?" She took hold of her hand and squeezed.

"The doctor said she's fine, but she might not be able to fight for a while, right, Doc?" Atreides didn't want her fighting any more battles for now.

"Yeah. I need to check on her again before I can declare her fit for fighting." The doc said, "I'll return if you need me in the meantime. Just let me know."

"Thanks, I will."

"I know we got all the rogue hunters, but would you mind if I stay here until Selena has recovered?" Rosa asked.

"Absolutely you can." He had planned to take care of her himself, but he wouldn't deny her sister's request to stay with them to watch Selena recuperate. If he needed to be away for clan business, he would leave some of his men with Rosa and Selena.

"Bernard said the other hunters saw a wolf chasing one of the rogue hunters and that's when the League hunters caught up with him," Rosa said.

"The wolf?" Selena said, stirring from her sleep.

"Ohmigod, Selena, how could you just run into the room and get shot up like that!" Rosa scolded her.

"I didn't realize they had guns until it was too late. Was it the wolf? Quail?" Selena asked, sounding drowsy.

"That's what Colt said. He saw him too when he was still in mist form and thought he was the same one that you had described. I wonder why he likes to show up as a wolf," Rosa said.

"Then he helped us at the last," Selena whispered.

Atreides kissed her forehead. "Sleep, Selena, we can talk about this later."

"Did we get all of them? Are Daniel and the two huntresses turned, and the other hunters all right?" she asked.

Atreides smiled at her. "They are all fine."

But Rosa was frowning.

"Who isn't fine?" Selena asked her sister.

"Daniel was shot, but he's going to be good. He wasn't hurt as badly as you. He was talking all the way to the car the other hunters carried him to. They figured they would meet a hunter ambulance on the way. It would be quicker that way."

"Okay, good."

"But naturally, he's worried about you." Rosa took a video of Selena. "Tell him something so he won't worry about you when he gets out of surgery."

"Hey, Daniel, thanks for coming to help us with this. Sorry you got shot too. Love you."

Then Rosa sent the video to their brother. "Now another for our parents. They are frantic, once they heard you were hit twice. And of course they wanted to know why I didn't protect you better, being the older sister."

Selena offered a sleepy smile.

"We should let you rest after this," Atreides said.

Selena said to her parents as Rosa recorded the video, "Love you, Mom and Dad. I'll be fine in no time. They gave me anesthesia so I'm a bit groggy, but I'll snap out of it soon."

Then Rosa sent the video to their parents. "They said they went to see Daniel at the hospital since I was with you."

"Tell them they can come to see Selena any time they want." Atreides wanted to make sure they understood that even though they hadn't had the official break-the-ice dinner with them, he wanted them to be part of his extended vampire family. He supposed it was time to tell his brother that he was mated and how that had all come about.

"We could do dinner with them tonight," Selena said.

"No way," Rosa said. "You need to rebuild your strength." Rosa got a call and smiled. "Uh, yes, she'll be fine. Okay, she just got out of surgery and is still a bit sleepy. All right, thanks. We're glad too." She handed the phone to Selena. "The president of the Council."

CHAPTER 20

"Well, you did it. You and the rest of your vampire and League hunter team," the president of the League Council said to Selena.

Selena hadn't expected the president to think of this as her team. They were just a bunch of vampires and hunters who had come together to fight the worst kind of evil. "Thank you. It was a joint effort on everyone's part."

"We heard about the other huntresses who had been turned and how they had helped to turn the tide against these men. We want them to join your special team. Since you're in charge of it, it's up to you if that will work for you. Just let them know if you want to 'hire' them and we'll make it happen. Full pay and allowances."

"Thank you." She couldn't believe the League would set up a team that she would be in charge of, or that the women would even consider working with her. Not when they were happy to live on the fringe. But they had more in common with her than not, and she thought they might have changed their minds about living on the fringe once they were fighting the rogue hunters.

Here, she'd thought she would have been a virtual outcast. She couldn't believe it.

She was glad Rosa was sitting beside her when she woke again, and she was now in Atreides's bed. "Where is he?"

"Taking care of business. Mom and Dad want to see you tonight. He has invited them over for dinner, even if you can't eat with us. He couldn't wait to meet them, and they couldn't wait to check on you and see how you're doing."

"What about Daniel? How is he doing?"

"He's doing well. If you can believe it, three huntresses are at his bedside at the hospital, mooning over him."

Selena chuckled. She could just envision it, and then the huntresses being miffed with each other if he decided on one to date. But then she was thinking of how—when she had killed Cliff's brother—a rogue just as much, she wasn't treated in the same way at all. The vampires had to come to her aid. *"Atreides, what are you doing?"*

"I'm trying to locate the wolf vampire. I want to thank him for helping us eliminate the last rogue hunter and killing the two rogue vampires. Are you feeling better?"

"I am. Wait, two rogue vampires?"

"Yeah, he found the twin brother of the one who had turned you. His brother wanted to turn huntresses, like we suspected, to have them do his bidding. His brother thought the huntresses turned could be real trouble so he was following him this last time to end you before you could be turned. He got away before Quail could eliminate the vampire, but now he's dead."

"Oh, good. I'm so glad. I was afraid that would be our next mission. You had invited my parents for dinner, Rosa said." She was glad he had. The sooner they met him and accepted him in the family, the better it would be for all of them. And it would validate, with the other hunters, that what Selena had done was acceptable.

Atreides appeared in the room. "Yes. I want to meet them. I

knew they wanted to see you. I figured it was the perfect opportunity to do all three."

"All right, well I'm coming to dinner." She wouldn't miss this for anything. And she did have the notion, if her parents were uncomfortable around Atreides, maybe she could make them feel better about him.

"If you are feeling all right. I don't want you to relapse and neither do your parents."

She loved how protective Atreides was of her. "I won't. I'll be fine." Though she felt like staying in the bed forever and never moving from it. Hopefully, she would heal enough by the time it was dinner, that she could get her lazy bones out of bed. "We did it. We eliminated the rogue hunters. How do your people feel about it?"

"Elated. Grateful to you and your kin and the hunters who came to help. I've talked to them about the two huntresses turned who want to work with you. They are eager to meet them. I talked to them about how you were feeling, and they want to meet with you as soon as you're able to. They realize that they won't be going on missions always, but it looks like they're moving out of the border town."

"Why? They haven't been ostracized by the fringe hunters, have they?" She'd been hoping they could have someone to contact in the border towns if they had trouble with the fringe hunters. But now they wouldn't. Though if it were something they truly wanted to do on their own, she would be happy for them. They deserved happiness, like she did, after all they had been through.

"They've had several hunters interested in dating them. League hunters. It's pissed off the fringe hunters."

"Oh." She hadn't expected that, but she was glad for them!

"And there are some vampires, like Colt and Renault and Basil, who are interested in dating them. So that doesn't help their status on the fringe either."

That she hadn't expected either! She smiled. "I'm glad they are seen as valuable additions to our worlds—both in yours and mine."

"Mine is yours as well."

"Are you going to tell Daemon then about what has happened?"

"No. Not until he returns home. He would most likely cut their trip short, not trusting that everything was wrapped up neatly in a bright red bow."

She sighed. She wished Atreides would just get it over with so they could deal with the repercussions, if there were any. "All right. I hope he's not too shocked by all that has happened. You know, he might not like it that a new vampire to the clan has a contract with the hunters to work within the clan."

"If it helps our people, that's all that will matter to Daemon. Oh, it's time to work on the meal."

"What are we having?"

"Grilled steaks. I've got to get them started."

"You? Grill steaks?"

"Colt taught me. It's raining, if you didn't notice, but the grill is under the large patio cover and I want to make this myself."

"Rare for me."

"Are you sure you're coming to the dinner?"

"If you don't cook a rare steak for me, I will be showing you my extended canines."

He smiled. "Rare for you and your parents and sister said medium rare for them. Your brother is coming too. He didn't want to. He was getting so much attention for his injury that he wanted to stay and enjoy it, but your father said this was a family dinner with your new mate, and a celebration for the mission we accomplished."

"Thank you for saving my life, Atreides. I can't remember if I told you that."

"You were pretty out of it, but I love you too."

She smiled. "Okay, I'm going to close my eyes for a little bit longer. But don't you dare let me sleep through dinner."

"All right." But the way he said it made her think that he would do just that if she were sleeping heavily.

She knew he would only have her best interests at heart, but she wanted to be there to celebrate her mating and see just how receptive her parents were toward Atreides. She hoped he charmed them as much as he had won her over.

Rosa said, "You look sleepy. Go to sleep and we'll wake you when everyone is here, and dinner is ready. I'll stay with you just in case you wake and need anything."

"I'll just close my eyes and rest them," Selena said, not intending anything more than that. She was going to dinner no matter what, though she might have to retire early after eating with her family and her mate.

He kissed her and she kissed him back, then closed her eyes and hoped he would wake her and if he didn't, she hoped she wouldn't be too angry with him.

* * *

As soon as Selena's family arrived for dinner, Atreides greeted Daniel and Selena's father and mother for the first time. "How are you doing, Daniel?" Atreides asked.

Daniel smiled. "Really good." Because of the huntresses' interest in a heroic, wounded hero?

"Selena is sleeping, and Rosa is watching over her for now. I'll go check on her." Atreides would have just transported to the room to see if she was awake and wanted to join them for the meal, but her parents and Daniel decided to come with him to see how she was faring for themselves. So far, everything had been cordial between them.

Selena was sound asleep. Atreides had mixed feelings about it.

He was glad her injuries weren't keeping her awake, but he knew how much she wanted to be with the family right now.

Rosa stood when they walked into the room and whispered, "She fell asleep right away after you finished talking to her, Atreides. She's worn out."

Her mother kissed Selena's forehead and then her dad kissed her cheek. Daniel squeezed her hand, but no one said anything to her, not wanting to disturb her if she could sleep through Rosa's whispered words.

"Let's eat," her dad said, definitely sounding like he was in charge of the situation.

Atreides was actually glad Selena's dad would do that so that she couldn't argue about it. At least he didn't think she would.

They left the room then and sat down at the dining room table. Atreides felt bad that he hadn't woken Selena, but her parents hadn't wanted her awakened either. But he knew Selena would be upset with him if she missed out on her dinner and attending the family gathering.

"Are you really all right?" Rosa asked Daniel, his arm bandaged up.

"Yeah." He winked at her. "Better than all right."

"So tell us how you met Selena," her dad said to Atreides.

He knew Selena had told them what had happened. Was he trying to get verification that it had all happened that way? He told them all that he had seen, but not about the dance he'd had with Selena. "I was afraid she was after a rogue vampire," he said. "I was afraid she was going to just stir up trouble."

Her dad smiled. "Yeah, that sounds like Selena. Once she has it in mind to do something, nothing will stop her."

That could be a good thing and bad, Atreides was thinking. He just hoped Daemon was as happy about him mating her as Atreides was.

"You're the right man for her," her dad said.

Atreides was relieved her father would feel that way about

him. He didn't want to be the wedge between Selena and her family.

"I knew it right away when you took care of her when hunters wouldn't." Her dad gave his son a chastising look, well-deserved, Atreides thought. Her dad also cast a reprimanding look in Rosa's direction. Also deserved.

Though Selena's sister and brother had apologized to her, it still was true. Not only were they hunters who hadn't watched out for her, they were her family, which made their reactions worse.

"Dig in," Atreides said, wanting everyone to enjoy their meal before it got cold.

"I agree with my mate," her mom said.

Atreides had hoped Selena's mother would feel the same way about him as her father did, so this was good tidings.

"We can see how she feels about you. You are perfect for her. How does your brother feel about this union?" Selena's mother asked.

"I'm sure he'll be fine with it."

"You haven't told him about it yet?" her dad asked, pausing to take another bite of steak.

"I didn't want to upset their vacation," Atreides said, making a mistake in saying so. "I mean, if my brother had known all the trouble I've had, not with Selena, but with the rogue hunters, he would have returned right away with Tezra."

"Tezra," her mother said. "She will help Selena make the transition as well."

"That's what we figure."

"We're glad for you both," her dad said then. "But we want to know if things change when Daemon returns home."

So they weren't fooled by Atreides's attempt to try and show that he believed Daemon would be fine with him and Selena mating.

Selena suddenly appeared in the dining room, arms folded

across her chest, and frowning at Atreides. She'd startled everyone and four hunters had their swords drawn. Her parents hadn't seen her using a vampiric mode of transportation yet, so it was probably sinking in a little more that she wasn't exactly like them any longer.

"It was my decision, Daughter," her dad said. "Join us before you fall down."

Atreides was already helping her into the seat beside him, trying not to smile at her dad's words, or appear too grateful her dad had made the decision for her and wouldn't hear another thing about it.

"I told you I wanted to eat with everyone."

"You are, Selena," her mother said. "Just a little late. You were tired, sound asleep, and even Rosa's talking to us in your room didn't wake you. What were we to do? You are a bear when you are tired. And after being injured so? You needed to rest further."

Selena was already eating her steak. It appeared she hadn't lost her appetite, though halfway through her meal she sat back in her chair and looked sleepy all over again. He wanted to carry her back to bed, but he suspected she wouldn't go for it and they would have their first fight as a mated couple.

Instead, everyone talked about the battle, what worked, what went wrong while Selena made the greatest effort to stay awake. Atreides appreciated that they were trying to keep the subject off how tired she appeared. The way she was so lethargic, reminded him of when she'd been so savagely attacked before. Atreides was dying to ask her if she wanted to return to bed, but she could return herself there, so he knew she didn't want to.

All her family members were glancing at Selena, looking at her with worried expressions, feeling as Atreides did. That she needed to be in bed, sleeping, to recover from her wounds faster. They finished the meal, all but Selena, and Atreides saved the rest of her steak for her for later. Then he carried her to the couch and his housekeeper brought a blanket and pillow for her.

They all took seats in the living room where they continued to discuss hunter strategy, while Selena rested her head on Atreides's shoulder and was fine like that for a while. The next thing he knew, she was lying on the pillow on his lap and was sleeping soundly. Everyone seemed pleased to see the way Atreides handled the situation with Selena and were comfortable with her being there.

He still wanted to take her to bed, but he suspected he would wake her and as long as she was happily sleeping there while they all discussed issues, he would do so.

He was surprised to hear her family speaking about hunter strategies though, since he was a vampire.

"So what do you think about the change in this game?" her father asked.

He wasn't sure if her father meant the business with having huntresses who had been turned working with them or—

"The gun issue," her father clarified.

"The vampires can dodge bullets, vanish, as long as we're not hit before that happens. Selena didn't stand a chance because she entered the apartment first to invite me in, was shot, not expecting it, and then had to transport to somewhere safe—the extra bedroom. She was unconscious for a few minutes before she could invite me in and then I immediately came to her aid. I wanted to take her out of there right away, but she was insistent that we take down the hunters, so they didn't get away from us and kill some more."

"She's persistent when she's after a rogue," her mother said.

"And she was right in taking down the hunters before they could kill any more innocents," her dad said.

"If we have trouble with this in the future, those who have to hunt rogues down of this nature, might have to wear bulletproof vests. We all heal faster, but if we bleed out before we can get to safety, it could be bad news for those who are newly turned or who are hunters. As far as it goes for us, the ancient vampires, it shouldn't be an issue. If that's the case, the League might have to call on us to come and help out against hunter rogues. Or rogue vampires who might decide that's the way to go. In a way, I would have liked to have kept this news from the press, so to speak. But there was no way to keep it under wraps because of the injuries Daniel and Selena had suffered," Atreides said.

"I agree," her dad said. "When it comes to a situation like this, we need to be aware of what had occurred anyway, to decide how to handle it best. If we don't, and it occurs again and we're wholly unprepared again, that's not good either."

"True." Atreides stroked Selena's dark hair.

"The hunters were staying in a bad part of town. Do you think they had the guns for that reason?" her mother asked. "They wouldn't have been successful against gunmen if they were using only swords."

"No," her father said. "If that were the case, they would have used swords in an honorable fight. They wouldn't have drawn guns and used them against a huntress. They knew who Selena was. Rosa. Daniel. They might not have known the huntresses turned, but they knew enough of the hunters that they should have dropped the guns and grabbed their swords to fight. They didn't because they planned it that way."

"Did they even have swords in the apartments?" Rosa asked. "We were in such a hurry to get Selena out of there, we never looked."

"The hunters who investigated the crime scenes found their swords near their bodies. They were armed with both. Maybe in the event vampires came after them and they knew they would have to kill them with a sword to the heart or remove their heads," Daniel said.

They were talking for about an hour when Selena suddenly groaned and sat upright, groaning again. When she saw her whole family sitting in the living room, she let out her breath. "I thought you had gone home."

"No, we didn't want you to think we had abandoned you. We were visiting with Atreides. Are you finally ready to retire to bed?" her mother asked. "We are. We've had a delightful time, and next time, we would love to have you both to our home for dinner."

"We would love it," Atreides said, glad her mother said they were ready to go home. He enjoyed visiting with them, but he really wanted to take Selena to bed where she belonged, and he suspected she wouldn't retire to bed until he did.

"Oh, yes, that would be great," Selena said.

"We have an early hunter meeting to go to," her dad said, standing and stretching.

"I have some calls to make," Daniel said. "Great dinner, Atreides."

"Thanks, we'll do it again sometime."

"I need to get my beauty sleep after all the hunting we've been doing at night. I have been burning the candle at both ends," Rosa said.

"I need to return to bed," Selena said.

Atreides knew everyone agreed, though they didn't say so.

Then they all left after giving Selena hugs and kisses, and even Selena's mom and Rosa gave Atreides a hug. Except for Selena and Tezra, well, and her younger sister, he hadn't had hugs from huntresses.

"When Daemon returns, we'll be sure to have you over again and let him meet everyone," Atreides said.

"Yes, we would like that." Then her dad and the others went outside, Daniel taking Rosa home and their parents driving their own car.

Atreides shut and locked the door, then grabbed Selena up in his arms. She wrapped her arms around his neck, and he carried her back to bed.

"Are you staying with me?" she asked.

"Yes. What startled you so when you were sleeping on my lap on the couch?"

"I had a nightmare about being assailed by a barrage of bullets. That has never happened to me before. Fighting a vampire that suddenly appears is one thing, and I'm usually prepared for that. Except for when the vampire attacked me."

"I'm sorry. I will always regret I wasn't able to protect you better."

She kissed him. "You couldn't have. I shouldn't have been so brash in running into the room to fight them all on my own."

"That's normally your way, sword out and ready for a fight. No one would have expected them to begin shooting," Atreides said.

"True. So what did you think of my parents?"

"I highly respect them. As far as I'm concerned, your family is my family. And they were completely accepting of me and of our relationship. "

"I'm so glad for that. I'm so sorry about the steak. It was delicious. As fast as my family scarfed them up, I know they loved them too. I just couldn't eat all of it."

"I saved it for you."

"I thought you had said that. Thank you."

"You're welcome." Then he kissed her.

"Make love to me."

He smiled. "When you are all better." He wasn't about to hurt Selena no matter how much she wanted this. Later, he would surely take her up on it.

* * *

TWO DAYS LATER, Daemon and Tezra flew in from their vacation in the middle of the night, and Atreides went along to pick them up, as was their custom, their driver driving the limousine. Maison and Voltan were with them. Atreides had wanted to go alone, to iron things out between his brother and him, and not have Selena in the middle of it. He wanted his brother, for the first time to meet her, to be as gracious toward her as her parents had been toward Atreides.

"So how did everything go?" Daemon asked, his brows raised.

"Everything was fine."

"You are seeing a new woman," Daemon said. "Someone I don't recognize."

Atreides should have realized they would smell Selena's scent on him as much as they hugged and kissed each other as new mates.

"About that," Atreides said.

"We know all about it," Daemon said, shocking the hell out of Atreides.

He'd been trying to find the words to tell them what had happened that wouldn't make his brother too angry with him.

"Who told you?" Atreides asked as the driver drove them home.

"The president of the League, Selena's father, her brother, her sister, King of the fringe hunters, Iconia. And a vampire who has come into our territory, though he often runs as a wolf, Quail, who has asked me to allow him to join the clan."

Atreides closed his gaping mouth.

"Why didn't you bring Selena with you?" Tezra asked, smiling at him. "I have met her before, and I know we will become best of friends."

"I wanted to tell you what had happened first." Atreides appreciated that his brother and his mate would trust in him enough to let him accomplish the mission without interfering. "When you learned of what was going on had you wanted to return and take over the clans to resolve the situation?" He had to know the truth. He couldn't imagine Daemon being fine with what had been going on.

"I was having too good a time with Tezra. We needed this

time alone. And you needed to prove to yourself that you could handle the difficulty, no matter what."

Atreides was having a difficult time believing that his brother hadn't been chomping at the bit to return home and straighten everything out. It wasn't exactly that Atreides felt Daemon didn't trust him to do the right thing, but that he was always ready to take care of a crisis, whatever it took, and leaving it to his younger twin brother to handle wasn't something he would normally do.

Then Tezra channeled her telepathic communication to Atreides privately, *"Yes, he was dying to return home to oversee things. But he knew you were handling things just the way he would have done, and there was no sense in him returning early from our vacation when you were getting a handle on it."*

That's what Atreides figured. He wasn't sure Daemon felt that Atreides was handling things just fine. He suspected Tezra had a hand in convincing him to leave well enough alone. And he appreciated her for it.

"How is Selena and her brother?" Tezra asked.

"Her brother is milking his injury for everything it's worth—getting lots of huntresses' attention. Selena is getting much better. She wants to meet you tomorrow night. She figured you would be tired from your journey home, and she would have another day to rest up." Which was true, but Atreides knew she had made the suggestion because she knew how unsure he was about speaking with his brother about this whole situation. Though he thought her resting up for another day was a good idea too.

"That works for us. Did you want to have dinner at our house then?" Tezra asked.

Atreides hesitated. He hadn't thought they would want to have dinner right away after they got home from their vacation and he was wondering if Selena would prefer to be in the comfort of their home, or in Daemon and Tezra's.

"At our house," Daemon said. "She needs to visit with us there since she has never seen the place. We'll prepare dinner. She has been through a couple of ordeals. Let her rest up and we'll treat her to a feast."

"All right. At your house then." Atreides was so relieved all of it was out in the open, even though he thought he was going to have to do a lot of explaining.

"We're proud of you," Tezra said, "Aren't we, Daemon?"

"Yeah, I couldn't have done a better job than you did."

Atreides couldn't have asked for better praise from his brother and he felt so much better about it now. "Thanks. I didn't want to trouble you when I knew I could handle it." Which Atreides knew for sure, but he just hadn't been so sure his brother would have wanted him to take care of matters. Well, he was actually sure his brother wouldn't have left it up to him to do. Especially if Tezra hadn't had a hand in it. He would have to thank her later. But he had to know, had anything he had done been in secret? "Was everything I was doing reported back to you?"

It bothered him that there were spies in the clans who might have been reporting every little thing back to Daemon. Which reminded him of the dance he'd had with Selena and what all was said about that! And the *way* he had danced with the fiery huntress before she'd even been turned!

"No. You'll have to fill us in on all the details," Daemon said. "The League Council contacted me so that I knew they were working with us now, and they wanted to make sure it was fine with me. Iconia told me about you protecting a huntress and taking her home with you. But then she told me later that it didn't matter, everything was fine, Iconia and you had broken up and she was happily seeing Ragnar. I pressed her about the huntress, but she just said all that had been handled."

Atreides appreciated that Iconia had made a complete turn-around where Selena was concerned. He didn't expect the women to become fast friends, but anything was possible.

"We want to meet with Selena's family as soon as possible also," Tezra said. "Since I'd lost most of mine, it will be great to expand our family."

"It's going to really work out well, I think, with having ties to the League and they're coming around with working with the fringe hunters too. But I'll let Selena know you want to meet with them too," Atreides said.

The rain started and pelted the car as they drove to their home. Tezra gave Atreides a hug. "We're so glad you took charge so we could have our vacation."

Daemon hugged him also. "You did good. You know what this means, don't you?"

"You're going on more vacations?" Atreides was hopeful Daemon felt that he and Tezra could now.

Daemon smiled. "Yeah, and if I need to help out others in need, like even the hunters turned against the rogue vampires in Florida, I can do it without worrying that you can manage things on your own. You've made some real changes that should benefit all our kind. You've made me proud."

* * *

"How was it?" Selena asked as Atreides climbed into bed with her. The flight was so late that night, that Selena had a hard time staying awake for Atreides, but she couldn't sleep until Atreides had come home to her and she knew what had happened between him and his brother.

"I thought you would be asleep. I told you not to wait up for me." Atreides kissed her cheek and pulled her into his arms, then kissed the top of her head.

This was what she had needed, him with her, snuggling. "No

way. I had to know if you and your brother were cool about this after you told him about it."

"They already knew a lot about what was going on."

"I figured they might. It would have been hard to keep something like what had happened a secret." Then she frowned. "But are they all right with it?" Everything had worked out well, in the end, she thought. But it didn't mean Daemon would agree with it.

"Yeah, they said we did such a good job, they're inclined to take more trips and leave me in charge. Daemon said he was proud of me."

She heard the well-deserved pride in Atreides's voice and knew just how much that meant to him and someday she wanted to tell Daemon how much that had meant to his brother. "Hmm, I could have told them you would be fine." She was so pleased with the way everything had worked out.

"With you at my side, yeah." He sighed as he cuddled with her. "I have to admit, I'm ready to enjoy some down time with you."

She smiled. "Do you think we'll get any?"

Daemon communicated with the two of them, *"Thanks for taking care of my brother. He needed you in his life and we couldn't be happier."*

* * *

ATREIDES HADN'T EXPECTED his brother to talk to them both right now. He really hadn't figured he'd be talking to him again until dinner tomorrow night. It had to be important, he figured.

"We...you have a mission. Two fringe vampires found an injured vampire girl who is one of our clan in their border town. It's your job to learn who she belongs to, who injured her, and how she ended up in the border town."

Atreides looked down at Selena and raised a brow.

"We're right on it," Selena told Daemon. *"And I needed Atreides in*

my life just as much." She leaned over and kissed Atreides. "I love you."

He sighed. "I love you too. I just thought with Daemon back, we could have some downtime."

"If, Selena, you're up for it, considering your injuries," Daemon added and Atreides knew his brother only meant for him to have to go on the mission.

"I'm ready," she said.

"Thanks, if the two of you need any help, let me know," Daemon said.

"We will," Atreides said, glad that his brother trusted him with the mission as they ended the telepathic communication.

Selena was already out of bed and getting dressed in a hurry, as if she were afraid Atreides might change his mind and leave her behind to recuperate further.

Atreides quickly dressed too and then Selena telepathically said to her huntress turned friends, *"Eliza, Brittany, we could use your help."*

He was glad the women had become her friends. And then Selena and Atreides were heading to the border town.

When Atreides had seen the huntress Selena walk into their vampire cub, he never would have believed where that would have led, but he couldn't have been gladder to have resolved the issue of the vampiress murders and the rogue vampires turning huntresses or attempting to murder them and that he would have found a mate who was a huntress too. He was thrilled everything had worked out as it had and was glad his brother had been proud of how he had managed things. Now he was off on another mission with his mate, and together, he knew they would solve it. He just hoped that she was truly recovered enough to be with him, but he was glad she would be at his side.

* * *

EVERYTHING HAD TURNED UPSIDE DOWN for Selena on a mission to find her sister, Rosa. Not only did she end up locating Rosa and helping to solve a rogue hunters' crime, she had learned who had bitten her, turned her, and she had found a mate. Not a hunter, like she had always assumed she would have. But one hot vampire who heated her blood with primal desire. She had hoped when Daemon had returned, she could have spent more time with Atreides in mated bliss, but this was important too—taking care of the innocents of the region was their top priority—and the other would have to wait.

They arrived in the town, saw a hunter coming at them with a sword raised, two more joining him and they prepared for the fight. She didn't recognize any of the hunters—out-of-towners? Fringe hunters? They weren't local League-sanctioned hunters, that's all she knew.

Her huntress turned friends suddenly appeared beside Selena, evening up the odds. Together with Atreides and her new friends, she knew they would be victorious.

EPILOGUE

A *Thanksgiving family celebration, three months later at Daemon's house*

Selena couldn't believe how great it was to be with Atreides and his family along with hers at a big family celebration. They didn't do big vampire bashes with a mix of her family and the vampires, yet, nor did she take Atreides to hunter bashes, though she hoped in the future it would be a mutual thing they could share. For now, they enjoyed their small hunter-vampire family gatherings, and even though she thought it should not be a topic of conversation, they often talked about how they had taken down rogue vampires, and then Atreides and Daemon would talk about how glad they were that the hunters had.

And even the vampire Quail in his human form, not a wolf's, had been invited to the dinner because of his saving Selena from the rogue vampire after she'd been so brutally attacked.

"I felt guilty that I had forced you to walk back to the club that night, though I'd had the best intention," Quail said. "I knew you would be the only one to help us out of the mess we were headed toward—a war between vampires and hunters—because you had taken a stand to protect a vampiress that the hunter vowed to kill. I hadn't had time to prevent the vampires attacking you. And for that I'll forever be sorry."

"Don't be. I might not have returned to the club and we wouldn't be where we are today," Selena said, squeezing Atreides's hand. "Thank you for killing the rogue vampire for me. You saved my life."

"And countless others," Daemon said, agreeing. "We're glad to have both of you in the clan."

One thing that seemed to be causing a bit of trouble was the fact that Eliza and Brittany were getting so many offers of dates from both vampires, who insisted the hunters turned should be with them, and the hunters, who wanted to have a huntress turned in their court. As mates, they could really use the special vampire conditions the newly turned vampires had. But the problem was that the vampires lived such long lives that the hunters lost out in that regard. And a vampire, even half, mated to a hunter meant losing him at some point in their mated lives.

Which was another reason Selena was glad she had a vampire to love. She didn't have to drink blood very often, but it didn't bother her at all like she thought it would. She hadn't bitten anyone other than her mate yet, and she was just as happy about that.

The fringe vampires and hunters were more receptive to the rules of the vampire clans and League of Hunter's council, though they still didn't want to join either force. But communication was better.

And the issue with the three hunters she and Atreides and her hunter turned vampire friends had to deal with in the border town? The hunters were history. Rogues beware—whether they were hunters or vampires. They would be swiftly taken care of.

"So what do you think?" her mother asked Selena.

Selena realized her thoughts had been a million miles away as they all sat down to the Thanksgiving feast and she wondered what she'd missed out on. "About?"

"What you're going to shift into," Daniel said. "You said you've been trying to shift into something, and we were just curious as to what."

"Mist." Not that mist was the form she was shooting for, but it was the only thing she'd managed this early on after being turned.

"Can you do it?" Rosa asked, her eyes wide.

"Sure."

"Show us," her dad said, sounding just as intrigued.

So she did, turned into mist at the table, drifted off and around them, seeped under a door and seeped back in, then returned to her seat and didn't shift back. Damn it. She knew she shouldn't have shown off. At least she was nearly done with her food.

"That is so cool," Rosa said. "You can shift back now."

She wished. She couldn't even telepathically communicate with Atreides when she was in this form.

"It might take a few minutes," Atreides said, attempting to reassure her family, and her.

She knew it could. Or sometimes hours, like the first time she'd shifted into mist. She'd ended up having to sit next to Atreides on the couch binge watching a vampire series, which he said was not at all realistic, and she would have told him it was supposed to be fiction, but of course, she couldn't say anything.

Everyone continued the conversation around her, eating and drinking and being merry. That would teach her to turn into mist at the dinner table from now on. Atreides smiled at her as if he were truly seeing her sitting there, and then just right when dessert was brought to the table: pecan pie and pumpkin pie and even a chocolate cream pie, she shifted back.

Her mother smiled. "The chocolate did it."

Selena wondered. Atreides kissed her. She felt foolish that she had showed off and couldn't shift back right away, but her mother only smiled at her and said, "Well done."

Selena was glad her parents had been so approving of all the changes in her life when she truly had believed they would feel differently. But maybe they had been because it had opened up a new world to all of them. One in which they might have a better handle against the rogues—either hunters or vampires.

Rosa and Daniel were both enjoying their new status with the vampires and hunters. But there were still those on either side who didn't like the way things were changing.

Suddenly, she heard a faint heartbeat coming from inside her belly, and Atreides glanced down at her belly, then his gaze met hers. He smiled. She was pregnant?

Just when she thought she was beginning to get the hang of things—fighting as a huntress turned, shifting—as mist, anyway for now. She wanted to be a wolf. Getting to know everything now that she'd been turned.

A baby? In the middle of all this?

Everyone had grown quiet as he placed his hand on her stomach and smiled. Their baby. No telling what it would be—vampire? Hunter? A mix of both? But born, not turned?

Then she smiled. "It looks like Atreides and I are pregnant." Which meant no champagne for her. For whatever reason, when Daemon was serving it, she'd felt chilled and couldn't drink any. Was her body warning her not to drink it? She remembered her mother couldn't drink alcoholic beverages before she learned she was pregnant. Even the thought made her ill. Iced tea too, which, now that Selena thought of it, she hadn't been able to drink for the past few days either. Not iced tea, but hot tea.

Everyone had a glass of champagne to celebrate the happy occasion, though Cook brought her a glass of milk before they dug into the pies.

"Congratulations to yet the newest member of our family—in a few months," Daemon said, rising to his feet and toasting them.

Everyone followed suit—her mother wishing their first grandbaby the best health, her father vowing to turn him or her into a fine hunter, her brother saying he couldn't wait to teach him a hunter trick or two, her sister telling them she would outfit the baby prince, or princess, to the nines, and Atreides promising to be the best father ever—including changing diapers. Daemon was ready to give the new prince, or princess, his or her first set of wheels—a tricycle, and Tezra and Rosa said they would help Atreides and Selena decorate the baby's room.

But they would have to wait until they learned what the baby's sex was.

Atreides wrapped his arm around Selena and gave her a hug. "I love you."

"I couldn't have found a better mate than you," Selena told Atreides and kissed him. "I love you, Atreides."

* * *

ATREIDES KISSED HER BACK, thinking on the day he had first seen her, proud, head held high, ignoring the vampiresses who had exposed their fangs to her, taunting her, hissing at her, and something deep inside him had wanted to get to know the huntress better, when he knew he should have let well enough alone. He never would have wished a rogue vampire to tear into her like he had, but Atreides was glad he had danced with her and she had felt enough of a connection to him to come to him for help.

Now, he was having a baby with her—then he listened, thought he'd heard something else, but he had to be mistaken. Just as soon as he heard it, Selena's jaw dropped, and she turned her attention to him.

He leaned over and listened to her nearly flat belly and then heard what he thought he had heard. Everyone had gotten quiet again, watching him, waiting to hear what was wrong. He lifted his head, beaming. "Two babies. Twins."

Everyone cheered again.

He wasn't surprised at the news. He and Daemon were twins, though his brother was the first born.

Daemon immediately left the dining room and brought in another couple of bottles of champagne.

Life had gotten just a little more uncertain and a whole lot busier.

Atreides knew they would have a big vampire bash to welcome the first royal babies to the clan in centuries. He glanced at Tezra, wondering when she and Daemon would have babies of their own.

"We were waiting for my sister to finish hunter school," Tezra said, as if she could read his mind. "She wants to live with us, hunt, and help with the baby."

Atreides thought with the long vacation she and his brother had had when Atreides had been left in charge, they would have surely been making a baby. And he was certain his brother would want to have one first.

But when it came to Tezra, Daemon often did anything to make her happy, and Atreides had admired him for it.

"But we're having one anyway. You know what they say—babies will come, sometimes when you least expect it."

Atreides noticed then that though everyone had been drinking champagne, he hadn't poured any bubbly into her glass. She'd been pretending to drink toasts!

"We were going to tell everyone within the next couple of days because we wanted this celebration for Selena. But it seems silly now that she has baby news, we don't share ours also," Daemon said.

Atreides smiled at his brother. "The whole year next year will be a cause for celebration."

Smiling, Daemon inclined his head to him.

They would rule on, Atreides thought, unless someone else objected. But should anything happen to Daemon and him while fighting rogue vampires or rogue hunters, their offspring would carry on. Though this time, they would be hunter-vampires and able to be out during any sunny day. At least he hoped so.

Though they stayed up late, visiting family, it was finally time to take his mate back home and the hunters left to enjoy the rest of their evening, the same as Daemon and Tezra.

"We have to go back to the vampire club and dance like we did before—and before I get too pregnant that I can't make those kinds of moves," Selena said.

"We will, and instead of alcoholic drinks for you, I'll make sure we have milk on hand."

"Okay. That sounds good. I want to change into a wolf," Selena said, when he thought they were going to bed to make love.

"Think of being a wolf," he said, helping her to remove her clothes. Once she was naked, he began to take off his own clothes, thinking she would help him and they would make love, but she began pacing, frowning, and he wondered what was wrong.

And then she was a wolf in the blink of an eye. His lips parted in surprise. She looked up at him, startled and he stared at her in disbelief. He smiled. She did it! But then he frowned. He hoped she wouldn't get stuck at it like she did when she turned into mist. And she'd be disappointed or upset.

She suddenly vanished. Damn it. He was trying to remove his clothes so fast, he nearly fell. Then he was naked, shifting, and vanishing, appearing in the general vicinity where she'd gone.

He saw her off in the distance and he woofed, then tore off to join her. He could have vanished and reappeared, but he loved running as a wolf and hadn't done so since she had come into his life because she'd wanted to so badly and couldn't seem to do it.

She nipped at him in play, woofed, and tore off through the woods. He raced after her, loving her, glad she was his mate, and could even shift into the wolf, that she was having his babies, and he knew the choices they had made had been all the right ones.

ACKNOWLEDGMENTS

Thanks to my beta readers, Darla Taylor and Donna Fournier, for jumping out of the world of wolves and into the world of vampires to help me catch my bloopers. I couldn't do it without you ladies, so thanks for all the help!

ABOUT THE AUTHOR

USA Today bestselling and award-winning author **Terry Spear** has written over eighty paranormal romance novels, young adult, and medieval Highland historical romances. Her first werewolf romance, *Heart of the Wolf,* was named a 2008 *Publishers Weekly's* Best Book of the Year, and her subsequent titles have garnered high praise and hit the *USA Today* bestseller list. A retired officer of the U.S. Army Reserves, Terry lives in Crawford, Texas, where she is working on her next werewolf romance, shapeshifting jaguars, cougar shifters, vampires, hot Highlanders, and having fun with her young adult novels and helping to take care of a granddaughter and soon a baby grandson. For more information, please visit www.terryspear.com, or follow her on Twitter, @TerrySpear. She is also on Facebook at https://www.facebook.com/TerrySpearParanormalRomantics. And on Wordpress at:

Terry Spear's Shifters

http://terryspear.wordpress.com/

And her Wilde & Woolley Bears, award-winning teddy bears, that have found homes all over the world: www.celticbears.com

ALSO BY TERRY SPEAR

Heart of the Cougar Series:

Cougar's Mate, Book 1

Call of the Cougar, Book 2

Taming the Wild Cougar, Book 3

Covert Cougar Christmas (Novella)

Double Cougar Trouble, Book 4

Cougar Undercover, Book 5

Cougar Magic, Book 6

Cougar Halloween Mischief (Novella)

Falling for the Cougar, Book 7

Catch the Cougar (A Halloween Novella)

Cougar Christmas Calamity

Saving the White Cougar, Book 8

* * *

Heart of the Bear Series

Loving the White Bear, Book 1

Claiming the White Bear, Book 2

* * *

The Highlanders Series: Winning the Highlander's Heart, The Accidental Highland Hero, Highland Rake, Taming the Wild Highlander, The Highlander, Her Highland Hero, The Viking's Highland Lass, His Wild Highland Lass (novella), Vexing the Highlander (novella), My Highlander

Other historical romances: Lady Caroline & the Egotistical Earl, A Ghost of a Chance at Love

* * *

Heart of the Wolf Series: Heart of the Wolf, Destiny of the Wolf, To Tempt the Wolf, Legend of the White Wolf, Seduced by the Wolf, Wolf Fever, Heart of the Highland Wolf, Dreaming of the Wolf, A SEAL in Wolf's Clothing, A Howl for a Highlander, A Highland Werewolf Wedding, A SEAL Wolf Christmas, Silence of the Wolf, Hero of a Highland Wolf, A Highland Wolf Christmas, A SEAL Wolf Hunting; A Silver Wolf Christmas, A SEAL Wolf in Too Deep, Alpha Wolf Need Not Apply, Billionaire in Wolf's Clothing, Between a Rock and a Hard Place, SEAL Wolf Undercover, Dreaming of a White Wolf Christmas, Flight of the White Wolf, All's Fair in Love and Wolf, A Billionaire Wolf for Christmas, SEAL Wolf Surrender (2019), Silver Town Wolf: Home for the Holidays (2019), Wolff Brothers: You Had Me at Wolf, Night of the Billionaire Wolf, Joy to the Wolves (Red Wolf), The Wolf Wore Plaid, Jingle Bell Wolf, Best of Both Wolves

SEAL Wolves: To Tempt the Wolf, A SEAL in Wolf's Clothing, A SEAL Wolf Christmas, A SEAL Wolf Hunting, A SEAL Wolf in Too Deep, SEAL Wolf Undercover, SEAL Wolf Surrender (2019)

Silver Bros Wolves: Destiny of the Wolf, Wolf Fever, Dreaming of the Wolf, Silence of the Wolf, A Silver Wolf Christmas, Alpha Wolf Need Not Apply, Between a Rock and a Hard Place, All's Fair in Love and Wolf, Silver Town Wolf: Home for the Holidays (2019)

Wolff Brothers of Silver Town

Billionaire Wolves: Billionaire in Wolf's Clothing, A Billionaire Wolf for Christmas, Night of the Billionaire Wolf

Highland Wolves: Heart of the Highland Wolf, A Howl for a Highlander, A Highland Werewolf Wedding, Hero of a Highland Wolf, A Highland Wolf Christmas, Wolf Wore Plaid

Red Wolf Series: Seduced by the Wolf, Joy to the Wolves

* * *

Heart of the Jaguar Series: Savage Hunger, Jaguar Fever, Jaguar Hunt, Jaguar Pride, A Very Jaguar Christmas, You Had Me at Jaguar (2019)

Novella: The Witch and the Jaguar (2018)

* * *

Romantic Suspense: Deadly Fortunes, In the Dead of the Night, Relative Danger, Bound by Danger

* * *

Vampire romances: Killing the Bloodlust, Deadly Liaisons, Huntress for Hire, Forbidden Love, Vampire Redemption, Primal Desire

Vampire Novellas: Vampiric Calling, The Siren's Lure, Seducing the Huntress

* * *

Other Romance: Exchanging Grooms, Marriage, Las Vegas Style

* * *

Science Fiction Romance: Galaxy Warrior

Teen/Young Adult/Fantasy Books

The World of Fae:

The Dark Fae, Book 1

The Deadly Fae, Book 2

The Winged Fae, Book 3

The Ancient Fae, Book 4

Dragon Fae, Book 5

Hawk Fae, Book 6

Phantom Fae, Book 7

Golden Fae, Book 8

Falcon Fae, Book 9

Woodland Fae, Book 10

The World of Elf:

The Shadow Elf

Darkland Elf

Blood Moon Series:

Kiss of the Vampire

The Vampire…In My Dreams

Demon Guardian Series:

The Trouble with Demons

Demon Trouble, Too

Demon Hunter

Non-Series for Now:

Ghostly Liaisons

The Beast Within

Courtly Masquerade

Deidre's Secret

The Magic of Inherian:

The Scepter of Salvation

The Mage of Monrovia

Emerald Isle of Mists (TBA)